WHAT A
DEMON
WANTS

What a Demon Wants

Kathy Love

BRAVA

KENSINGTON PUBLISHING CORP.
www.kensingtonbooks.com

BRAVA BOOKS are published by

Kensington Publishing Corp.
119 West 40th Street
New York, NY 10018

All Kensington titles, imprints, and distributed lines are available at special quantity discounts for bulk purchases for sales promotion, premiums, fund-raising, educational, or institutional use.

Special book excerpts or customized printings can also be created to fit specific needs. For details, write or phone the office of the Kensington Special Sales Manager: Kensington Publishing Corp., 119 West 40th Street, New York, NY 10018. Attn. Special Sales Department. Phone: 1-800-221-2647.

ISBN-13: 978-0-7582-3195-6
ISBN-10: 0-7582-3195-4

First Kensington Trade Paperback Printing: February 2010

10 9 8 7 6 5 4 3 2 1

Printed in the United States of America

For Kate.

This book was a struggle without you.
You will be deeply missed.

SPECIAL THANKS

Julie Cohen—thanks for all the plotting help. And for driving, too.

Erin McCarthy—just for answering her phone. Always.

F. Paul Wilson—for all the weapons info. All mistakes are my own. . . . Oh—thanks for the sweet websites, too.

The Tarts—for being there.

Megan Records—for her patience and hard, hard work.

And for Emily—my life.

Prologue

Where the fuck is it?
This was the second time going through her shit. Her computer, her notes, her books.

He grabbed one of her *New York Times* bestsellers off the shelf, where it sat with eight others in the series. Fantasy, fiction. But not all fiction. He knew that all too well.

And this was the one. The one that had brought him to this place.

He flipped to page 128 where, in innocuous Times New Roman print, italicized of course, as all her spells and incantations were, was the one spell that had brought him to this lowly state. Intolerable state.

He didn't reread the passage. He'd read it dozens of times before. He had it damn near memorized. The goddamned spell. He shoved the book back onto the shelf. Then his rage overtook him. With a sweep of his arm, he brushed all the books off the shelf. Then another shelf. And another.

But with each crash, each thump of the falling books, his rage didn't lessen. It only rose until it strangled him. Blinded him.

He turned on her desk, attacking that with his fury.

When he was done the room looked as if a violent storm had hit, leaving destruction in its path.

He was breathing heavily, his chest puffing up and down with his exertion and his anger. Another wave of rage filled him. He was weak and pathetic now. He couldn't stand this . . . not a moment more.

But how? How did he reverse this spell?

He stepped forward, walking on her books and papers as if they were nothing but trash. Then, in the moonlight filtering in through the French doors, he saw something.

A single sheet of lined paper with neat, precise handwriting listing ingredients and chants. Something about those tidy words drew him. He leaned down and carefully picked it up. Something told him he needed to be calm now. To focus.

He zigzagged his way through the mess until he stood in a direct beam of moonlight. The full moon illuminated the page, so the words were bright and clear even to his inferior eyes.

A Spell of Escape.

His heart, not fully recovered from his fit of anger, sped up more. This could be it. This could finally be his ticket out.

Escape. Freedom.

He read the words.

This would work, he realized. This would release him from the awful bonds he'd been stuck in for months. He'd be strong again. He'd be free.

Relief and excitement made him almost giddy, replacing the anger that had seemed to simmer within him for weeks.

He'd be free!

He read the spell again. It was really quite a simple incantation. Some herbs and other sundries created into a powder that he would dust over himself. Then he would read the invocation aloud. There was only one part that could be tricky.

While dusted in the charmed concoction and saying the chant, he had to commit a human sacrifice.

A smile turned up his lips. Lips that hadn't smiled sincerely in weeks.

Hmm, who to kill?

He glanced around the office that he'd just ransacked. Well, that was a no-brainer, wasn't it?

"Found dead today in her New Orleans home was Ellina Kostova, the reclusive author of many highly successful fantasy novels."

He laughed as he carefully folded the paper in Ellina's own handwriting, her handwritten death warrant, and exited her home through French doors that led into her courtyard.

Chapter 1

"Why would a demon need a bodyguard?" Ellina Kostova pushed her relentlessly unruly hair out of her face and attempted to give her brother her most formidable look.

Maksim ignored her and continued to thumb through the papers he held, pulling out one and tossing it on her desk.

"*You* need a bodyguard, and I have a man coming here today to meet with us," he said.

"Maksim, you are being ridiculous." She didn't bother to look at the paper, which she knew was probably the equivalent of a bodyguard résumé. It struck her as sort of amusing. What would a résumé like that say? *Took a bullet for so and so in 2005. Roughed up so and so in 2007. Fended off crazed paparazzi in 2009.*

"And you're overreacting," she added.

Maksim lifted an eyebrow. "You do realize you live in a fantasy world?"

"If I can't live in a fantasy world, who can?" She pushed the paper back toward him, trying not to disturb any of her notes. She'd just finished researching *The Ritual of Restraint*, which was a particularly involved incantation for binding the most powerful of demons, and one she was using in a key place in her next Jenny Bell, Demon Hunter, book. So she did not want to get her notes out of order.

And she prided herself on her accuracy. She might write fiction, but her demon knowledge was correct. It should be; she was half demon, after all.

She glanced back to her brother. Of course, she couldn't always be totally accurate. Some things humans wouldn't necessarily buy. Like how sullen demons often were.

Oh, they were evil and manipulative, sure. But oversensitive and cranky . . .

That just didn't make for good fantasy adventure.

Her brother scowled.

Or maybe it would. His glare might border on cranky, but it was certainly dark enough to be seen as menacing too.

She ignored it.

"You are reading way too much into a few coincidences," she said.

"Broken into. Not once, but three times." He held up three fingers just in case she wasn't clear on how many times that was. "In fewer than as many months, I might add. Your books and research missing. You call all that a coincidence?"

She shrugged. "I'd call it unlucky. Or maybe lucky, because I wasn't home any of the times it happened. And nothing irreplaceable was stolen."

"And the strange phone calls?"

"They've stopped," she pointed out.

"Yes, about the same time the break-ins started. Coincidence?"

"This is New Orleans. I mean, crime happens. Come on, weird stuff happens here all the time."

Maksim shook his head, the desire to shake her clear from his grimace and his clenched hands.

"And you were just nearly run down by a car?"

"Again, this is New Orleans. Drinking and driving definitely happens."

"Ellina, you have to be smart about this. You are a famous author. What if this is some crazed fan? Or some religious fanatic who doesn't like that you are writing about demons? Or worse yet, some other demon who doesn't like you writing about demons?"

She'd thought about all these things too. She wasn't that clueless, but a bodyguard? In her house?

It was a known fact that she was a bit of a recluse. A reclusive writer who created fantastical worlds filled with monsters and demons and the inexperienced, yet fortuitously savvy, cake decorator turned demon hunter who protected humanity from them.

She liked staying in her charmed and fictional world of writing, and while Maksim didn't know why, it was necessary.

But lately it did seem that the altogether too real outside world was determined to come into her safe little haven.

"And what about being trapped inside a cat? For several months?" He raised his eyebrows, daring her to argue that one.

Well, that hardly seemed like the "real" world, but it had happened. And it was disturbing, to say the least.

Ellina sighed. "Well, that one's a little harder to explain away."

But actually she had; she figured it was one of her other half brothers. The twins, maybe. They loved practical jokes. Neither Andrey nor Pasha had owned up to it. Even after Maksim bullied them, and Maksim was a professional when it came to bullying—now being a perfect example. She definitely liked it better when he bullied someone other than her.

He glared at her, clearly frustrated.

"I think it was the twins," she said as she had many times before. "You know they aren't particularly fond of me. They love to mess with me."

"They aren't fond of anyone. But I don't think they put you in the cat. They seemed altogether too disappointed that they hadn't come up with the idea."

She could imagine they would have seen that as a missed opportunity. But their disappointment still didn't clear them. It's not like either of them could be labeled the embodiment of truth. And while they tolerated Maksim, because he was a more powerful demon than they were, they didn't have to be so careful with her. They somewhat tolerated her, because Maksim insisted they do so, but she certainly couldn't rule them out as the culprits of the cat fiasco.

Being trapped in a cat was something she'd rather not repeat, but it hardly warranted a bodyguard. Okay, all the things he mentioned put together did perhaps necessitate something to keep her safer. An alarm system. A dog maybe. But a bodyguard?

She didn't want some burly lunkhead following her everywhere. She had too much work to do. She liked her privacy.

Not to mention she was far behind on her deadline for her publisher, who was already calling every other day to see if her newest Jenny Bell book was close to completion. Which was great, because her publisher was excited about her books, but it wasn't even close to being done. And how did one explain that the reason she was late on her deadline was because she'd been stuck in a cat for nearly six months?

Her editor loved the books and all her demon ideas, but she didn't think Ellina was working from experience. She certainly didn't know that Ellina was half demon. Like she'd believe any of it anyway.

So Ellina just had to buckle down and get the book done as quickly as possible and with as few distractions as possible.

Maksim pushed the paper back toward her.

"You might as well look it over. I've made up my mind about this."

Ellina stared at paper bullet-pointed with dates and past jobs. Nothing about "taking a bullet." How good could this guy be anyway?

"This is ridiculous," she said.

"Maybe. But better safe than sorry."

Ellina snorted, knowing the sound was inelegant—and so undemonlike. "Better safe than sorry? That hardly sounds demonlike to me."

He ignored her. "Jo thinks it's a good idea too."

"What do I think is a good idea?" Jo said, appearing at Ellina's office doorway, her very pregnant belly showing just slightly before the woman herself.

Maksim was immediately at his wife's side. "Did you walk here?"

The wind-mussed hair and flushed cheeks answered for her, even as she said, "No."

Clearly Maksim didn't believe her any more than Ellina did.

"You shouldn't be walking," he said, his dark scowl now directed at Jo.

"Of course I should walk," Jo said, undaunted by his frown. "It's nice and cool outside. And my back has been bothering me all day. Walking helps."

"Your back hurts?" His glower was replaced by a frown of concern. He instantly began to rub a place low on her back that he'd obviously rubbed for her in the past.

Jo sighed, closing her eyes.

Ellina smiled at her brother's protectiveness and attentiveness. He'd gone from the ruler of the eighth circle of Hell to a complete worrywart and a pretty great husband.

"I'm fine," Jo told him after a few moments, touching his

cheek, which seemed to pacify him. Unfortunately, because he only studied his wife a moment longer, then tugged her over to Ellina's desk.

"Tell her," he said to Jo. "Tell Ellina she's being stupid, she needs someone around. That the things happening lately aren't just coincidences."

Jo pursed her lips, giving Ellina a pained look as if to say she didn't want to think the worst, but . . .

"I do think you should have someone around. At least until you find out who pulled the cat trick." Then Jo smiled as if to buffer her words and gestured to Ellina's hair. "I like this new color. Blond suits you."

Ellina touched her newly colored hair. "Thanks."

Maksim rolled his eyes.

Ellina rolled her eyes back, then returned to the topic at hand. "But we may never discover who did that. And I'm not having someone hanging around all the time. My work requires *alone* time. To write. To research. No."

She shoved the paper back across the desk at her brother, this time disregarding her orderly, printed-out notes.

Maksim growled, frustrated. "Don't even get me started on all your alone time."

Ellina frowned. This was a topic she didn't want to talk about, but she couldn't stop herself from saying, "I like my life the way it is."

"How can you like . . ."

Jo stepped forward, raising a hand to stop the tirade she saw coming. "Ellina, just let Maksim hire someone for a couple weeks. If nothing else happens, then you can let him go."

Maksim made a noise as if he was going to argue the plan, but Jo waved her hand again, silently shushing him.

"And you know with the baby nearly here, Maksim won't be able to watch out for you himself. And he will worry."

Well, that was great. Now they were guilting her for not

taking around-the-clock security. And sadly, it was working. Darn it.

"What can it hurt?" Jo added, driving in the last nail of the coffin of her will.

Ellina looked at her note-cluttered desk, then her computer screen with a Word doc opened and reporting a mere twenty pages finished.

What could it hurt?

Her career. Her deal with her publisher. Her future deals.

Then she glanced back at her brother and sister-in-law, and selfishness created a sinking feeling in the pit of her stomach. Both of their expressions showed how worried they were. And they had a baby due to arrive any day.

What could it really hurt? It would calm Maksim down and allow him to fully focus on Jo and their new baby, and it did only have to be for a little while. She could suffer through it for a little while, right?

Once Maksim realized he was paying someone for nothing, she'd be back to her normal life.

"Fine," Ellina muttered, but waved the unwanted résumé at Maksim.

Maksim frowned but accepted the paper. "Don't you want to look it over more?"

"I'm assuming he's already your choice," Ellina said, not bothering to hide her irritation with being railroaded.

"Well, I do think he's the best, yes."

Ellina made a *well there you go* face at him.

"Now," she said, turning her attention back to her computer, "why don't you give me a little time to—"

A loud, abrupt rap echoed through her apartment.

Ellina glared at her brother.

"That's him," Maksim said with a smug smile.

So much for work now.

* * *

Jude stood in the doorway of a shotgun cottage that looked as if it had fallen out of the pages of a fairy tale. He half expected children in lederhosen to answer the door.

But instead of Hansel or Gretel, the door was jerked open by a tall man, fit and tough enough to be a bodyguard himself.

"Jude Anthony?"

Jude nodded. "Yes."

The man extended his hand. "Maksim Kostova. I'm the one who contacted you on behalf of my sister."

Jude had guessed as much. He accepted the man's hand, giving it a brief, firm shake. As he released it, he fought the urge to wipe his hand on his pants as if there was something thick and slimy clinging to his fingers.

Demon. That particular preternatural aura affected him more than some others. The energy from Maksim was strong and heavy, coating Jude's palm and fingers, creeping up his arm like a living thing. The Blob from horror movie legend.

Damn, he hated that sensation. He flexed his fingers, trying to subtly shake the sensation off.

Maksim raised an eyebrow, obviously aware that Jude had had some reaction to him, but he didn't inquire. Instead he stepped back, opening the door wider.

"Come in."

Jude moved past him, keeping a good distance between them. This male was clearly a powerful, high-ranking demon. Jude could even feel his aura just in passing.

Jude steeled himself to the sensation, but was pleased to step into a fair-size sitting room. More space was always better.

He could do this. Just a few more jobs, and he'd be done with this life. No more paranormal creatures. No more of this existence. He would reinvent himself.

With renewed determination, he turned his focus away from the demon and to the room they'd just entered. His impression again was that of being in a fairy-tale world. Lavender walls, gold brocade furniture, and beaded lamps gave the room a feeling of a princess's private parlor.

But the woman who entered the room was no fairy-tale character. Not unless fairy tales had changed greatly since he'd last read one. She was hugely pregnant, making her hard to miss. Her belly protruded, almost comically large when compared to her slight frame. Then his gaze moved to the tall, blond-haired woman who followed the waddling pregnant one.

She was stunning. Definitely princess material here . . . except instead of a flowing gown she wore a faded concert T-shirt that clung to her small, pert breasts and slender midriff.

Dark washed jeans encased her long legs, accentuating the flare of her hips and cupping what he had no doubt was a great ass—not that he could see that, but he just knew. Pale bare feet with her toes painted cherry red peeped out from under the cuffs of her jeans.

Jude's body tensed, very aware of her.

Just observations, he told himself. What he was paid to do. Notice—things. But his body told him it was more than a detached inventory. He reacted. Instantly. Viscerally.

Don't let this be Ellina Kostova. Please don't let this be her.

He tried to ignore his response, relieved when Maksim spoke. "Jude, this is my wife, Jo," Maksim said, gesturing to the very pregnant woman, drawing Jude's attention away from the beauty.

His wife stepped forward and offered her hand. The briefest touch revealed she was human. A welcome sensation after making contact with her husband. No supernatural residue there.

But of course, Maksim redirected him back to the other woman. "And this is Ellina, my sister. The one you will be protecting."

Shit. He'd been hoping this wasn't her. She certainly didn't fit his image of Ellina Kostova—the reclusive, eccentric author who preferred to stay in her world of demons, monsters, and other things that went bump in the night.

He hadn't expected her to be so young . . . or so lovely. She had an almost ethereal quality to her features. Full lips, large pale eyes, creamy skin.

She moved closer and offered a hand to him. Her fingers were slender, elegant. A beautiful hand.

But she was paranormal, he reminded himself. So really, would she be anything less than perfection? On the outside, at least. That was the way of preternaturals.

He reached for her hand, waiting for the same clinging, distasteful aura to encompass him. The aura that would remind him that not all things were as beautiful on the inside as they were on the outside. He knew from the information her brother had given him that she was only half demon, but half was all it would take for his preternatural awareness to kick in.

But instead of that sickening, clinging, creeping sensation, her touch sent tingles up his arm. Tangible, electric pulses. Pulses that were anything but unpleasant.

As if in utter synch, they released each other, both stepping back.

Unlike him, Ellina didn't show any outward reaction to the touch. Her lovely face was as serene as that of a mannequin. Certainly she didn't show any indication she'd felt the same shock waves passing between them. Instead her pale eyes roamed over him, taking very obvious inventory, although her expression revealed nothing of her thoughts. Just an assessment. Testing his musculature, his strength. Like appraising a horse about to be purchased.

Except he was no stoic equine. His body tightened further—his mind imagining what her fingers would feel like moving over him. Those tiny pulses radiating from her fingers into him.

His spine straightened, and he forced his attention, and his reaction, away from the woman who'd managed to affect him more with one fleeting brush of her fingers than hundreds of paranormals before her.

He turned to Maksim. "I'm sorry. I'm not the right man for this job."

Chapter 2

Well, he wasn't a lunkhead.

That was Ellina's first thought when Maksim escorted the man who was to be her bodyguard into the room. Nope, not a lunkhead at all. No bulked-up shoulders and chest that hid any hint of a neck. No military crew cut or arms the size of small battering rams.

Really, the only way to describe him was—perfect. Very tall—6'5" maybe. Lean, powerful muscles like those of a swimmer, hair that bordered on shaggy. Sexy, but not because he intended it to be that way.

His touch had been very nice too, his palm slightly callused and warm, his fingers tapered and strong. And she'd felt a wave of something, so she'd released his hand.

He did appear—well, perfect.

That was until he spoke.

"I'm sorry. I'm not the right man for the job."

What? Ellina frowned, all of her pleasant surprise and interest disappearing in a rush of irritation.

What? How had he come to that conclusion in just a few seconds? Ellina knew it was silly, but damn it, she was insulted. She was supposed to be the one deciding whether she wanted to hire him. Not the other way around.

Maksim started to say something, but Ellina cut him off.

"What do you mean you're not right for the job?" she asked sharply, which was probably what Maksim was going to ask too—although maybe a tad more tactfully.

The man, who was rapidly becoming the lunkhead she'd expected, didn't react right away, didn't even act as if he'd heard her speak. Another bad response on his part. But after a moment, he shifted to face her.

"I just don't think this job would be a good fit for me."

She raised an eyebrow and placed her hands on her hips, feeling further insulted.

"And you came to that conclusion how?"

He again didn't respond immediately. As if he was searching for the right words.

Lunkhead.

She frowned at him, fighting the urge to tap her foot as she waited.

Why was she reacting this way? Because *she* was supposed to be the one who was reluctant about this. But instead he hadn't just been reluctant, he'd *refused* to work with her. And it was . . . it was insulting. Why wouldn't he want to work with her?

"I—" He snapped his mouth shut.

She'd been right, he was trying to find the appropriate words, and he was struggling. That wasn't particularly comforting, frankly.

What was it about her that made him decide he couldn't work with her? And that quickly too? She was easy to get along with. She was downright enjoyable to be around. Ask anyone. Well, ask her brother. Or her sister-in-law. Maybe her editor.

Whatever! Plenty of people thought she was just lovely.

Her right foot started to tap, and she stopped it.

"I just don't think I'm right for this job."

All that careful thinking, and that's all he could come up with?

Her foot tapped again, and again she caught herself, keeping her bare foot pressed to the worn floorboards.

"I've already discussed the details of this job with you. You said it wouldn't be any problem," Maksim said, impatience coming out in his voice rather than his foot.

Jude shifted back to her brother, the action so swift, she got the impression that he was relieved not to have to interact with her any further.

She gritted her teeth. This was ridiculous—and in a different way than she'd expected.

"That is true," Jude said. "But—"

"But what?" Even Maksim seemed insulted on her behalf.

"I can usually tell right away if I'll be the right for the job or not. And in this case—I just think it wouldn't be a good fit."

"So you've said," Ellina couldn't help saying to his profile. "But you seem unable to explain why."

Jo made a noise from beside her, but Ellina didn't stop glaring at the once-perfect-now-lunkhead in front of her to see if her sister-in-law was laughing or just making a sound of agreement.

"Sometimes these things can't be explained," he said, turning to meet her gaze, although she couldn't read his eyes. Just blank. "In my work, I've become pretty good at following my gut."

Ellina made a face, letting him know exactly what she thought about his gut, then asked, "Well what could your gut possibly tell you about me? In less than two minutes?"

From the corner of her eye, she noted that Maksim's reaction changed from irritation to bemused amusement. She had no doubt that he found her reaction quite humorous, given that she'd adamantly said she didn't want a bodyguard and now she was fighting with the man to have him.

Well, not have him. But not be disregarded by him.

She paused. What was she doing? She had become far too careful to become agitated. She knew what could happen when she felt anxious. She'd spent years perfecting her ability to remain calm. But she could feel herself slipping. And how long before this lunkhead saw it too?

Who the hell cared if he did? She didn't want him here anyway. She should be pushing the man right out the door. He was giving her a perfect out.

The only thing still perfect about the guy.

She started to open her mouth to say that he should probably go, then snapped her lips shut.

She couldn't help it. She wanted an explanation as to why he didn't want the job. Breathing in deeply, she calmed herself down. A method she'd mostly perfected over the years.

"Why can't you work with me?" she asked again, this time keeping her voice steady.

"Well, I'm pretty certain you are difficult," he said, his voice wry.

"She can be," Maksim agreed.

Ellina glared at her brother. *Breathe.*

"But difficult clients can't be that unusual to you," Maksim added, oblivious to Ellina's glower. "You know as well as I do that this isn't the typical security position. Ellina needs some pretty special abilities to keep her safe. And you have those abilities. This is exactly the type of job you said you take."

Jude didn't say anything, but a muscle in his jaw jumped slightly as if he was clenching his teeth.

"Special abilities? What special abilities does he have?" Ellina asked Maksim, already aware that she wouldn't get a direct answer out of the lunkhead.

Maksim frowned. "If you'd read his résumé, you'd know that he's more than capable of handling any situation, whether it be from human causes or otherwise. And he knows what you are too."

"Oh. Right."

Of course he'd have to be paranormal. All bases had to be covered, didn't they?

And, of course, Maksim would have disclosed that she was a freak. Half human/half demon. Not a part of either world. She could deal with that most of the time, but there were moments when she struggled with being okay in her own skin. This was beginning to feel like one of those times—even now that she'd gotten her agitation under control.

Still, did the half-breed thing bother him? She knew it was off-putting for some preternaturals. Maybe he was one of them. But Maksim told him all about that before he even agreed to come here. So . . . what was it?

She studied Jude. And if he could protect her, then clearly he wasn't a normal guy either. So what kind of creature was he? What made him such a great candidate to protect her?

She couldn't sense anything about him, because she didn't have that ability. Her brothers could sense preternatural beings at fifty paces. Ellina couldn't tell a demon from a human from a wererabbit—if there were such a thing.

To her, Jude was nothing more than an unusually good-looking—and irritating—guy. But he must be something pretty powerful. A demon too? A very old vampire? Except he was out in the daylight, so probably not.

Was he put off because he was such a strong preternatural and she wasn't?

"Is it the half demon thing?" she heard herself asking, wondering why it mattered.

* * *

Jude clenched his teeth again. Did she have to look so wounded when she asked that? He didn't like the way her frown and searching eyes made him feel. Like a real jerk. And he was pretty good at doing that to himself without any outside help.

Maybe because she'd hit on something that was true. He didn't like preternaturals. Hypocritical, he knew. But that wouldn't stop him from taking a job. Obviously. Money was the only thing that factored into why he took a job.

But his likes and dislikes aside, why did it matter why he didn't want to work with her?

She still watched him, hints of hurt darkening her pale eyes to a steely gray. Clearly, it did matter. She was taking his refusal personally.

For a moment, he considered telling her it *was* the demon thing, but knew he couldn't. He'd already assured Maksim that he was quite comfortable facing off with other preternaturals. Any kind. And the same went for protecting them. A job was a job.

Of course, he hadn't expected his first face-off to come with the person he was supposed to be protecting.

He pulled in a deep breath, trying to decide how to get out of this without causing even more wounded looks from the stunningly beautiful woman in front of him.

Stunningly beautiful. And that thought right there was why he needed out of this job.

Then Jude managed to gather his scrambled, distracted thoughts. "I should have mentioned this on the phone," he said quickly, "but I'm also considering another job."

Which was a lie. This was the only job he had lined up. The only paying gig to get him closer to where he wanted to be. Done with violence, done with preternaturals. Free. And in charge of his own life for the first time in centuries.

"Listen," Maksim said, "I've already told you I'm willing to pay you anything you ask."

Maksim's wife moaned softly, and Jude supposed that offering their money so freely might not sit as well with her.

"Name your price," Maksim said.

Jude wanted to groan too. He was so close. This job, especially if he could set any price, could be enough to allow him some semblance of a normal life.

His gaze flicked back to Ellina's lovely face. He flexed his fingers, which still tingled from when he'd touched her, a warm and arousing sensation.

He didn't know if he could be around this woman. This *demon*, he told himself as if that reminder would somehow negate his instant reaction to her. And that reaction was dangerous. He just knew it.

But the money . . .

"Truthfully, you are our only option," Maksim said.

Ellina snorted. The indignant sound should have sounded out of place and graceless coming from such a pretty woman, but somehow even her snort worked for her.

So dangerous, Jude told himself. So, so dangerous.

But it was the noise that then came from Maksim's wife that jarred everyone out of their conversation. A shuddering breath that turned into a full-out cry.

All eyes turned to her. The woman hunched forward, her arms wrapped around her distended abdomen like she was hugging a beach ball to herself.

"Jo!" Maksim was at her side at once, his demon abilities making the movement unnaturally quick. But the way he braced his arms around his wife, trying to take her weight and her pain, was purely human. Jo curled into him, her pain seemingly made more manageable by his nearness.

Jude's chest tightened, and he found the interaction hard

to watch, but he did, waiting to see what he could do to help, if anything.

"The baby?" Maksim asked, his voice bordering on panic. Another jarringly human reaction.

For a moment another woman, swollen with child, and another man, thrilled and terrified at the prospect of his first child, flashed through Jude's mind.

He shook his head, shoving the image aside.

Those thoughts were better left in the past. For a very short time, he'd believed he could atone for his past. He could have a full life again. Then he realized he'd never be anything other than a monster. And monsters didn't deserve redemption. All he wanted now was peace.

"Should I call your doctor?" Ellina asked, joining Maksim at her sister-in-law's side.

"I think—" Jo struggled to pull in a calming breath. "I think I'll be all right."

"Yes," Maksim said, as if his wife hadn't spoken. "Call this number." He fished a cell phone from his jeans pocket, rifling through the numbers in his phone book with one hand, the other still around Jo's back.

Jo shot her husband a look somewhere between irritation and amusement. "I've only had a few contractions, and they weren't terribly close together."

"You've been having contractions?" Maksim looked hurt that she'd withheld that information from him, but he shook the emotion off. "I don't care how close together they are, call the doctor."

Maksim waved the cell phone toward his sister. Ellina took it, and he returned his attention to his wife.

Jude watched as Ellina pressed the button to connect with the doctor, seeing the excitement in her eyes. There was something else there that caught his attention. A change in the color of them? In the shape? Even her features seemed somehow different.

She told someone on the other end of the line what was happening, referring to Jo for more information, which Maksim felt the need to repeat as if Ellina wasn't right there to hear Jo.

"Dr. Kelley said that you probably have hours to go yet," Ellina told them after she hung up the phone. "Just time the contractions. Walking will help. Or a bath. And call her when they are coming in regular five-minute intervals."

Jo started to nod, then another contraction hit her. She groaned and hunched forward. Maksim held her again, talking to her in low, hushed tones. But Jo only groaned louder.

"We're going to the hospital," Maksim announced as soon as the contraction lessened and Jo could stand upright.

"But—" Jo started.

"No," Maksim said, all frazzled expectant dad, "I'll feel better if we are there. Please."

Jo smiled at him, oddly calmer than her demon husband. "Okay. I guess I would too, actually."

They started toward the door, when Maksim seemed to remember Jude was still there.

"I'll pay you whatever you want. Whatever—you name it. But you can't leave. I don't know how long I'll be gone. And I don't want Ellina alone."

Jude hesitated, then found himself nodding.

What the hell was he doing? He couldn't do this. Being here was too much. It was a situation that was making him feel strange things. And remember things he didn't want to think about again. Ever again.

He'd learned long, long ago the best way to be an effective bodyguard, killer, machine, was to feel nothing.

Maksim searched Jude's face, and Jude knew the other

man was looking for something to assure himself he could trust him. A virtual stranger.

Then Maksim nodded, apparently finding the answer he wanted. Although Jude didn't know how or what he found. *He* didn't know if Maksim could trust him, or if he could trust himself.

"I'll call you from the hospital," Maksim said to Ellina.

"Okay. Let me know if you need anything. Love you both." Ellina followed them to the door.

"Call Maggie and Erika," Jude heard Jo say from outside the door.

"I will." Ellina waved, waiting in the doorway until Jude heard Maksim's car start and speed away from the house.

After the whir of activity, the sudden silence in the small cottage was harsh and unnerving. Then Ellina turned to him. Her face wore that serene mask he'd seen when he first entered her house. Nothing odd about her eyes. Nothing amiss, and he now wondered if he'd just imagined some strange change in her.

"Thanks for agreeing to stay, but you can go."

Jude didn't respond for a moment, surprised by her abruptness, but considered taking her up on the invitation.

"No, I'm staying."

He couldn't go.

Ellina stared at him for a moment, then shrugged.

"You are one odd dude," she said, then strode out of the lavender living room, disappearing down a hall the color of blue cotton candy.

"You have no idea," Jude muttered to the empty room.

Chapter 3

Ellina fled straight to her office and closed the door. She knew her comment and abrupt departure were rude, but she had to put some space between herself and this guy. This very annoying and confusing guy.

Not to mention, she'd felt herself losing control. Jo's starting labor had unnerved her. Ellina didn't know nothin' about birthin' no babies. But she'd gotten control back quickly. Normally something like that wouldn't distress her, so it had to have been the combination of her interaction with Jude and then the surprise of Jo's contractions.

Usually it was only two things that made her agitated. Crowds. She had a hard time controlling herself in crowds. And arousal.

And she refused to believe arousal played a factor here. Yes, Jude was good looking, but she'd long ago learned to quash attraction. For everyone involved.

Still, her hasty exit was rude. Then again, what was the proper etiquette for having a bodyguard in your house? Especially one who one minute didn't want to be there, and the next insisted on staying? Did she show him around her place? Did she tell him to make himself at home?

Or did she just hide until he changed his mind yet again and left?

Of course, he'd changed his mind when money had come up. So he was only staying for the cash.

That didn't smooth her ruffled ego. Ruffled ego? This was all so silly.

Ellina actually giggled to herself at their whole exchange. Then she giggled even louder. She'd always had a terrible habit of laughing about things that really weren't funny. She suspected it was because she was always so aware of being controlled. Something had to give.

She moved around her desk, composing herself. Sitting down, she checked the hallway for shifts in the shadows to see if he'd followed her. She noticed nothing and only silence filled her apartment.

Still watching the door, Ellina nibbled her lower lip and debated what to do. She could pay him off to leave, but she knew she likely couldn't meet the price Maksim would pay. She had plenty of money, but Maksim had demon powers. Money was no issue. And why was she giving up her hard-earned money to get rid of someone she didn't even want to hire in the first place?

Seemingly, she'd have to suffer with this guy—at least until Jo had the baby, then she'd pressure Maksim to forget this silly idea. Hell, plead if she had to.

So what to do in the meantime?

"Well, the most obvious answer is work," she muttered to herself. The odd bodyguard could do what odd bodyguards did without her assistance. And she needed to get this chapter done. Today.

She wiggled her computer mouse against her Hello Kitty mouse pad, waiting for her monitor screen to flicker to life, jarred out of sleep mode. The chapter, half-done, stared at her. She forced herself to reread the last words she'd written and get her thoughts back to the next section of her book.

That's right, Jenny had just found a strange man in her bakery. That was appropriate, wasn't it?

She glanced back at her door. She wondered why the other job he'd mentioned was more appealing to him. And what had turned him off from the moment they met?

Who cared?

She didn't.

She turned back to the sentence she'd started, reading it again. And again.

Making an irritated noise low in her throat, she shoved back her chair and stood. She headed to the door, pausing with her fingers on the handle.

She just wanted to know if he was still here, right? It was unnerving not to know. That was probably the reason she couldn't concentrate. Once she knew that, then she could get back to work. And she should probably tell him to make himself at home. She didn't have time to entertain him.

Ellina started to push down the handle, but paused again. She had to admit hiding out in here was more appealing. But he was her employee, so she needed to give him some ground rules. She didn't have a clue what those rules were, but . . .

"I can't just leave him standing in the living room. He needs some sort of directions, right?"

Taking a deep breath, she tugged open her door. As soon as she did, a large body loomed in front of her, blocking her from leaving her office.

Ellina yelped and stepped back.

"Are you okay?" Jude stood there, arms crossed over his chest, legs slightly apart.

"What are you doing out here?" she managed to snap, even as her thumping heart stole her breath.

"Guarding you."

She frowned. So much for being able to tell if he'd followed her down the hall. Clearly he'd been standing here the whole time.

Had he heard her talking to herself? Worse yet, had he heard her laughing? That had to have seemed slightly crazy, at best. She didn't ask, not sure if she wanted the answer, so instead she asked, "So this is what you are going to do? Just stand around in the hallway all day?"

"And night," he added, his tone bland.

Her frown deepened. Well, that answered one question. He clearly hadn't decided to leave again in the last ten minutes.

"Money makes the world go 'round," she murmured.

"Pardon?"

She ignored his question. "I can't concentrate knowing that you're lurking out here."

"I'm not lurking. I'm guarding."

"Well, whatever you're doing, I can't concentrate. You want to leave. And I want you to leave, so why don't you just go now. I'll even tell Maksim you did stay for a while."

"That would be a lie."

Ellina gritted her teeth. "My brother is a demon. He enjoys a good sin every now and then. And you can't tell me that a guy like you cares about a lie every now and then either."

She tried to read his reaction to that assessment, but aside from a slight tic in his jaw, his expression told her nothing.

"I'll *even* pay you to leave."

Still no reaction. Nothing.

"I don't need a bodyguard," she added once she realized he didn't intend to answer her. "My brother is a bit of an alarmist. An interesting fact, that. Many demons overreact. I've even written about it."

Jude leaned one shoulder against the wall, looking decidedly disinclined to go anywhere. And, frankly, a little bored with her.

So it surprised Ellina when he said, "I've read your brother's report about the incidents that have happened to you. They sound a little suspicious to me. Definitely reasons for concern."

"Yeah, well, then you're probably an alarmist too."

Jude quirked his lips in a gesture that Ellina couldn't exactly label as a smile. More a smirk. But the curl of his lips hinted at a dimple in his left cheek that had remained hidden until that moment.

"I think you're confusing alarm with caution," he said.

Ellina made a face, frustrated that they were talking in circles. "Listen, you don't want this job. And I don't want you here. So please just go."

Jude knew he was being handed his out—again—but he couldn't do it.

Money. Maybe even enough money to make this his last gig.

Keep your eyes on the prize, buddy.

Plus he *had* read the report, and either someone was out to get this woman, or she had the worst luck of anyone he'd ever encountered. And given that he had some pretty crappy luck, Jude felt pretty confident no one's luck was quite that bad.

No, he couldn't leave her alone. She could be in real trouble. That wouldn't be . . .

He stopped his train of thought. That wouldn't be financially wise.

"I'm staying."

Ellina glared at him, the flash of irritation in her pale eyes making them more brilliant, this time making them glint like polished aquamarines. The firm set of her lips did nothing to diminish their fullness.

He forced his eyes to a point on the wall over her left shoulder, telling himself his notice of those things meant nothing. Just like he was now noting the small nail hole that marred the paint and plaster, right there beside her. Something must have once hung there. A painting? A photo?

But the notice of the nail hole wasn't what pulled his muscles taut, or caused his blood to speed up to a low hum in his ears. No, that was all the woman in front of him.

He had to get a grip on his disobedient body. This woman was a job. If she wasn't a job, he'd have to leave immediately.

Just focus on the cash. On the future finally within your reach.

After several seconds lost on regaining his perspective, he realized Ellina hadn't reacted to his last statement, but neither had she moved. When he looked back to her, she simply stood, watching him. Those pale eyes searching for something.

Actually he was surprised by her silence. He'd expected her to argue. To get more irritated. But her probing look made him uncomfortable. *More* uncomfortable. He, a man who'd been in dozens, maybe hundreds, of awkward and awful positions, yet this woman's penetrating stare made him want to turn and leave. To run away.

Like the coward he really was.

She studied him a moment longer, then sighed. "Okay, obviously I'm not going to win this. So what do we do? Because I'm on a deadline, and I can't be worrying or wondering what you are doing."

"You don't have to do either. I'll just be here in case something goes wrong."

She nodded, then smiled. Her full lips turned up in a wide smile, revealing perfect white teeth. The smile lit her eyes.

His breath seized in his chest like stepping out into arctic air. He wished that freezing effect would reach the rest of his body, which burned at the simple gesture.

"Can you wait for something to go wrong while hanging out in the living room? Does it require you standing in the hallway?"

He forced his attention away from that literally breathtaking smile. Back to the nail hole. Maybe there'd been a hook there once. Or a clock. A mirror?

"I can remain in the living room," he said after a second, his voice calmer, cooler than the fiery rush in his veins. "But leave your door open. I need to be able to hear you if you need me."

He would be able to hear her anyway. His hearing was highly developed, but staying in the living room was a concession to them both. For her work, and for his mental health. Normally he didn't like to be that far away from a client, so having the door open seemed like a good compromise.

"I'll be quiet," he added, when he stole a quick look back to her and saw she was nibbling at her lower lip, debating his request. He quickly looked at the wall again. A small shelf, maybe?

"Fine," Ellina said. He could feel her eyes on him a moment longer, then she turned back to her office. Out of habit, she started to close the door behind her, then stopped, making a slight face that was even appealing in its cuteness, as she realized what she was doing.

He wanted to groan.

"Sorry," she said and pushed the door open, then headed toward her desk.

Jude didn't linger, realizing she wouldn't appreciate that. And frankly, he didn't want to watch her lithe body strolling across the room. He turned and strode away from the door-way—and her. He needed space too.

As soon as he was in the living room, he pulled in a steadying breath. He had to stay focused. He had to see this—and her—as like any other gig.

Of course, if he was really treating this post like any other one, he wouldn't have actually left his position in the hallway. Maybe he'd have moved away a little, but he'd have stayed there. Close by.

No, agreeing to wait in the living room was more for himself than her. And that wasn't a good approach. He should never come first over a client. But he needed a moment to refocus. To get his head screwed on right. Both heads, he added, trying to ignore the one that still stood at half-mast.

Breathing in deeply, he glanced around the room. The whole cottage was small. He'd definitely hear if anything went wrong. And he could be to her in a fraction of a second if necessary.

All great justifications, buddy.

If he was dealing with a paranormal attacker, then it was always best to be as close as possible. He was fast, but he'd learned the hard way there was always someone, or something, faster.

He paced the room again, then decided if he was going to take the coward's way out and keep space between them, he should at least do something productive. He hadn't explored the house, and he needed to know where all the points of entry and other danger zones were.

He had a fairly good idea of the layout. It was a typical shotgun cottage, popular in Louisiana, and they all followed the same basic floor plan. But this one had obviously been modified, probably when plumbing and the bathroom had been added.

He walked down the narrow hallway, stepping into a galley-style kitchen. The whole space seemed miniature. A two-burner cooktop with a small oven below. A dorm room–size fridge located under the tile counter. Even the sink was smaller than average size. Above the counter were three cupboards, painted lemon yellow, adding to the colorful, whimsical theme that Ellina seemed to favor.

While Jude made note of all the kitchen's features, or lack thereof, what he concentrated on was entries and exits. The lack of a window was good. Not that a preternatural attacker would need a window or a door to enter her place, but he still liked to know where the vulnerable areas were.

And even without an easy outside entry, the kitchen was still not a very safe place. Because it was so confined, Ellina could be easily cornered here. He made a note of that.

The next room was the bath, which was larger than he expected, and with only one window, high on the wall and not big enough for anyone but a child to get through. The bathroom had three doors; the one he'd entered through came from the hallway.

Three doors were good and bad. Easier escape for Ellina, but also easier access for an intruder.

One of the doors stood ajar; he pushed it farther open to find a small bedroom. A double bed took up most of the space, and the lack of personal items on the nightstand and small chest of drawers made him think this was a guest room. The door on the other side of the bed must lead back to the living room.

Behind bathroom door number three had to be Ellina's bedroom.

He turned the knob and slowly pushed it open. It indeed led to her bedroom. The first thing to greet him was a huge, four-poster bed, covered in a fluffy pink comforter like a billow of cotton candy.

She sure did like pastel colors. He wandered to a window on the far wall and fingered the sheer mint green panel that covered the panes.

The room was surprisingly large, and given the smallness of the rest of her place, clearly an addition. It looked newer than the rest of the building, with its modern windows and highly polished hardwood floors.

Another window stood on the same wall, also covered by mint green sheers. The curtains would be opaque enough to stop anyone from seeing clearly inside, but they wouldn't hide Ellina's silhouette as she moved around the room, especially at night.

Jude parted the curtain. Her room backed up to a small rectangular courtyard surrounded by a six-foot privacy fence twined with oleander and jasmine. An easy fence to scale. A small café table and chairs sat to one side of the flagstone patio. A lounge chair was off to the side. He recalled the door to enter the courtyard was in Ellina's office.

That would have to be locked at all times. He made a mental note to tell her.

He turned back to her cotton-candy room. On the other side of her bed, beside the door that led back to her bathroom, was another door. A closet, he suspected.

He hesitated, debating whether he should open the door, then grimaced. This was part of his job. He had to know the layout of a place. The potential hazards, the pitfalls, the places that Ellina needed to be aware about too.

He crossed the room and jerked the door open, the old hinges making a squeaky protest. A warning should anyone hide in there.

The closet wasn't a full walk-in, but it was big enough for someone to hide. Searching for a light, he discovered a piece of blue yarn hanging down from an exposed bulb on the ceiling. He tugged, and the metal chain at the base of the socket scraped against the old porcelain fixture as the closet flooded with light.

The closet must be part of the original structure, he noted.

Jude shifted some of the neatly hung clothes aside, again noting that the hangers scraped on the metal rod. Another warning should someone try to sneak out of there.

The back of the closet was deeper than he first thought.

Definitely room for a full-grown man—or preternatural—to hide, unseen behind the clothing.

He started to drop his hand away from Ellina's garments, when his fingers brushed against something smooth. Soft, silky.

Against his better judgment, he pushed the other clothes back to inspect the scrap of satiny cloth. And scrap was exact. It was a small nightgown, black, smattered with tiny white polka dots. The thin straps clung to the hanger, revealing a neckline that plunged low and was trimmed in black lace.

"Is going through a person's closet how you usually protect your clients?"

Chapter 4

Jude dropped the nightgown, shutting the door with more force than necessary. He turned to find Ellina standing in the center of her bedroom, her jeans and vintage-looking Beatles T-shirt at odds with the frilly room. She crossed her arms tightly over her chest, then tilted her head, waiting.

He wasn't sure if she had seen exactly what he was doing, but she knew he'd been doing something.

"Your closet is a potential vulnerability," he stated, trying to sound as stern and unshaken as he could.

"Why? Are you tempted to cross-dress?"

He ignored her comment, trying to get control of the situation, and to forget that tiny little nightgown, and how it would look clinging to her tall, gently curved body. *Job. She's a job.*

"You do realize someone could hide in your closet."

Her lip curled up at one corner as if she was suppressing laughter—and she was losing.

"You know, I never really thought about it. But I'm pleased you did. Are you planning to guard the closet now?" This time she smiled fully, pleased with her ribbing.

He gritted his teeth, not knowing how to deal with this

woman. Demon. Demon woman. So far she seemed either to be irritated with him or amused by him.

He could handle the first one much better. Smiling really did very distracting things to her mouth.

"I'm here to protect you."

Ellina sighed, tightening her arms across her chest. "Right. And I'm sure with you here, I'll be perfectly safe."

That was the theory. But sometimes that wasn't the case.

"So what is the other job?"

Her question caught him so off guard, he didn't respond.

"You know," she prompted, "the one that's a better fit."

"Weren't you supposed to be working?" he said, realizing his words sounded terse, rude. But he did not want to talk about this.

She surprised him again by smiling wider.

"Yes. Definitely. I just wanted to tell you to help yourself to whatever you can find in the kitchen. I don't have much, but anything you want is yours."

Anything you want is yours.

An image of her in that wisp of silk flashed in his mind. He gritted his teeth for a moment, forcing the tantalizing picture away.

"Thanks," Jude managed, though his voice sounded rough, guttural.

She didn't seem to notice.

"So that job?" she asked again.

God, she was tenacious.

"That's not really something I can discuss." Since there was no other job.

She nodded, but clearly was not dissuaded from topic. "Is that because of client confidentiality, or just because you don't like to explain anything?"

He had to give it to her, she was tenacious, and she didn't beat around the bush.

"It's a matter of client confidentiality," he said. That sounded plausible.

She nodded again, but he could tell that answer didn't satisfy her. He hadn't known her long, but he was already detecting a pattern. Nodding, in her case, didn't mean acceptance.

"I don't just do bodyguard work," he found himself saying in an attempt to beat her to the punch.

"Really?" Her eyes sparked with curiosity, and he regretted his effort. *Great, here come more questions.*

"What else do you do? Besides closet inspections?" She smiled, yet again pleased with her joke.

His eyes fastened on those full, pink lips.

"I do a lot of things," he said, forcing his eyes back to hers. "Basically if you need someone paranormal to deal with something paranormal, then I'm the one for the job."

She tilted her head, considering that. "And this other job, it's not working as a bodyguard?"

"No." He'd leave it at that.

His gaze returned to her lips. They didn't look any less appealing in a contemplative frown.

"So what kind of job is it? I mean, give me a vague idea. You know, without going into specifics. After all, I wouldn't want to overstep the client's privacy."

Like a dog with a bone. He shook his head, his emotions somewhere between annoyance and amusement.

"Somehow I don't think you're that concerned with my client's privacy," he said.

Ellina widened her eyes as if she was offended, then she shrugged. "You're right. I'm not."

A smile tugged at the corner of his lips, the sensation almost foreign to him.

Her pale eyes locked on his mouth, homing in on that slight smile.

Then she stepped back from him, as if she suddenly needed

to put more space between them. And again her line of conversation switched abruptly, which seemed to be commonplace for her.

"You probably should go with the other job. Really. I have friends I can call should anything happen. And I know how to dial 911."

He didn't answer, and she didn't wait for him to do so.

"I've got to go write." With that, she left the room.

Jude had to give it to her—Ellina's departures were as abrupt as her questions and subject changes.

She was right. He should just go, but he couldn't, even though he knew this job was dangerous. And probably not worth any amount of money.

Breathe. Breathe.

This was so bad. Bad, bad, bad.

She hurried into her office. Ignoring her promise to Jude, Ellina shut her French doors, then leaned against them.

Damn it. She was finding her reluctant bodyguard attractive. Extremely attractive. Like heart-racing, skin-tingling, parts of her body growing moist attractive.

Which would be fine, if her physical reaction stopped with the heart-racing, skin-tingling parts of her body growing moist part. But her reaction didn't.

She carefully lifted her shirt, peering down at her bared stomach. Then she jammed the shirt back down and groaned loudly, letting her head fall back against the door. She waited a moment, eyes squeezed shut, then lifted her shirt again.

Red scales replaced the pale skin that usually covered her stomach.

She groaned again.

Men got erections. Some women's nipples hardened. When she became aroused, she got scales, horns, and glowing eyes.

She made a frustrated growl low in her throat and walked

over to the window that looked out at her small, enclosed courtyard. She rested her forehead on the cool glass, breathing slowly, willing away her reaction to him. When that didn't work, she opened the French doors that led outside, letting the winter air waft over her, breathing it deep into her lungs, willing the chill to drive away the heat in her body.

Gradually the low burn faded, taking the scales away with it.

She studied her garden. Her hanging flowers had gone by, the coolness of the winter months withering the colorful blossoms to shriveled brown. But much of the foliage clung to the hints of sunlight, remaining green.

She knew it was not strange or abnormal to find a man attractive. In fact it was very normal. But given what she was, and how her demon side had chosen to manifest itself, crushes, love, and sex had never been a realistic option for her.

Just like the green vines and bushes in her garden clinging to the sunlight, even in winter, Ellina'd once longed for a real relationship. She'd had a seed of hope. But now she thought she'd honestly given up on that idea, especially since she'd never found preternatural creatures attractive. And they were the only ones she could expect to understand and accept her little oddity.

Oh, she could easily see that demons and vampires, even werewolves, were stunning creatures, but it was exactly their physical perfection that turned her off. It wasn't real. It was an illusion, a creation of their supernatural nature.

She much preferred human men. Human men with imperfections. Real smiles with the occasional crooked tooth. Glasses. A few gray hairs. Realistically handsome.

She wasn't perfect—being half demon/half human wasn't even close to perfect, so she didn't feel like she could ever be comfortable with perfection. She wanted normal, average.

But therein lied the trick; she wasn't normal. At all. And

she couldn't have a human man. It would take a pretty extraordinary guy to understand what she was.

Sure, her brother had found a human partner, but he didn't have Ellina's little—issue. Okay, big, big issue.

So she'd accepted that a relationship wasn't going to happen for her. Most men quickly lost interest when they learned sex was off the table. And who could blame them?

She lifted her shirt, and her pale smooth skin had returned. She let out a breath, then closed the doors, blocking out the cold air, turning her back on the bits of garden that clung to the hope of warmth and summer sun.

So why this guy? A man she didn't even want in her house. And she was using the term "man" very loosely, because she didn't even know what he was. But he wasn't human.

Maybe her reaction was due to cutting herself off from everyone. For several years now, she'd kept herself closed off, in the safety of her home, because here she could control her demon side.

Maybe she would be attracted to any man . . . male . . . whatever.

But Jude? Really? First of all, he wasn't exactly warm and fuzzy. He clearly didn't have a great affinity to her. And he was really too uptight.

But it was that smile of his. It had just briefly and very unnervingly hinted at a more human side to the huge, rigid, humorless bodyguard.

Human side. Hmm, that was probably exactly what appealed to her. Aroused her.

All she had to do was remember he wasn't human. He wasn't normal. And she *did not* need any more unusual in her life.

Feeling calmer, she moved around her desk to her computer. With a self-control she had managed to groom over the years, she returned to her book. What was the word for how she had dealt all these years? Sublimation.

She was a pro at sublimating—and she'd deal with this strange little reaction the same way. Redirect her desire into her writing.

So he was attractive. So what?

Jude finished his evaluation of the house, avoiding Ellina's office. He wasn't ready for another run-in with his interesting client. Then he headed back to her lavender and gold living room. Easing down on one of the chairs, he let his tense muscles relax as much as he could.

He wasn't going to be able to do this. If he was smart, and he liked to believe he was, he'd try to find someone else for this job.

But still Jude didn't rise to leave.

Really, how could he? He didn't know anyone to contact, and he wasn't the type to trust someone else to do the job right. And what if something happened . . .

He was stuck.

He leaned back in the chair, resting his hands on either arm. The brocade material was oddly rough and satiny all at once under his fingers, the cushions firm, but comfortable. A weird paradox like the house itself. Like its owner.

He sat still, silent. Just listening. Just taking in the feel of the house.

He could hear Ellina moving. The faint creak as she shifted her chair. The tap of her fingers over her keyboard. Noises that reached him across a distance as if he were drifting off to sleep and they might be real or they might be a dream.

He wondered how he could still recall that somnolent state, that place between reality and slumber, considering he hadn't slept in hundreds of years. Funny the memories that never faded. Even over centuries.

He listened to Ellina's steady rhythm for—well, he didn't really know how long.

Suddenly the even, lulling tempo stopped, but before he could barely register the break, a small, sharp cry broke the sudden silence. Definitely real.

Jude leapt to his feet and was down the hall in one fluid, instantaneous motion. When he reached the office doorway, he saw two men standing in center of the room, their tall frames blocking Ellina from his view.

Both men turned when they heard him at the door, and Jude was struck by the strangeness of their looks. They were identical, except they seemed to be negative exposures of each other. One had black hair, a true black with no hint of any other color in the locks, and the darkest eyes—like bottomless caverns—Jude had ever seen. Both his hair and eyes seemed to eat the light, absorbing it like a black hole.

The other had white hair, pure white like newly fallen snow, and the palest eyes, his irises only a shade or two darker than the whites of his eyes.

Both men had ivory skin and dark red lips the color of de-oxygenated blood.

Clearly not human. And the vibe in the room was not one of affability.

That was all Jude needed to register before bracing himself and inventorying his best plan of attack. The dark one was closest to him, and if Jude went low, he could possibly knock him off center and into the lighter one. That was, of course, if he could still get the element of surprise.

He suspected that aspect was gone.

Judging from their sizes, he'd be okay on sheer strength, even with two of them, but that was assuming they didn't blindside him with some supernatural ability.

Not the best scenario. He wished he had his Benelli. A few large pumpkin-ball slugs with rock salt added for even more pain would slow them down enough for Jude to get the upper hand. But his shotgun was still in his van. He'd been stupid not to bring in his weapons as soon as he'd decided to take the job.

Was he decided then?

Jude frowned.

Not the time to continue that debate, buddy.

From the looks of the strange guys in front of him, he was in the midst of the job. He remained coiled, trying to read their slightest movements, their expressions, and also trying not to be distracted by the strangeness of their looks.

Two he could definitely handle, but not if his attention was being drawn back and forth between them. Damn, their appearances were disconcerting.

But neither man, or rather creature, seemed inclined to move toward him. Instead, in unison, they turned back toward Ellina, who Jude managed to catch a glimpse of between their broad shoulders.

Jude couldn't tell from his position which one of the weird twins spoke, but he heard the words clearly.

"Who's the dude, sis?"

Chapter 5

Ellina glared at her brothers.

"You know I hate it when you just appear like that," she stated, ignoring their question. "Can't you come to the front door like normal people?"

Pasha leaned a hip on her desk, which Ellina noticed brought Jude farther into the room, his gaze shifting back and forth between her brothers, gauging their slightest actions. It was on the tip of her tongue to tell him it was okay. That the odd-looking twosome were her half brothers. But something stopped her.

"We aren't normal," Pasha said drawing her attention back to him. Boredom tinged with condescension filled his nearly white eyes. Not an unfamiliar look from her *loving* brother.

"And we aren't people," Andrey added, moving to browse her bookshelves with the same disparaging demeanor as his twin. Again, nothing new.

Ellina fought the urge to roll her eyes. *Ask a stupid question . . .*

"So who's the guy?" Pasha asked again, gesturing to Jude with a jerk of his white head.

Ellina ignored the question, realizing why she hadn't explained who they were to Jude. Then she'd also have to explain who Jude was, and she had no desire to tell these two that Maksim had hired her a bodyguard. They'd think it was a riot. Their silly half-breed sister who couldn't take care of herself.

But this time, when she didn't answer, Andrey stopped feigning interest in her books and turned directly to Jude, his black stare pinning the other man.

"Maybe you'll tell us who you are, since our baby sister doesn't seem so inclined."

Jude stood rigid, his arms down at his sides, but he still looked poised to strike, and Ellina had no doubt he would, if necessary. That was what he was paid for, after all.

She also had no doubt he'd tell her brothers exactly who he was, and they'd find it all highly amusing.

But before Jude could answer, she piped in.

"He's my boyfriend."

What? *Boyfriend?* Had that really just come out of her mouth?

Wincing, she looked at Jude, expecting to see surprise, irritation, perhaps general disgust on his face. But instead he regarded her evenly, his sea-green eyes unreadable, his features placid, as if she hadn't just said the most outrageous thing ever.

Then his features transformed again—and into another expression she was not expecting. He smiled. A full smile that revealed white teeth and that dimple, deliciously deep, at the side of his beautifully sculpted lips.

Jude offered his hand to Andrey.

Andrey stared at the offered hand, then turned to gape at Ellina. She sensed Pasha's equally stunned look, even as her eyes remained locked on Jude. She was sure her own expression matched theirs.

She waited for him to deny it, even though his smile didn't indicate he planned to contradict her preposterous claim.

"Well, well. A boyfriend." Pasha tilted his head, so his paleness blocked her view of the still smiling Jude.

Not that the image wasn't ingrained on her mind. That smile. Wow. The smile was almost as overwhelming as the craziness of her lie.

Ellina blinked, forcing her attention on her brother. She managed a smile of her own. "Y-yes. A boyfriend."

She glanced around Pasha, questioning Jude silently with her eyes.

Jude moved away from the brothers, coming toward her, nothing in his expression answering her wordless question. In fact, he looked totally serene, as if what she'd said was nothing less than the truth.

He stopped beside her, close enough that she could feel the heat radiating from his large form.

She glanced up at him, and he smiled down at her. God, not the smile again. It was—stunning. Lovely. Sexy. Yeah, they all fit.

She tried to collect her scattered thoughts, centering on his eyes, but they unnerved her just as much. Clearly they were causing her to hallucinate, because she could swear there was actually something akin to possessiveness in their green depths.

Bright green, now, like polished sea glass. A sigh escaped her, and she leaned toward him.

What the hell was she doing? What the hell was Jude doing? How were they going to pull off this stupid lie?

Ellina straightened away from him, determinedly keeping her attention on her brothers' still bemused looks.

"When did this happen?" Andrey said, stepping closer to the other side of the desk. His perceptive gaze had shifted from surprise to suspicion.

Ellina glanced up at Jude. She wasn't sure what to say.

Okay, this was her fib . . . but it wasn't a well-planned one. What did she say? What sounded even remotely believable?

But Jude didn't even miss a beat, flashing another one of those dazzling smiles at her and then at her brothers.

He had to stop that if he expected her to follow along with this tall tale.

"It's been kind of a whirlwind."

Ellina blinked. Oh, he was good; whirlwind would be the most accurate description she could give of their relationship thus far.

"It's really all very new," she added.

Ellina could feel Jude looking at her, but she ignored him.

"Where did you meet?" Pasha asked, raising an eyebrow, the movement appearing nothing more than a shift of shadows, and Ellina could tell he didn't believe this story one iota.

"In the living room," Ellina answered automatically, then tried not wince at the stupidity of her response.

Okay, leave the story to Jude.

"I don't think that's what they meant, darling." Jude shone another smile down at her.

She blinked again.

Mush. Brain mush.

Which was working in her favor—she was so muddled her demon side didn't seem to be threatening an appearance.

"We were introduced through Maksim," Jude said easily, turning his attention back to the twins, which allowed Ellina's mind to function once again.

Both Andrey and Pasha nodded in that eerie unison that they often had. Again, Ellina got the impression they still didn't believe a word. But she didn't think it was her lame response that had them doubting. They were suspicious by nature.

Plus, given Ellina's track record, why would they believe she had a boyfriend? Then again, why would they care?

Because they were meddlers. Troublemakers. Prankster demons.

And they seemed to live to torment their half-sister.

"I've known Maksim for a while," Jude said. "I've been doing some work for him."

Ellina tried not to react to that. Jude was getting pretty darn close to the truth, and she knew her half-brothers would pry.

"Really. What kind of work?"

Jude didn't even hesitate. "I worked on the nursery for him. I'm a carpenter."

Both brothers lifted their heads slightly in acknowledgment like synchronized swimmers surfacing out of the water. But plastered-on smiles weren't part of their act. Doubt still shadowed their eyes as they studied Jude.

So she was surprised when they nodded again and suddenly lost interest in Jude, turning their full attention back to Ellina.

"Have you talked to Father?" Pasha asked.

Ellina frowned, confused by the shift in conversation. Or maybe it was because she was all too aware of each subtle shift of Jude's body standing so close to hers.

"No. Why?"

"Daddy is not pleased with you," Andrey said, toying with the edge of one of her piles of research notes. Ellina reached across the desk and slid the notes away from him. The movement not only protected her valuable, time-intensive research but also created a little distance between herself and Jude.

Her brother raised an eyebrow, but didn't attempt to touch the stack of papers again. Instead he slipped his fingers casually into the front pockets of his jeans.

"Why? What's going on with Dad?" Ellina asked, not really sure if she wanted the explanation in front of Jude or if she even wanted to hear it herself. Her father forever had issues with her.

"He's not pleased with you," Pasha said, his tone smug.

"In fact, he's very angry," Andrey added, his tone matching his twin's.

"About what?" Ellina said, unmoved by their words and their self-satisfied expressions. They really were like naughty children, enjoying every minute of someone else getting into trouble.

"What do you think?" Pasha said, smiling smugly.

Ellina didn't have to think too long or hard about that one. He'd been pretty clear in the past on what he thought of several things in her life. But one in particular really bothered him.

"Is he on another kick about my books?" she asked.

"Oh yeah," Andrey said, a smirk tugging at one side of his lips. His midnight eyes twinkled.

These two did so love meddling, and Ellina would bet money their father hadn't sent the twins here to inform her of this not-so-new news. They'd just taken it upon themselves.

But why? She was well, *well* aware of what their demon daddy dearest thought of her chosen career path.

"Well, I'll take his opinion under advisement," she said, then waited for her brothers to leave. After all, there didn't seem to be any other reason for them to stay.

Both of her brothers just regarded her, tattletale glee still written on their faces.

Finally, when she realized they were content to do this indefinitely, she asked, "So why didn't he come here to tell me in person? Sending lackeys doesn't seem like Dad's style."

She waited for their smug smiles to disappear. The effect was almost instantaneous.

"Lackeys?" Pasha sputtered.

Their self-satisfied smiles transferred to her. She couldn't hold back her grin. She knew that comment would get their goats.

"No need to be so sensitive," she said, her smile widening. She knew it was petty, but she loved using one of their favorite placations back on them. How many times had they told her she was too sensitive about their often cruel little practical jokes? Her comment hardly compared to their open mockery over her half-breed status.

"We are no one's lackeys," Andrey said, his midnight eyes somehow growing even darker, as if his pupils were eating up the light around him.

Ellina knew she should stop, but instead she shrugged. "Sure seems like it to me."

Pasha's anger grew evident too, his pale skin also absorbing that light around them until he practically glowed. Both brothers glared at her, more than mere irritation filling their eyes.

Some of her satisfaction dissolved.

Okay, when would she learn? She should have kept her mouth shut. Not that she'd ever been great at that.

Now her brothers were beyond goaded, they were furious. Even Jude could tell that. His arm brushed against hers, as he positioned himself even closer to her, preparing himself to block her from attack, if necessary. She wasn't sure it wasn't going to be necessary

"How dare you, not even a full demon, say something like that to us?" Pasha said, although his voice no longer sounded exactly human. It was more like a guttural rumble echoing through her office like thunder.

"Have you forgotten who we are?" Andrey asked, his voice taking on the same unnatural quality. "What we are?"

That was a ridiculous question. How could she possibly forget? The demon half of her family never let her forget that she wasn't a real demon, while the human half never let her forget she wasn't a real human either.

But she didn't say that. She'd pushed them too far, and it wouldn't make things better to keep going. She knew the best course of action was to just let them rant and then, with any luck, they would leave.

Unfortunately Jude didn't know the plan.

"Is that some sort of threat?" He moved forward just a bit.

Ellina elbowed him, but the subtle jab didn't seem to register. Instead he continued to scrutinize the two demons, his expression calm, his muscles coiled.

Ellina should have been relieved that her brothers' attention moved from her to her faux boyfriend. But she wasn't. This couldn't turn out well. Not unless she convinced Jude to zip it.

"It's okay, Jude," she said quickly, touching his arm. "Just a little sibling rivalry. Just harmless ribbing, really. Right, guys?"

She turned pleading eyes toward Pasha and Andrey. Her pained, worried expression seemed to please them, because the air shifted, some of their anger ebbing away, like water slowly swirling down a drain.

Well, a clogged drain maybe. And unfortunately Jude wasn't taking her cue.

"Maybe you two should just go," Jude said. "I don't appreciate your veiled threats."

Rage rose up in the air again. And now the drain was totally stopped up. Great. Ahh, if only there was such a thing as emotional Liquid-Plumr.

"You know, I think you should mind your own business," Pasha said, his pale gaze eerier than usual. Iridescent and snapping with anger

"Ellina is my business." Jude stepped away from her, coming around the desk to be on the same side as her brothers.

She followed, again touching his arm.

"Jude, you're really making too much of this. It's all fine. Right, guys?"

She gave her brothers another desperate look. This could be bad. Pasha and Andrey wouldn't fight fair, and really, this situation wasn't worth a brawl. They'd come here to taunt her—for reasons she still didn't comprehend—and she should have let them do it and be done with them.

No good ever came from defending herself with these guys. Not that she ever learned that lesson. She always felt the need to get little digs in whenever she could. Maybe that was proof she was their sibling.

But she'd clearly learned she should just keep her mouth shut, especially with Jude here.

"I can't believe you're threatening a demon," Andrey said almost conversationally, moving around the room, acting as if he was just casually pacing the room as he talked.

More fear crept up Ellina's spine, and she couldn't suppress the shiver that ran through her as her gaze shifted back and forth between Jude and her brothers. Apparently feeling her worried looks, Jude glanced at her, just a quick flick of his eyes toward her, but that was all it took for Andrey to make his move.

He lunged, his attack nearly invisible, a barely there whir of motion. But to her amazement, before her brother's lightning strike could even make contact, Jude threw a hand up, capturing Andrey by the neck.

With only one hand and no sign of exertion, Jude lifted Andrey off the floor until his feet dangled inches above the ground as if he was nothing more than a limp rag doll. Certainly not a tall, leanly muscled demon.

Andrey didn't react immediately, clearly shocked. Then he dematerialized from Jude's grasp like vapor disappearing through his fingers. Her brother reappeared on the other side of the room, his anger still intact, but now her sibling was visibly shaken.

Andrey started to lift a hand to his neck, then caught himself. He wouldn't give Jude the satisfaction of that much reaction.

Ellina glanced to Pasha, who looked equally as wary of Jude, but his pale eyes still snapped and glowed.

"What are you?" he asked Jude.

Jude's expression was calm, almost blank. He didn't answer the question, but he did reply, his voice low and even. "I won't let you hurt Ellina."

Something unfamiliar curled through Ellina's chest. A feeling between relief and something else she couldn't quite pinpoint. Maybe a need to trust this man she barely knew. A longing to have someone to trust.

Pasha's jaw tensed as if he was grinding his teeth. Clearly not the answer he wanted.

"What are you?" he repeated.

This time Jude didn't answer at all.

Pasha and Andrey stared at Jude for several moments, the air in the room almost suffocating. Tension and male aggression seemed to be sucking the oxygen out of the enclosed space.

At least for the sole female.

"You know, I think we've all just gotten off to the wrong start here," Ellina finally said, when it appeared that the men were going to be satisfied to just stare at each other indefinitely in some silent challenge.

It was almost on the tip of her tongue to add, *Can't we all just get along?*

She suppressed one of her inappropriate laughs at the thought of throwing out a "where's the love" sort of platitude. Now that would really piss all of them off, wouldn't it?

"I think you need to leave," Jude finally said, further positioning himself so she was shielded.

"I think you need to rein in your boy toy, Sis," Andrey called to her over Jude's broad shoulder. His eyes narrowed into disturbing black slits.

The laugh she'd already been repressing broke free in a startled burst. Boy toy? Really?

She knew the situation wasn't funny, but boy toy? Could this whole encounter get any more absurd?

From her angle, Ellina couldn't see Jude's expression. But she noticed his muscles seemed to bulge under his skin as if he was itching to attack. Maybe being called a boy toy was a fighting word for him.

For whatever reason, that idea struck her as amusing too. This whole thing was crazy. Bratty brothers, fake boyfriends, the bandying about of terms like *boy toy*. It was all nuts.

And what was the point of these three men hell-bent on this stupid standoff like feral dogs, hackles raised, teeth bared? It was all ridiculous, really.

Ellina giggled, despite herself, and found all three men's attention suddenly riveted on her.

"I'm sorry," she said, which also struck her as amusing. What was she apologizing for? She didn't even understand what was going on. But she did manage to keep her laughter in check. Just barely

Clearly the long writing hours and the new member of her household were pushing her to the edge. She clamped her lips tighter together.

"I'm glad you find this all so amusing," Pasha said.

Andrey raised an unimpressed eyebrow.

Jude just frowned at her as if she'd lost her mind.

As she gazed from face to face, more laughter bubbled up in her.

All this machismo. And for what? Her giggle spilled over, sounding more like a strangled squeak than a laugh.

Of course, she must look quite mad. But it *was* ludicrously funny.

Well, briefly.

Then it wasn't.

Out of the corner of her eye, she caught the vague swish of Andrey lifting his arms in an abrupt upward motion.

And with that simple gesture the room flew into utter chaos. Her many meticulously organized notes swirled into the air, eddying around her office like trash in a windstorm. Books soared off the shelves, hitting the floor and the opposite wall like cracks of thunder.

Ellina screamed, ducking, as a hardback, possibly her first bestseller, nearly hit her in the head. Jude grabbed her arm and half dragged/half threw her behind her desk, pushing her down to her knees.

But even with the barricade of the large desk, Ellina still had to cover her head to protect herself from the papers, pens, paper clips, and all the other odds and ends that had once been on her desk that now whipped around them like office supply projectiles.

A stapler glanced off Jude's shoulder, but rather than falling to the ground it launched back into the air like a self-propelled torpedo. She cried out as several paper clips hit her arms, stinging like bees as they connected with her bare skin.

Jude positioned himself around her like a human cage, blocking further attack, but she could hear the items whacking the desk. The walls. Jude.

"Stop it," she cried.

As if on her command, although she wasn't naïve enough to believe it really was her doing, everything collapsed to the ground with a whooshing thud. The maelstrom vanished completely as if it never happened. The quiet was almost as jarring as the sudden eruption.

Jude didn't move immediately; he stayed crouched over her, his large body protective, his heat warming her fear-chilled skin. And when he did move away, she oddly missed both feelings.

He gestured for her to remain down behind the desk.

After a moment, he said, "They're gone."

Slowly Ellina stood, taking in the mess around her. Her brothers appeared to have left, but they had the last word. As always. Of course, this wasn't the first time she'd seen her office in such overwhelming disarray; it was becoming a pattern.

She stared at her destroyed office, her completely jumbled research notes littering the floor. All her hard work, strewn around, like nothing more than garbage.

She didn't feel like laughing now.

Chapter 6

Jude watched as Ellina stumbled around the desk. She stood in the middle of the room, looking around as if she didn't know what to do first. Finally, she knelt down and began picking up the papers that were strewn everywhere, nearly blotting out the oriental carpet and mahogany-stained wood floor. Her movements were slow, automatic, and her demeanor concerned him.

Jude didn't speak. Instead he joined her, crouching down and gathering up the papers. Pages and pages, some handwritten in small, precise lettering, others computer printouts. None of them were even close to being in order.

They worked silently, until Jude realized she'd stopped and sat amid the papers. He couldn't see her face; her thick, unruly hair falling forward shielded her expression from him. But her slumped shoulders and the collected pages cradled in her lap told him she was distressed.

He continued to clear the floor, casting looks in her direction as he worked. Finally, when she hadn't moved for several moments, he stood and placed the papers he'd gathered on her desk. Carefully, almost reluctantly, he picked his way through the mess to stand next to her.

He stood there, trying to decide what to do, hoping Ellina

would just say she was fine and they could get back to cleaning up this mess. But she didn't. She remained still, her head bowed.

He cleared his throat, feeling more out of his depth than when facing off two bad-tempered demons.

"Ellina?"

She didn't respond. Although he thought he detected her shoulders shaking, just barely.

Damn. What if she was crying? He couldn't deal with crying.

But still he moved closer, dropping to his haunches. She breathed in, the sound a deep, shuddering sigh and the only sign that she might be aware of him. Or crying.

Please, no crying.

Before he even realized what he planned to do, he touched her arm, her skin warm and bare under his fingers. A jolt passed through him; again he was stunned that it was not like the touch of other preternaturals. Not a sticky, distasteful feeling. Quite the opposite, and more unnerving.

He jerked his fingers away from her, and she followed the sharp retreat of his hand, then lifted her head to meet his gaze. Her pale eyes looked flat, hopeless. But no tears.

Jude opened his mouth to ask what was wrong, then hesitated. He could see what was wrong, and what could he say to help her? He didn't know how to offer comfort. Protection, yes, defense, yes. Consolation, no.

And he knew what was wrong. Her brothers were dicks, her office was in a shambles, and she was understandably upset.

Still, he should say something.

Before he could summon up some sort of response, Ellina pulled in a deep breath, straightened, and turned her attention back to the scattered papers.

"This is a real mess," she said, injecting airiness that she clearly didn't feel into her tone. She started back to work.

He watched her for several moments, then joined her. They worked side by side, neither speaking. He focused on the books, placing them back on the shelves. Books that were obviously a source of friction in her family.

So why did she write them? What drove her to continue something that might cause her actual danger—from very dangerous demons?

Finally the floor was cleared, but now her desk looked like a couple dozen books had exploded on top of it.

"Well at least they didn't ruin my computer," she said, her voice filled with feigned optimism. Aside from the keyboard and mouse, the computer hadn't moved.

She booted up her computer, then tested the keyboard and mouse. "Good. Working fine."

She smiled, but he could see her discouragement; her shoulders were slumped as if she had more burden on them than she could possibly handle.

The urge to cross the room and pull her against his chest suddenly and distressingly filled him. Jude remained motionless.

"I'm sorry," he said instead.

Ellina forced another smile that didn't lessen the defeated look in her eyes. "My brothers always like to make my life difficult. And I shouldn't have started anything. I should know better."

Jude didn't think she'd done anything to merit all this, but the twin demons obviously had hair-trigger tempers. He also got the feeling they were willing to do more than make her life difficult; they were dangerous.

But he said nothing. Warnings wouldn't help her right now. She was already overwhelmed.

"Is this research for another book?" he asked, gesturing to the clutter of pages.

Her eyes remained locked on her desk, then she sighed. "Yes. Hours and hours of it. And now it will take me just as long to sort it out."

She sighed again.

Jude couldn't explain why, but he felt helpless. She looked so forlorn. But he wouldn't be any help with sorting through her notes. No more than he would be trying to comfort her. And frankly, he was pretty certain she didn't want either from him anyway.

Still he asked, "Can I do anything?"

She shook her head, just as he knew she would. "No. It's just going to take time to get this all straightened out." She sighed. "A lot of time."

"Okay, well, I'll let you get to work."

She nodded, picking up one of the papers, then dropping it back to the pile as if she didn't have any idea what to do with it or where to start. He lingered a moment longer, his helplessness making him reluctant to leave. He was a man of action. He didn't like this feeling.

Then she began sorting, and he decided it was best to just leave.

Just when he reached the door, she spoke, stopping him. "Why did you go along with my stupid boyfriend explanation?"

Jude closed his eyes for a moment at her question. Why had he gone along with that? He faced her.

"I thought it was a good cover so they wouldn't question too closely who I am or why I'm here."

"Oh, they'll question. They already are. And soon more members of my illustrious family will start asking questions too."

She returned to her papers.

Jude studied her for a moment. Why would her family be so surprised by a boyfriend? Ellina was stunningly lovely. Surely she'd had many male admirers. Maybe she already had a boyfriend, and that was what had her family so shocked. The sudden appearance of a new man in her life.

Which led him to another question . . .

"Why did you say I was your boyfriend?"

Her fingers paused on her papers.

"I—I just didn't want them making fun of the fact Maksim had gotten their silly sister a bodyguard." She made a face. "Stupid, really. Because they'll make fun of me anyway."

Jude wanted to ask if the *they* she was referring to was just her brothers or if this was aimed at her whole family, but she was again focused on her work. Something about her stance, her expression, told him she wasn't in a mood to talk anymore.

And in truth, neither was he. He needed a moment to process what just happened.

Ellina could have chosen anything. Why boyfriend? And how were they going to pull that off believably?

He started to step out of the office when she said, "Sorry for the awkward choice of cover."

Could she read his mind? Her thoughts seemed to follow the same track as his.

"You can't even stand to touch me," she added with a dry, humorless laugh.

Now *that* he hadn't expected. Had she noticed his reaction to her when he'd laid a hand on her arm? Obviously.

It was on the tip of his tongue to tell her that wasn't why he'd pulled away, but then thought better of it. He'd already learned enough about this woman in a few short hours to know she wouldn't accept that answer without further questions. Questions he wasn't prepared to answer or ponder too closely.

"Well, it's our cover now," he said, again wondering why he was sticking with this plan.

"Bad choice," she said without looking at him as she continued to sort through her papers.

He couldn't disagree with that, but not for the same reasons.

This time he did leave her office but paused in the hallway, out of sight, but close enough to hear another of her sighs. Hopeless, tired.

He waited, listening. The creak of her leather office chair as she sat down. The shuffle of papers. A couple more sighs.

Again, he felt that tug, that longing to help her, but he couldn't. She had to concentrate and get her work done and so did he. He needed to keep his mind on the job and figure out what was really going on here. Because something was going on. His gut told him that, and he wasn't often wrong about such things.

But as he made his way to the living room, he kept hearing her parting comment.

Bad choice.

That remark summed up this whole situation, didn't it? Backing up the boyfriend lie. His choice to stay. Pretty much every choice he'd made since meeting this woman.

Demon woman, he reminded himself. Remember she was a preternatural—just because she didn't affect him like other preternaturals wasn't reason enough to lose sight of what she really was.

But now he knew one thing was definite. Leaving was out of the question. Not after the run-in with Ellina's brothers. Jude did not trust the photo negative twins. Not one bit.

Ellina might think they were just troublemakers, pranksters, but he didn't believe that for a minute. They'd come here for a purpose and not just to taunt her. There had been a point to their appearance. They had made it known their father wasn't pleased with her. But why? Was Ellina's father the real threat?

He needed to research the twins and her father. Fighting

demons was always tricky—no two demons had the same strengths and weaknesses.

He exited her house, moving with his usual stealth. The street was quiet, even though it was a fairly warm afternoon. His black van was parked a couple houses down the street. Sun glinted off the darkly tinted windows, making it impossible to see inside the vehicle.

He strode to the rear, disengaging the alarm system with the keyless remote, then unlocking the double doors. The back of the van was set up as a makeshift living space. A mattress took up the side behind the driver's seat; the bed was made up neatly. Several bins were piled up behind the passenger's seat: one filled with clothing and others with dry goods and canned supplies. A couple gallons of water sat beside the plastic tubs.

But it was his computer case and two duffels close to the back doors that he reached for, slinging the computer and one duffel over his shoulder. The other he carried at his side.

He slammed the doors closed, locked them, and engaged the alarm again. He silently reentered Ellina's cottage, again stopping to listen. He also tuned his body into the vibe of the house. Nothing prickled at his skin or caused a creeping sensation along his spine. The house was fine for the moment. But he'd already discovered demons could pop in at the snap of his fingers.

He didn't want to make that mistake again. Getting caught off guard even for a second could be bad news for Ellina . . . and him.

He dropped the duffel bag in his hand next to the sofa. The canvas bag filled with clothes made a muffled thump against the hardwood floor. He was much less cavalier with the other two bags, setting his computer case on the polished coffee table. The other bag he placed carefully to the side of the sofa, out of the way.

He listened again. Concentrated. Ellina was in her office. He could sense her there. And she was fine. He dropped onto the couch and reached for his computer case.

While his computer booted up, he pulled out the file Maksim had faxed him. Jude had already read through the notes, but he scanned them again, focusing his attention on the mentions of Ellina's twin brothers.

Andrey and Pasha.

Maksim stated in his notes that he considered these two capable of being a real threat to Ellina. After that meeting, Jude agreed.

He placed the papers beside his computer and typed in his password. Within moments, he was connected to the Internet. Fortunately Ellina had unsecured wireless. She should have it password protected, but for his purposes now, he was glad she didn't.

He pulled up his favorite search engine, then typed in "demons Pasha Andrey." The search returned almost instantaneously with dozens of results. He'd half-expected to get nothing—suspecting that twins' human names weren't their demon names, which was true.

They were better known as Andras, the demon of quarrels, and Pyro, the demon of falsehoods. But their human names were close enough, making the search easier than he expected.

Jude read through the descriptions of them, making notes. They were primarily, as Ellina had described them, tricksters. Relatively low-level demons deriving most of their powers from causing rifts and misunderstandings and meddling.

But Jude didn't disregard them. Anyone could be dangerous. Anyone could kill—especially demons. More likely, since they were low level, it was possible that they could be working for someone else.

Ellina's father. The twins had mentioned him and said he wasn't happy with his daughter. Were they working on his behalf? Could a father—even one who was a demon—want his daughter dead?

Of course.

Jude had seen far more disturbing things in his two thousand years.

Jude continued to review Maksim's notes and research on the other demons he'd mentioned, including Ellina and Maksim's father, who was a very strong demon. He was not as easy to research. Higher level demons did much better jobs of keeping their identities and abilities unknown. They spread conflicting information themselves, making it hard to know what was fact and what was fiction.

If only they had a snopes.com for demons.

By the time Jude finished his research, the living room was dim with graying shadows. He checked the clock on his computer. A little after seven o'clock.

The house was quiet expect for the occasional faint sound from Ellina's office.

Jude straightened away from his laptop, rotating his shoulders to get the kinks out. Leaning over the coffee table to type wasn't ideal, especially not at his height. Being immortal didn't exclude him from minor aches and pains. There'd been many a fight in his past that had left him hurting afterward, he just didn't hurt as long. And, at least as of yet, he hadn't died.

He stretched again. Ellina must be sore too, hunched over her papers. His stomach rumbled. And she had to be hungry as well.

Dinner. That's something he could do to help her. Cooking would help settle his thoughts and would allow him to work through all the information he'd just found.

He rose and headed down the now dim hallway toward the kitchen. Ellina had turned on a lamp in her office, and muted light filtered out into the hallway from her doorway.

He moved silently, stopping outside the door to check on her.

She sat at her desk, her attention centered on piles of papers. She scanned one, then debated between the multiple stacks, a frown creasing her brow as she considered her next move.

She chose one of the piles and placed the page on top. She looked back to the next page in front of her, her eyes moving from left to right over the words. Her brow was furrowed, and strain pulled at the corners of her mouth. Yet her obvious focus and stress didn't lessen her loveliness.

Jude watched her a moment longer, noticing that she'd pulled her hair back into a messy bun. Her skin glowed buttery gold in the lamplight. She worried her bottom lip as she concentrated on her reading.

Jude's body reacted instantly to the sight. White teeth biting into soft, pink flesh. He stepped slowly away from the doorway as if carefully backing away from something that could lunge at him. Something that could attack.

Attack. That wasn't the threat Ellina presented, but she was a threat.

No. His reaction to her was the threat, but he could control his reactions. Yes, she was a beautiful woman. Yes, he was attracted to her. Any male would be. But he didn't have to respond to that attraction.

Bad choice.

Ellina had unwittingly made a comment that applied to so many things at the moment.

He turned away from the door, away from the light, as if even seeing the warm glow could lure him back like a helpless insect drawn to a hot flame.

Stupid, he told himself. He could control himself. Control had been key to his existence, and he was good at it.

Still he hastened his pace, putting space between them. He paused just outside the darkened kitchen, letting the shadows encompass him as if the darkness could mask his response.

Then he pulled in a deep breath.

Without looking back toward the office, he forced his attention onto what drew him away from his computer. Food. Food always captured his attention easily enough. He flipped on the light inside the doorway of Ellina's miniature kitchen and began perusing her cupboards for dinner staples.

After just a few moments rooting, Jude found dried red beans and rice, and in her mini fridge, he also found chicken breasts. He could make a good meal out of this, and it would allow him to focus on something other than Ellina looking frazzled and lovely.

Food was always a good distraction. Even for other types of hunger.

Was there any hope of getting these notes back into order? Ellina thought, tossing down yet another bit of her research. What a mess.

She hadn't numbered some of the pages. Others were numbered, but with the same numbers as other spells and incantations.

Note to self, number consecutively. Or better yet, keep things in a binder. Had she learned nothing from the break-ins? This was her third time sorting these things out.

And frankly, she was damned tired of it.

With a sigh, she picked up the page in front of her. *Page 2—* and only one of six others she had piled in front of her. What spells did this one go with? Which pages 1 and 3 did it go between? She didn't know—some of this research she'd done months ago and she just couldn't recall the sequence of the spells.

It was frustrating, exhausting, and making her tense. Having a sister-in-law in labor, brothers angry at her, undoubtedly an impending visit from her father ahead of her, and a stranger posing as her boyfriend in her house wasn't helping her tension.

Ellina pushed her chair away from her desk and stretched, reaching her arms over her head and up toward the ceiling, telling herself to just focus on the task at hand.

A noise, metal against metal, paused her stretch. She listened again, now hearing a faint movement in another part of the cottage.

Then she realized a smell filled the room. An appetizing scent that made her stomach growl in a loud appeal. She dropped a hand to her complaining belly and frowned toward the door.

What was the smell? It was wonderful.

She stood, following the scent out of her office toward the kitchen.

Food, she realized. The smell of cooking food, emanating from her kitchen. Now that was a novel idea.

When Ellina reached her kitchen, she was surprised again. Jude stood at the counter, his large frame taking up most of the width of the galley-style room. His back was to her, and she could see the subtle roll of his muscles under his T-shirt as he stirred something.

Leaning on the door frame, she didn't speak, just watched him work. He finished mixing whatever was on the stove, then turned to the counter, quickly and precisely chopping what looked like garlic.

Garlic? Where did he get that? Did she even have garlic? Without seeming aware of her watching, he returned to the stove, adding the possible garlic to something sizzling in a pan.

"It's almost ready," he said, and for a moment she wasn't even sure he was talking to her. But when she didn't respond, he glanced at her over his shoulder.

"I hope you like Cajun."

Ellina nodded, still bemused by the sight of this huge guy, a paid bodyguard, doing something as domestic as cooking.

"I love it," she said.

He turned back to the sizzling pan. Ellina watched him a moment longer, then snapped out of her amazement to ask, "Can I help? I should warn you, I'm a disaster in the kitchen, but I could probably chop or stir something."

He immediately shook his head. "I'm fine here. I opened some wine."

He gestured to the counter. A bottle of Riesling sat on the counter with two wineglasses already waiting.

"Pour yourself a glass and go relax. I've got things under control here."

Something about the way he said the last bit, tightly, as if he had his teeth gritted together, caught her attention, but when he gestured again to the wine, she couldn't see anything in his expression to back that impression. He looked utterly composed.

She glanced at the wine. "That does sound good."

She poured herself a glass, then raised the other one toward him. "Want some?"

Jude nodded, his eyes staying on her for just a moment before he turned back to his cooking. This time, Ellina did see a change in his expression. A sort of longing.

And she wasn't sure it was for the wine.

She poured him a glass, then crossed the tiny space to place it on the counter next to him.

"Here you go."

He reached for the glass, their fingers touching for just a fraction of a second, a mere brush of skin, barely there. But totally there.

So totally there. She could feel the tiny contact throughout her body. She could feel the budding of arousal simmering up in her belly, spreading. But before she could pull away, afraid of her body's reaction, he snatched his hand away, sloshing wine on himself in the process. He shifted away from her as much as the confining quarters would allow.

He didn't like her touch.

She'd sensed that before, but now it was almost ridiculously apparent.

She stepped back too, forcing a smile. "Thanks for all this." She waved a hand at the stove and the wineglass clenched in her other hand.

He nodded, this time not quite meeting her eyes.

She nodded too as she exited the stifling small kitchen.

As she walked almost aimlessly toward the living room, she wondered what it was about her touch that bothered him so. And why it upset her so much that he was bothered.

She should feel relief. It wasn't like touching was an option for her. Not really.

Chapter 7

Jude took a deep breath as soon as Ellina left the kitchen. Then he took a gulp of his wine, nearly emptying his glass.

How could her touch affect him so? And why couldn't the reaction be like the one he had to every other paranormal creature? Wow, he never thought he'd wish for that. Why was it different? Why did he want more of it? Even now he craved her fingers moving against his skin.

He polished off the rest of his wine, then moved to refill the glass. The wine wouldn't impact his senses, at least not his reaction time to intruders or other threats, but he prayed it would calm him a little. His body tightened with hypersensitivity. His skin sizzled with awareness, ready to explode.

He downed that glass, then pulled in another deep breath. *Control. Control.*

He turned his attention back to his cooking. The chicken was nearly done. And the rice and beans simmered nicely. He breathed in again. The wine did seem to be helping. He turned to the rather peaked-looking lettuce he'd found in the fridge, wondering if he could salvage enough for a salad.

See, he could focus, he told himself as he put the lettuce in a bowl and filled it with cold water. He then moved back to the stove to turn the chicken one last time before lowering the heat.

"Sorry."

At the sound of the voice directly behind him, Jude spun, jutting the spatula out in front of him like a weapon.

Ellina jumped back, gaping first at him, then the spatula, then back to him.

He opened his mouth to apologize for his jumpy response, but before he could say a word, she started to giggle. Her laughter filled the room like a measure of joyous music.

She made a small noise, trying to suppress her laugh, then managed, "Sorry. I just wanted to steal a little more wine. I wasn't prepared for your kitchen utensil kung fu."

Another giggle sneaked past her lips.

He glanced at the spatula still held out in front of him, then placed it on the counter.

"You . . ." He frowned. "You caught me off guard."

She shot him a quick smile as she filled her glass, and he could see she was still struggling to keep her amusement in check. "I'm sorry. I didn't mean to sneak up on you."

His frown deepened.

She tried to sober even more and added, "Please forgive the laughter. I have this terrible habit of finding the most inappropriate things funny. It's always been a problem."

When he didn't respond, she clearly mistook his silence for annoyance, because she quickly finished filling her glass and excused herself again.

Jude still didn't speak as she disappeared out of the room, looking decidedly uncomfortable, probably with both their reactions. But he couldn't stop her, couldn't reassure her that his silence wasn't annoyance, but rather shock.

No one could sneak up on him like that. *No one.* Not even stronger and older paranormals. So how the hell could one little half demon? And she'd actually startled him. Unheard of.

What was going on? He hadn't even been in this woman's presence twenty-four hours and she'd managed to unnerve him more than anyone in years, decades . . . hell, centuries.

He glanced at the nearly empty bottle of wine. Maybe it was the wine. Maybe it had more effect than he realized. Not that two glasses of any alcohol should affect him so. It never had before. And the wine certainly wasn't the cause of the sensations that radiated through his body when they touched.

He grimaced, frustrated that his body—the one thing he'd always been able to trust—seemed to be betraying him.

Then something reached him . . . a scent.

He turned, realizing the smell was the chicken. Burning.

"Shit," he muttered, yanking the frying pan off the lit burner.

Well, his body hadn't failed him on this minor disaster, but then again, he didn't need to keep Ellina safe from scorched poultry, now did he?

Ellina winced as she heard Jude's muttered curse and the clatter of pans. She shouldn't have laughed, but she really did have a hard time controlling her inappropriate giggles. And the way he'd whipped around and waved that spatula had startled her, then struck her as funny.

She giggled again at the memory. He'd looked as surprised as she was. She certainly seemed to make the man uncomfortable.

But as soon as that thought reappeared in her mind, her amusement was gone. She took a sip of her wine and collapsed into one of her living room chairs

Why was she even worrying about his unease with her? Wasn't that simpler for both of them? He didn't appear to like her much, and she got the sneaking suspicion she could like him too much. Well, be too attracted. She had no idea if she'd actually like anything about him aside for his looks, which she really did like.

She closed her eyes for a moment, telling herself she had to let her attraction go. Get a grip on her much-neglected libido.

And really, leave it to her to be attracted to someone who was clearly not attracted to her. Revolted would be a better word, really.

Shaking her head, she opened her eyes and took another sip of her wine. Over the rim of her glass, her gaze landed on all the items set up on her coffee table. His stuff.

A new looking laptop computer was open with a notebook, also open, beside it. A duffel bag sat on the floor beside the sofa.

Somehow seeing those items made her decision to just get over her attraction seem all the more daunting. Why should a canvas bag and a computer cause something akin to panic to swell up in her chest?

Because he was staying. Here—with her. And possibly for a while. Could she get really get a handle on her attraction with him living here?

Posing as her boyfriend of all things.

Ellina dropped her head onto the back of the chair. How was she going to do this? Focus on other things.

She opened her eyes, her gaze landing back on his stuff, specifically the open notebook. She straightened up, leaning forward, and although she could see small writing in blue ink, she couldn't make out any specific words.

Should she sneak a peek? His notes—probably related to her—were a distraction from him, right?

No. She wasn't comfortable with looking at his personal things—not without asking him first.

But she didn't lean back in her chair; instead she scooted a little closer to the coffee table. Maybe just a little look. After all, he had gone through her closet. Her whole house, she suspected. And without a doubt, these notes were about her case. Was that what she was? A case?

She glanced toward the door leading down the hallway . . . toward the kitchen.

She could hear him still in there, getting down plates from the cupboards. The clatter of utensils being taken out of the silverware drawer. Her attention returned to his notes.

Really, shouldn't she know what he knew about her? Maybe who he considered as a threat to her?

A threat to her.

She shook her head and leaned back in her chair. She was a case all right. A head case.

Was she actually starting to buy into Maksim's suspicions that someone really wanted to hurt her?

"Here you go."

This time it was Ellina's turn to jump. Clapping a hand to her chest, she shifted to find Jude beside her chair, a plate in one hand and the bottle of wine in the other.

She could tell by the slight rise of one of his eyebrows that he'd noticed the direction of her attention. His own eyes flicked to the coffee table and his notes, but he didn't reveal whether he was bothered by her interest in his stuff.

She dropped her hand and tried to look calm. Her voice was even steady as she said, "Wow, this looks amazing."

He didn't speak as she accepted the plate, so she couldn't tell if he was annoyed with her obvious interest in his work. He moved to the end table and refilled her wineglass, still saying nothing.

Although it shouldn't have, his lack of response unnerved her, and before she even realized what she planned to say, she blurted out, "I wasn't going to look at your stuff without asking you. I mean, I did consider it, but I wouldn't have."

He nodded, his expression unreadable.

Man, she hadn't known him long, but she already knew she hated that about him.

There. There, that was one part of him, outside of the

physical, that she could quite decisively say she didn't like—since she had considered the fact that she likely wouldn't care for him, if she really knew him.

And his inscrutability was definitely something that took away from his overall attractiveness. Well, a little. Actually, she thought grudgingly, in a weird way it sort of added to his dark good looks too, which was odd, because she'd never considered herself a woman who liked the aloof, brooding type.

Ellina stopped her mental debate when she realized he was leaving the room.

"Are you coming right back?"

She winced at the needy tone of her question. Where had that come from? Why had she even asked?

Jude paused, turning slowly to look at her.

"Why? Are you afraid you won't be able to resist?"

She blinked. Huh? Was he somehow reading her thoughts? Could he actually read minds? She knew some paranormal beings could. Great, had he been tuning into her private thoughts all day like some listener tuned into a gossipy talk show?

"Well—I—I mean," she sputtered, her previously "tell-all" mind going blank.

"Feel free to look."

She blinked again. What? But as if of their own free will, her eyes did roam down his tall, strong body. She did like looking at him, but how did that tie into what she'd been thinking?

Maybe it was his way of saying that was all she was going to be able to do with him. Just look.

"After all, all of it is about you. So you have the right to look away."

She frowned. Okay, she was lost. It was about her?

Then he actually smiled. The curve of his lips and that deep dimple transformed him from handsome to stunning.

"Seriously, look away."

Ellina blinked, then Jude gestured toward the coffee table with a jerk of his head.

"I think it would be good if you looked all the information over."

Oh. Right. He was talking about his notes. She could actually feel the heat of embarrassment creeping up her cheeks. Of course he was talking about that.

She nodded, the bob of her head a little too rapid, too eager. "Thanks. Maybe I will."

Jude's smile faded and his eyebrows drew together as if he was confused by her reaction, but he didn't say anything. Instead he headed back to the kitchen.

Ellina fell against the cushions of her chair. What a fool. How had her mind gone somewhere so completely wrong?

Get a grip, girl.

Still embarrassed, she remembered the plate she held. It looked and smelled delicious, and she needed a distraction from her own ludicrous train of thought. To actually think he'd been referring to himself.

A small laugh escaped her. Wow, it's moments like this when she knew she was meant to be a writer. Talk about an overactive imagination. She glanced at the notes, debating them as a distraction, but somehow looking at Jude's notes seemed a little too personal at the moment.

And, frankly, the food was already grabbing her attention. The presentation was that of a five-star restaurant. Not at all what she'd have expected from a bodyguard. She breathed in appreciatively. Scooping up a bit on the end of her fork, she tested it.

Scrumptious.

As she chewed, her eyes closed in pleasure. Wonderful. The spices, the way the rice and beans were cooked. Not too mushy, soft yet firm. Perfection. In fact it was better than most restaurant versions of the famous Southern dish.

She took another bite and another.

"Looks like you are enjoying it."

Ellina paused, the fork halfway to her lips. She looked down at her plate. It was well over half empty.

Sheepishly, she smiled. "It's so delicious, once I started, I couldn't stop. You are an excellent cook. I never would have guessed."

She took another bite, this time chewing slower, savoring the spicy favor. She was so lost in her enjoyment, she didn't immediately realize that Jude still stood in the center of the room, holding his heaping plate of food in one hand and a large glass of milk in the other.

She set down her fork on the plate. "Is everything okay?"

"Why wouldn't you guess I would be a good cook?"

Her frown deepened. That seemed like an odd question. She certainly hadn't meant it as a slight. Yet he looked almost . . . wounded?

"I'm sorry," she said, "I guess that was a presumptuous thing to say. I mean, I don't even know you."

He shrugged as if the answer didn't really matter.

Of course, if the answer didn't matter, then why ask the question?

But she didn't question him further, because he settled into the chair on the other side of the living room and began eating with a resolution that excluded any interest in her.

They both ate in silence for several minutes until Ellina found the dead air between them stifling.

"So are you from this area?"

Jude looked up, his expression almost startled, as if he'd

forgotten she was there. So much for him feeling the uncomfortable silence between them.

"No. Not originally. I've lived all over."

She nodded. "That must be interesting."

He nodded, not offering any more than that. That didn't dissuade her.

"I know you didn't seem too interested in answering this question when my brothers asked, but what are you? I mean, what kind of paranormal are you?"

He glanced at her, then took another bite of his chicken, chewing slowly, using his fork to toy with the rice and beans.

Just when she was sure he wasn't going to answer, he swallowed and said quietly, "I'm a mutt."

"A mutt?"

"I'm not just one thing."

Ellina considered that.

"Explain."

He looked dreadfully close to rolling his eyes. But he caught himself.

She smiled. Was it wrong to find his exasperation amusing?

He didn't speak again for a moment, then said in a rushed, almost uncomfortable way, "I'm half vampire/half werewolf."

"Really?"

God, he hated that question. And more than that question, Jude hated the reaction that followed. Ellina was fascinated and shocked like he was a freak on display in a traveling circus.

"How'd you become both vampire and werewolf?"

And even more than the reaction, he hated the inevitable flurry of *more* questions that followed that.

"It was a bit of an accident."

That was his standard response. And an utter lie. He'd planned to become what he was. He'd sought to become a freak. No, he'd wanted to be an unstoppable killing machine. Freak was just an unavoidable derivative of that.

"So how can you be out in the sunlight? Does the werewolf side somehow offset the vampire side?"

At least she hadn't gone to that horrible question yet. The why question. He wouldn't answer that one. He wasn't going to tell this woman—or anyone—what a selfish ass he'd been.

"Yes," he answered. "Although sunlight does bother my eyes, and I will burn badly if not protected."

"And clearly"—she glanced at his plate—"you don't have to live solely on blood."

He'd almost finished his mound of food, and he'd probably get another helping.

"Yeah, I've got the werewolf appetite, although I do like my steak very, very rare."

She smiled, but he could see her mind was still going, and more questions would follow, of course.

"And what about full moons?"

"I don't get claws and fangs and pointy ears, if that's what you mean."

"So you get nothing from your werewolf side? Aside from the eating habits?"

He hesitated. Damn, he felt dumb admitting this, but he knew she'd keep pressuring if he didn't give her something, and he wasn't telling her about some of the other side effects. One in particular, she'd never know about.

"My hair gets longer."

She blinked, then laughed. "Your hair gets longer? Just on your head? Or all over?"

He gritted his teeth. This was way too much sharing for him. "Mostly just on my head."

She laughed again, clearly pleased with this new side of

him. "Hmm, are we close to a full moon now? Does that explain the shaggy hair?"

"Yes." They were less than a week away. He was always aware of the phases of the moon. Since meeting Ellina, he was very aware.

She giggled again.

"I'm glad you find my oddities so amusing," Jude muttered roughly.

"They are fascinating."

"Is that so? And what about your oddities?" he asked, wanting her line of questioning of him. "What sort of quirks does a half human/half demon have?"

Her smile faded.

"None that are interesting."

She busied herself with her meal, fastidiously loading up her fork. Then she dropped the fork on her plate and rose.

"You know, I think I'll go give Maksim a call and check on Jo. Dinner was delicious. Thank you."

She hurried out of the room before Jude could even respond.

He filled his fork and took another bite of his food, watching the empty doorway. It seemed that both he and his client had some interesting traits of their preternatural nature. Traits that neither wanted to talk about.

He definitely found that interesting. Very interesting.

Chapter 8

Well, that would teach her to keep her damned nosiness to herself. Ellina should have guessed that they'd get back around to her and her demon side. Her bizarre, embarrassing demon side.

She should just learn to keep her mouth shut. She'd get into a lot less trouble that way.

Hastening her steps, she placed her dirty dishes in the sink and headed to her office. She did not want to get cornered in that small kitchen and asked more questions about her freakish quirks. One freakish quirk. A big one.

Disregarding Jude's request, she closed her office doors. Albeit quietly. She did not want him to hear and come to reprimand her. She needed some time to gather herself.

What would he think if she'd revealed her strange little secret?

Oh, my oddity? Well, it's nothing, really. I just happen to turn into a full-fledged, red, horned, scaly demon when I'm turned on. Yep, forked tongue, tail, and all. No biggie.

Yeah, right.

He was paranormal too, but somehow she didn't think he'd encountered anything like that before. That was too much information of the highest order.

Damn, she wished she remembered to grab her wineglass when she'd dashed out of the living room. She could really use a little more liquid courage. Or, in this case, liquid calm.

She glanced at the door and didn't see any shift in the shadows in the hallway. Not that that meant anything. She hadn't been aware of him standing in the hallway earlier.

Since she'd claimed her quick exit had to do with calling Maksim, she supposed that was what she should do. It had been hours. And while she knew labor could take a long time, she was worried. She'd expected Maksim to call when they got to the hospital just to let her know they were there safely.

She opened the top drawer of her desk, thankful that when Andrey pulled his little insta-tornado act, her cell phone had been in her desk where she often kept it.

She scrolled through her phone book to Maksim's name and pressed the button to dial him. As the phone rang, Ellina fought to get her mind off Jude's question.

He wouldn't pursue it further. He wasn't a "sharing" kind of guy. Of course, that probably meant she couldn't ask anything more about him either.

That was disappointing.

She frowned at her train of thought. Blast her and her nosiness. Why did she need to know anything more about him anyway?

Let it lie, Ellina Barrett Kostova.

Just then, Maksim's voice sounded on the other end of the line, snapping her out of her mental conversation with herself.

"Maksim?"

"I'm not available. So leave a message . . . or don't."

Ellina rolled her eyes at herself. His voice mail. She was trying to converse with her brother's voice mail. She really did need to calm down.

"Hey there," she said after the beep. "I just wanted to see if there was any news about my new niece or nephew. But since you're not picking up . . ."

Ellina paused as she saw a shift of shadows from the corner of her eye that seemed to change the whole feeling of the room. She glanced toward the French doors leading to the hallway, then the doors leading to the courtyard.

She sensed something. That odd, vague feeling of being watched. Funny how something so intangible could feel so real.

Still eyeing the doors, she remembered she was leaving a message for her brother. "Sorry Maksim . . . um . . . since you aren't picking up . . ."

That watched feeling intensified, prickling the back of her neck.

Jude? Or someone else?

She rose carefully, making sure her office chair didn't make any noise, then carefully stepped across the room. "I'm assuming you're a busy guy."

She peered at the office door, still trying to see any subtle movement of shadows through the small rectangular panes. "I hope things are going well. Call me."

She gently placed a hand on the handle. Holding her breath, she jerked the door open and rushed into the hallway, only to see Jude's backside disappearing into the kitchen.

It had been him. He had been there. Watching.

A loud beep echoed in her ear, making her jump. Then she realized she still held her cell phone to her ear, and apparently Maksim's cell got impatient with her inattention and broken message.

She hung up, then paused, still watching for the change of shadows from the kitchen doorway as Jude worked. Her heart thumped a rapid tattoo against her rib cage.

Why was she scared? So unsettled? She should have known it was Jude skulking around, checking on her.

But that realization didn't calm her, it angered her.

Ellina stormed to the kitchen.

"I really don't appreciate you lurking around," she stated to his broad back.

Jude turned around from the sink, a sponge and plate in his hand. "I don't lurk . . ."

"I know, I know. You guard. Well, don't do it like that. If you are going to check on me, just come to the door. I mean, how am I going to work with you creeping around? And you knew I was going to make a phone call."

He set down the item he was washing and reached for a dry dish towel on the counter. Wiping his hands, he regarded her, unruffled by her sudden tirade.

"I mean it," she said, feeling the need to repeat herself even though he gave every indication that he heard her and understood.

"Okay," he said, his tone calm, even.

And it managed to steal the air right out of her outburst. She frowned, feeling foolish, debating what she should do now. Now that, yet again, she'd reacted rather than staying composed. Like him.

"I'm sorry," she murmured. "I just had this feeling of being—watched and—"

"It scared you."

She didn't want to admit that was the truth of it. She'd already told him over and over today that she thought Maksim's decision to have him here was ridiculous. That she didn't need anyone here. Yet a nebulous, undefined sensation had her acting like a frightened, little ninny.

"I-I should get back to work."

Jude didn't try to stop her, but something in his eyes kept her from moving away.

"I'm sorry." He spoke in that same soothing tone. Ellina felt herself relax. "I'm here to make you feel safer, not scare you."

She didn't know what to say about that. She didn't even understand why she'd gotten spooked. But she couldn't deny she found having him close and so controlled eased her.

"Want to stay and help me?" He gestured to the dishes.

She nodded. She did want to stay with him. Just until her overactive imagination was in check. She entered the kitchen, again reminded of how tiny this room was with his large body taking up a goodly portion of it. But this time she felt no desire to put space between them.

"You wash? I dry?"

"Sounds good." He picked up the sponge and started right in.

Ellina reached into the drawer and pulled out a dish towel and waited.

He should be laughing, watching Ellina from the courtyard. Tiptoeing across her office, nervous as a helpless, little mouse, casting wide-eyed looks around her. She even peered toward the courtyard windows. But she couldn't see him, hidden in the shadows.

She'd sensed him, but he wasn't worried. Her awareness wasn't much of an accomplishment. The little nitwit could only sense exactly what a perceptive human could. The same as him.

Humorous, really.

But he wasn't laughing.

There was a guy staying with her. When he'd first seen the large man enter her house, he'd just assumed he was there to do some work for her. A repairman. Something mundane— and temporary—like that.

But the guy hadn't left all day. Then he'd had brought in a couple bags. Bags that didn't appear to contain tools or other work supplies. Bags that looked very much like he was planning to stay for a while.

Who was he?

Whoever he was, the dude was certainly fucking up his plans. Plans he'd so carefully laid out. Plans he'd intended to carry out tonight. Now he'd have to wait—yet longer.

He moved carefully, clinging to the shadows, then using thick vines to lever himself up and over the fence.

He glanced up and down the side alley. No one was around to see him. He started toward the street, walking as if he was doing nothing more than taking an evening stroll.

Patience. He had to remain patient. So now there was another factor. He'd figure out a way around it. The guy couldn't stay near her forever.

He turned right out of the alley, heading toward a small bar a block or so away.

Nothing would stop his plan.

Ellina Kostova would be dead. And soon.

"So how did you learn to cook?"

Jude didn't look at Ellina as he rinsed out a pan.

"I like to eat. And I tend to have a large appetite. So it made sense to learn to cook."

"Well, you are good at it. If you ever decide to give up your current line of work, you could probably make a great living as a chef."

She shot him a teasing smile, but he didn't manage one in return.

If he ever got out of his current line of work . . . She had no idea how close her comment came to his hopes.

"How did you get into this business anyway? You know, protecting paranormals from paranormals?"

He scrubbed at some cooked on chicken. "I just sort of fell into it."

She nodded, accepting his explanation readily enough.

"Because of what you are? Being vampire and werewolf

must make you very strong. And you must have amazing—senses."

"Yes." That's why he'd become what he was. To be the strongest, the most wily. Invincible.

Ellina finished drying the plate she held, then turned away from him. Jude slipped a look at her as she stretched up to place the dish in the cupboard. Her T-shirt pulled away from her jeans, giving him a glimpse of her slender back. And the jeans tugged against her perfectly rounded ass as if some invisible hands were molding to her. He'd known he'd been right about that ass. Perfect.

He imagined his hands there, shaping to her, moving slowly up to slide under her top.

The pan slipped from his hands, clattering against the stainless-steel sink.

Ellina smiled over her shoulder. "Soapy fingers?"

His eyes snapped up to meet hers.

"Yeah," he managed, although his voice sounded low and rough with hunger. Even to his own ears. He certainly wasn't feeling invincible at the moment.

But she was oblivious to his reaction. She turned back to the dish drainer and began wiping the flatware, placing it in a drawer beside the sink. That task brought her closer to him.

He could feel her energy snapping toward him, so strong that he was surprised the air didn't crack with static electricity. And while shocking, the vibe he was receiving wasn't uncomfortable like an electric jolt.

Well, only a little bit uncomfortable, he corrected, shifting slightly to accommodate the erection that pressed like a lightning rod against the unforgiving material of his jeans.

"So what are your notes about?"

"What?" He was so lost in his body's reaction to a mere glimpse of skin that he didn't follow her new direction in conversation.

"Your notes? What are you researching? Me?"

At the moment, more than she knew.

"Yeah. No. Sort of." How could he be so damned muddled? "I've been researching your—family."

Ellina made a noise that indicated she wasn't too pleased with that information, even if she wasn't surprised. She moved slightly, reaching for another recently washed spoon. Her shoulder brushed again his. His cock leapt as if it took the unintentional touch as a green light.

"And what are you thinking about them?"

He cleared his throat, trying to gather his thoughts into something remotely comprehensible. He placed the pan he'd been washing in the drainer, then leaned a hip against the counter, giving himself a little room away from her.

This was good. Focus on your reason for being here.

He watched her as she sorted the forks and spoons in the proper compartments.

Control, buddy. Control.

When he didn't answer, she paused, looking at him questioningly.

"You have an interesting family," he said.

She laughed slightly, even though he wouldn't describe the sound as truly amused.

"You can say that again."

She continued to sort. But something in her expression pulled his thoughts away from lust. Toward another emotion. And not one that made him all that more comfortable.

"Are you sure you want to talk about this tonight?"

She'd been nervous earlier, and while she seemed to have calmed down now, he didn't think his opinions on her family would do much to keep her in that state.

She frowned. "Sure. I think we probably should talk about it. It's why you are here, right?"

He nodded, partially in response to her and partially in reminder to himself. The job was why he was here. Protecting her was why he was here.

Not to lust after her.

"So what do you think about my family?" Ellina asked again, still not looking at him.

Jude regarded her a moment longer, then said, "I think that there are several members who could want . . ."

She stopped putting away utensils and met his gaze, her pale eyes widened, prompting him silently to answer. There was an innocence to those eyes somewhere between the lightest blue and the faintest gray.

"Want what?"

He gritted his teeth. He wished he didn't feel this way. But he did. And she needed to know.

"Want to kill you."

Chapter 9

Jude should have known his ominous words wouldn't get the response from this woman that he would expect. He'd been worried his opinion would put her on edge again.

Instead she laughed.

"I know this is your job, and you have to look for the worst, but I don't believe anyone in my family wants to kill me. Maybe give me a good shake every now and then. But kill? Nah."

Jude studied her, trying to decide how this woman, a writer, a preternatural—or at least half preternatural—who should be very perceptive, could be this oblivious. This unaware.

"But do they really consider you one of their own?"

Jude instantly regretted his blunt words. Ellina actually blanched, her skin whitening to the point that her eyes look huge as she stared at him.

"I just," she shook her head, "I just can't believe that."

Admittedly, he wasn't absolutely convinced either. But he did think she had to consider everyone. Even family. Maksim had made interesting observations about many of them. Ellina had rubbed several demons the wrong way, and mostly with her books.

The books essentially outed the demon world. Most of the demon world wouldn't appreciate that from a full demon, but from a half demon, that could be a real problem.

"Given what you write," he said, keeping his tone low, calm, "you certainly know how dangerous demons can be. And they cannot be happy with you exposing their secrets. Their weaknesses. Their strengths for that matter."

She laughed again. "I write fiction. Fantasy. I'm not exposing anything."

He crossed his arms over his chest. "That isn't what your brother led me to believe. When we talked, he said you use real spells in your books. Real incantations."

Her amusement faded into a frown. "I do. But these are fictional books. None of my readers would even consider that they could be real."

"Are you sure?"

"Well . . . no," she admitted, her frown deepening, more with consternation than irritation. "But the stories are so clearly fantasy."

"Your family knows that not all of it is fiction, don't they? And maybe other demons have figured it out too. Maybe humans, as well."

He watched the emotions at war on her face. She really had never considered the fact that someone human or inhuman might have discovered the facts scattered within her fiction.

"Why do you think your father doesn't approve of your books?" he asked.

Ellina blinked. "I know he doesn't like the ongoing storyline of a love affair between a demon and a human woman. I thought that he felt that was a little too close to home for him. You know, sort of writing the story of him and my mother, which did not turn out well."

Jude considered that. If that were the case, it didn't seem

likely her father would want her dead for being a little too candid about his romances.

"Maybe that is all it is. Or maybe it's more. And we have to assume it is something more."

"My father wouldn't hurt me," she said, her tone adamant, even though her expression was less resolute.

"But I think you really need to start taking the break-ins and the other incidents seriously."

Her gaze was distant and he wasn't sure if she was even listening to him. He knew she didn't want to hear any of this, but he had to discuss the possibilities with her. She *had* to start being cautious.

"I know you don't want to hear this," he said, wishing he didn't have to upset her so.

She came back from wherever her thoughts had been and met his gaze. "Did Maksim suggest all these possibilities?"

"Yes."

"Even the human risk?"

"He mentioned it. And I think we should consider it. You do have lots and lots of fans. And fans can be fanatical. Although I realize that a fanatical human doesn't explain how you ended up in a cat."

She nodded, looking distracted again.

Did she know something she wasn't telling?

"Ellina—"

Her eyes met his, but her gaze looked stricken, almost haunted.

"I need to get back to work."

She tossed the damp dishcloth she still held limply in her hand onto the counter, and moved around him, twisting her body to avoid contact as she passed.

She was doing it again. Jude had, even in this short time, learned one thing. Ellina ran away. When things got too much, she made a break for it and hid in her work. In a world of her own creation.

He understood that. Wasn't that all he wanted? To run and hide?

He caught her wrist.

"Ellina, wait. I know it's a lot to comprehend. And it's scary. But I'm here to help you."

Ellina's gaze locked on Jude's long fingers wrapped around her narrow wrist, his grasp gentle, his skin callused. Her breath caught at the intoxicating contrast, and her desperate, distraught thoughts faded.

His thumb brushed over the sensitive space on the inside of her wrist, just below her palm. She shivered.

Jude frowned, mistaking her tremble for more fear.

"We'll figure out what's going on here," he assured her, his voice low and husky. Velvety and rough. Another delicious paradox.

His thumb still stroked her, and the tiny caress seemed to reach deep inside her. Desire swelled and pooled, drifting lower and lower.

Desperation of a different kind filled her.

She tugged her arm away, panic making the action abrupt, anxious. She backed away from him.

"I-I know everything will be okay," Ellina said, the words rapid and tumbling over each other. "You know—um—I think maybe I'll just—just go to bed. It's been a long day."

He regarded her with that unreadable expression that managed to unnerve her further.

She said, "Make yourself at home, and feel free to move your stuff into the guest bedroom. The sheets are clean, and there are towels in the cabinet in the bath—"

A sudden wave of irritation washed over her as she realized how silly and manic she sounded, so she finished her ramble with, "Well, I'm sure you know where everything is, since you've investigated the whole place."

Okay, that sounded almost petulant. Not that it mattered at this moment. She just had to get away from him.

Her gaze dropped to the hand that had touched her. Long tapered fingers, a broad palm, with traces of scars, pale and white, on his knuckles. Masculine hands.

Hands that would feel so good touching her.

She felt her body reacting and backed away, bumping into the door frame in her hurry to escape.

"Okay. Good night," she said, keeping her eyes averted from him.

She didn't wait for him to reply. She simply turned and rushed toward her bedroom.

Once inside her "pretty in pink" bedroom, she closed the door and sagged against it, overcome with so many emotions. Too many.

After a few moments, she forced herself to straighten and cross the room to her bureau. She pulled out shorty pajamas and tossed them on the bed.

She started to tug off her shirt, but stopped and sat heavily on the edge of her bed. She dropped her head into her hands.

This was all too much.

Why hadn't she thought of what Jude mentioned tonight?

What if humans were reading her books and attempting the spells? Once he'd pointed out that possibility, most of his other concerns about her safety had fallen on deaf ears.

What if her books were actually causing harm? She'd changed her whole career path just to avoid something like this. That's why she'd stopped writing her "encyclopedias" of demons—because she realized they could be dangerous. Fortunately, her nonfiction books had been printed by a small press and the books didn't get the kind of circulation they needed to become big sellers. Now most of them were out of print.

So she'd stopped writing those and focused on the adventures of Jenny Bell. The fictitious adventures. And those her readers had to believe were all fiction, didn't they? After all, humans didn't attempt the spells in Harry Potter, did they? Or any other fantasy fiction?

Of course, how would she know? Maybe they did. And that didn't matter, because she'd bet money that J. K. Rowling's spells really were fictitious.

But hers . . .

She sighed, combing her fingers through her hair. She rose and paced her room.

"It is unlikely, right?" she said aloud.

The very idea terrified her. Some of the spells she'd included in her books were pretty powerful magic.

"You idiot," Ellina muttered. Why had she included real incantations? There was no point, really, but she just hadn't thought anyone would think they were real.

She hadn't really believed anything would happen either with her nonfiction books, but at least that seemed *more* likely.

She breathed in deeply, trying to calm the agitation that had her heart skipping and her blood humming in her ears.

This day was too much. She pulled in another breath and realized she honestly was drained.

She didn't have much hope she would sleep, but crawling into bed and covering her head seemed pretty damn appealing at the moment.

Stress, she told herself. Among other things.

Her mind moved from her worries about humans to Jude. He'd been almost—kind. He'd seemed genuinely concerned about her bout of nerves and also about discussing his trepidation about her family.

And when he'd touched her. His hands had been so big—so strong. The feeling she'd experienced when he'd defended her against her brothers warmed her inside again. The appeal of having someone on her side. Someone to watch out for her.

Then her thoughts turned to what it would be like to really be with a man like that. A protective man. A strong man.

She shivered, desire returning with burning force.

She peeled off her T-shirt, feeling every brush of the soft worn material against her stomach and even through the sheer material of her bra.

Almost reluctantly, she walked over to her bureau, looking at her reflection in the mirror. Her face, aside from the strain around her mouth and the tiredness in her eyes, looked normal. Her eyes had shifted back to normal. But her bared torso was another matter.

The scales were back. Red and iridescent in the low lamplight. A stark contrast to her pale ivory bra. She touched them, and they seemed to vibrate under her fingers.

She pictured Jude's hands moving over them. Not being distressed or repulsed by them. More scales appeared as she imagined him here with her.

She groaned. She was disgusted with her abnormality. Disgusted that even with her knowledge that her books had the possibility of harming someone, she was still thinking about her attraction to Jude.

Ellina strode to her bed and threw on her pajamas, covering most of the evidence of her utter lack of self-control.

She crawled into bed, determined to ignore her desire.

And she'd been so pleased with herself earlier in the evening. She'd stayed in her tiny kitchen and helped clean up the remnants of dinner. She'd been aware of him, attracted to him, but she'd kept her demon self in check.

She'd actually believed she could be around him and be fine. Be normal.

But, as always, that state was yet again elusive.

In the end, the only thing she'd managed to do with any success was keep her reaction from Jude. She felt confident he hadn't noticed any of her odd changes. She'd kept her eyes, which she knew had to have been glowing, averted from him.

The scales were a bit like hives. They tended to appear first on the warmest parts of her body.

She shifted her legs under the sheets, feeling scales in places that were . . . most embarrassing.

Groaning, she whipped the covers over her head.

This day needed to be over.

Jude heard Ellina's bedroom door slam shut, but he didn't bother to follow and tell her she should keep her door open. She was too upset, and he got the feeling she wouldn't comply anyway.

And frankly he needed time to regroup.

He turned back to the sink and started washing the last pan. The hot water on his skin only seemed to feed the need in him like pouring water on a grease fire. The need spread, intensified.

Just a mere touch. The innocuous skin of her wrist and he was practically mad with lust for this woman. What was wrong with him?

Was there something strange with this full moon? Was there an eclipse? An unusual alignment of the planets?

He finished cleaning the pan with quick, agitated strokes and left it to dry in the drainer. He dried his hands, then wandered out of the kitchen, trying to decide what he should do now.

Jude felt restless. After wandering around the house, he opted to go to Ellina's room. He stood outside her door and listened.

The room was silent, but he could sense she was in there. He could smell her, feel her. That touch, brief as it was, seemed to have created a link to her that wasn't easily fading. The electrical vibration pulsated through the air, through the door, the walls, reaching him.

Did she feel it too?

He gritted his teeth, biting back a groan.

Why had he touched her? Especially then when he'd been feeling so—so protective of her.

There was no avoiding that realization now. He was feeling protective of her—more so than normal for a client.

As they'd talked about his notes and his concerns about who could want to hurt her, he'd been worried about her reaction, but that concern had gone beyond the usual apprehension for a client in potential danger. His protectiveness was tinged with something else. Something far more worrisome.

He'd felt possessive. That feeling had only intensified when he'd touched her. Even now his desire, still there, was charged with that possessiveness. Like the electrical vibration in the air was a bond that somehow placed a claim on her.

He left her doorway, afraid of what he might do if he stayed. This had never happened with other jobs. He was a master of detachment. He did jobs. That was his focus. Not the actual individuals. Just the work and doing the work right.

Even when the full moon drew closer, in the past, he'd just gotten more aggressive, more aware, more willing to fight.

The next full moon was about five days away. It wasn't unusual for him to start feeling its effects, but this wasn't the usual result. Instead of alertness and the desire to fight, he felt jittery and—well, for a lack of a more eloquent term—horny.

Increased sexual desire wasn't odd. As the moon grew in the sky, his body seemed to pump more and more testosterone into his bloodstream. This wasn't just a drive for sex. This was an almost irrational need to have Ellina for himself. To possess her. *That* was not normal.

There had to be a reasonable explanation for this reaction.

When he reached the living room, Jude let out the groan that had been begging for release. Then he began to pace; his movements were tense and abrupt like those of an agitated, caged animal.

He sat down at his computer, trying to find some answers for what was plaguing him, but nothing he found sounded exactly what he was experiencing. Not that he expected to find answers. He was an anomaly—one of a kind. Werewolf lore didn't apply to him—neither did vampire.

Still, focusing on his research helped him calm down. He gave up on his searches and roamed the house again, checking the locks and windows. Probably pointless, but it made him feel like he was doing something. He wandered into her office.

He did feel calmer. He was sure the added space between himself and Ellina was helping too. That electrical bond had not totally disappeared, but it was becoming manageable. Less frenzied, less all-encompassing.

Determined to banish the foreign feelings even further, he returned to his computer. Work would help, even if it involved the object of his sudden, fierce lust.

Breathing slowing, a technique he'd used for years, centuries, to control his moon-inspired loss of control, he reopened his search engine. Then he typed in *Ellina Kostova*.

The results came up almost instantly. Thousands and thousands of results. All about Ellina and her books. Jude clicked the first one and began reading.

Over an hour and several dozen links later, Jude knew about her books, about the widespread popularity of them. There were nearly a million Jenny Bell novels in print—and by all accounts the New Orleans–based author was very private. He did find a few interviews, but they disclosed very little about Ellina herself.

In fact, he felt like in the brief amount of time he'd spent with her he'd learned more about her than was revealed in the dozens of articles he read.

One thing did stand out though. All the pieces he'd read

implied that Ellina had always shunned the limelight. Some even implied that she was agoraphobic.

Was she? He couldn't say why, but that wasn't something he would have guessed about her. She was too open. Too curious and vocal. She didn't strike him as someone who could be happy hiding from the world.

But he supposed she could be. Then he recalled Maksim had said she wasn't home when any of the break-ins occurred. So agoraphobia seemed unlikely unless it was a very mild case.

The other thing he learned was that if the person who was after her was a fan, there were literally millions of potential suspects. That was daunting.

Jude shut his computer down and packed it up in its case along with his notes, all the while still considering who could be threatening her. He wasn't really hired to act as a detective, but it sure as hell would help him keep her safe if he had some idea whom or what he was protecting her from.

He stood, stretching, and was relieved that his body had finally calmed. He headed down the hallway, checking the kitchen, then flipping off the light. He paused outside Ellina's bedroom door. He could hear her even breathing.

Asleep. That was good.

He didn't linger there long. That strange electric tingle reached out to him again like pleasing, luring, invisible fingers. So, so tempting.

But he needed to remain self-possessed.

He spun away from the temptation and strode into her office. Her computer still hummed and cast an eerie blue light against the walls. Jude didn't touch it, afraid if he shut the machine down, he would lose some of her work or some important research.

Her desk was still littered with her piles of papers, but

given the many neat stacks, it looked as if she'd made some headway.

He rechecked the door, even though he already knew it was locked. Staying at the door, he perused the courtyard lit by moonlight. Everything seemed quiet. That was good.

Turning to leave, his gaze fell on the bookshelves. He'd put all the books back, but hadn't really looked at them too closely. He stopped and browsed the shelves. Impulsively, he pulled down the first of Ellina's fantasy books, *Jenny Bell and Hell's Kitchen*.

Then he returned to the living room and picked up his bags, continuing to the guest bedroom.

As he had earlier, he surveyed the room again, making note of problems and benefits. The room was small and mostly taken up by a full-size bed, which would make quick movements a little problematic.

Of course, the fact that he didn't sleep gave him some advantage, and the fact that the room was connected to Ellina's via the bathroom made it easier to get to her from here than from the living room.

He set one of the bags on the side of the bed away from the bathroom door and clear of the door that led back to the living room. The other he set down on the bed.

Carefully, he unzipped the case. The sides parted to reveal a fairly impressive arsenal. To one side of the bag was his Benelli Super Eagle II shotgun, already loaded with what was known as the highway patrol cocktail—alternating double-0 shot and pumpkin-ball slugs. Of course, in his case Jude also added rock salt to the alternating mix. The double-0 shredded, the slugs let daylight through, and the rock salt, well that just added insult to injury—especially to evil spirits and demons. The ammo wouldn't kill the supernatural, but the wounds and rock salt would sure as hell slow them down.

On the other side of the bag was a sheathed katana sword.

The 26" high-carbon steel gave him the angle and power to cleanly behead a vampire or werewolf if he needed to do so.

Immortal was such a misnomer when it came to these two paranormal creatures. They wouldn't die of natural causes, of course, and they were fairly impervious to traditional accidents, but they sure as hell could be killed. Not many creatures lived through the loss of their head.

He removed the sword and placed it under the mattress of the bed, close enough to the edge that he could grab it easily.

In one of the padded pistol pouches he had a Kel-Tec P-II, but he didn't take out that weapon. Instead he reached for his Glock 21. His favorite.

He placed the pistol on the nightstand, then he refastened the bag and slid this one under the bed. Definitely not the type of luggage he wanted easily accessible to anyone other than himself.

Plus he instinctively knew that kind of weaponry would unnerve Ellina. It would unnerve most people, but he got the feeling it would really bother her. Probably because it would be another unwanted reminder that she could be in grave danger.

Despite the fact his theories had shaken her, she still seemed pretty determined not to believe.

He settled on the bed, moving the Glock to rest beside him on the mattress, easily within reach. He opened Ellina's book, but before he started reading, he centered his energy on the house, and again on Ellina.

All was fine. Calm.

Well, almost all was calm.

He flipped open the book, forcing himself to focus on the words in front of him. Ellina's words.

And he'd make himself remain in this calm, zenlike state.

Chapter 10

By the time the sun rose, Jude had read the first Jenny Bell book and snagged another one while doing an early morning house check. He could see why they'd gained the popularity they had.

Ellina's writing was snappy and clever; her plots took interesting twists, and even though he hadn't expected to like this type of story, he had to admit he was sucked in.

He made a note of the page number he'd just finished, then set the book on the nightstand. His stomach growled loudly, telling him that he'd stayed in bed long enough. Another endless night over.

During the night, he'd changed into just a pair of sweatpants. There was no sleep, but that didn't mean he shouldn't be comfortable. He debated dressing, but decided against it. His stomach was too impatient for him to worry about fashion.

He opened the drawer to the nightstand, noting that the only things in there were some books—mainstream fiction type stuff—and some tissues. He placed the pistol on top of the items inside, sliding the drawer closed.

The sun shone through the living room windows, glistening on the hardwood floors. The bright, cheery light even warmed and softened the fairy-tale colors of the walls and furniture. As he strolled through the room, he realized there was something very cozy about her place.

A sense of peace filled him—then instantly unnerved him.

Cozy was not something he ever considered. Of course, he'd find just about anyplace cozy after living in cheap hotels and his van.

When was the last time he'd had a real home?

Don't be nostalgic, buddy. No point.

Once in the kitchen, he began to scavenge—and scavenge was the right word. Ellina was not big on grocery shopping. That was clear. But he did find eggs, a small can of jalapeños, cheddar cheese, tomatoes, a little leftover garlic.

With the mishmash of ingredients in front of him, he considered what he could make. A recipe came to mind, and he started to work. He moved with the stealth of a cat burglar. It was still early and he didn't want to wake Ellina.

He knew she hadn't gotten much sleep last night. He'd gone into the bathroom around two A.M. and was surprised to see a faint gleam of lamplight glowing from under her bedroom door. She must have slept only a while, then woke up.

He'd remained on the other side of the door, listening. He'd heard the flip of a page. Then another. She was reading. Or from what he'd seen of Ellina, maybe working. The same greeted him at three A.M. and again at four A.M.

When Jude checked again at five o'clock, her light was off, and he could even make out the faint, even sound of her breathing. He'd stood there for countless seconds just listening to the soft, rhythmic sound.

He couldn't actually say his motives for letting her sleep were totally altruistic. He was enjoying the easy feeling of a quiet Sunday morning.

Oh, he could sense her. But it was a calm, steady sensation at the moment. Almost nice. He finished shredding the cheese, then chopped some tomato, then opened and drained the jalapeños. The systematic work was soothing as it always was to him.

Carefully he tapped an egg on the edge of the mixing bowl, then another and another. A soft metallic clack filled the room as he whisked them to a frothy, yellow liquid.

At first, he didn't register the faint noise over the whisk and his own serene thoughts. The sound was so subtle. Then it happened again, a little louder, and Jude realized it was not one of the normal "house" sounds that he'd become familiar with over the course of the night.

He set down the bowl and stuck his head out the kitchen door, focusing. But he didn't even need his keen senses to hear the distinct rattle and swoosh of the front door opening.

Instead of heading toward the sound, he turned out of the kitchen and ducked into the bathroom. Then, moving quickly, silently, he entered the guest bedroom. Keeping his movement as swift as he could without making any noise, he eased open the nightstand drawer and got his Glock.

Gun up in front of him, he stepped out of the bedroom into the living room just in time to see a man entering the hallway toward where Ellina slept.

"Okay, bitch," the intruder called out, "Get your lazy as—"

The man's words broke off with a sharp *oof* as Jude caught his arm, twisted it, and then shoved him hard against the wall. Jude kept the gun at his side. The stranger seemed to be putting up no fight, so there was no need for firearms.

Unless necessary.

"Who the hell are you?" Jude growled, his voice low as he used his own weight to keep the man pinned. The intruder, while tense, remained still. Wise choice. He wouldn't have any chance against Jude. The energy coming off him was human.

"Pete," the intruder said.

"Pete?" Ellina echoed.

Jude turned slightly, not lessening his hold to see Ellina

standing at the end of the hall, echoing his name. And she sounded even less pleased than the intruder.

She strode toward him, her lips pressed into a firm line, and Jude instinctively hid his gun, pressing it to the leg that was away from her. If she didn't like the manhandling, she really would hate the weapon.

"Jude. Let him go!"

Jude didn't.

"Who is he?" he asked instead.

"My neighbor," Ellina said, her irritation undeniable now.

Pete held his hands up.

"I'm the neighbor." His words were slurred slightly, because of the way Jude had his arm pressing the man's face to the wall.

Jude loosened his hold, but didn't release him totally.

"How'd you get in?"

"The front door," Peter said.

"He has a key," Ellina added.

She placed her hands on her hips, giving him a full view of her scant nightwear. He was instantly reminded of the tiny nightgown he'd seen in her closet. This outfit wasn't quite as tiny as that one, but damned close. A camisole top revealed her smooth, bare shoulders, and short-shorts showed just how long and shapely her legs were.

He blinked, realizing he was staring, and she was glaring back.

"Jude, let my friend go. Now."

Jude did—the action automatic, because he was so stunned by the sight of her, not because he agreed that he should.

As soon as Pete was released, he didn't waste a moment. He skittered away from Jude, moving closer to Ellina. Jude managed to tear his gaze away from Ellina and to the intruder—or rather Pete.

He was 5'10" or 11", only a couple inches taller than Ellina. He had an athletic build, not brawny but not wiry either. Pete's hair was somewhere between light brown and gray, which seemed to hint that he could be older than Jude, except his features were smooth and unwrinkled. Baby-faced, Jude guessed was the term that would be used for his look. All Jude knew was it made it difficult to estimate an age.

And Jude noticed for the first time that he also had small headsets in each ear. Hearing aids?

"Are you okay?" Ellina asked, turning all her attention on her friend. Her friend didn't do the same. He kept a wary eye on Jude.

"I'm fine."

Jude regarded him the same way. Maksim hadn't mentioned anyone named Pete on his list of potential threats, but Jude wasn't willing to dismiss him without knowing more.

Who was he? And what was his relationship to Ellina?

"Come sit down," Ellina said, looping her arm through the other man's, brushing past Jude and leading her friend to the living room. Jude didn't miss the look she cast him as she did so. He also didn't miss the easy way she touched the man. No reluctance like when he touched her.

A wave of the same overwhelming possessiveness from last night swept through him. His muscles tensed. His jaw clenched.

He started to follow, but as he did, she glanced at him over her shoulder, the narrowed glare warning him to back off.

Despite his gut impulse, he did what she silently asked. Or ordered, really.

Besides, he still held the gun, and frankly, at the moment, he didn't quite trust himself with something that could do some major damage to the mere mortal man at her side.

That she touched.

Jude didn't move out of the hallway, and he heard Pete ask in a hushed tone as they disappeared into the living room, "Who is that?"

"Long story," was Ellina's response, and she sounded none too happy.

Jude lingered in the hallway, then decided there was no point. Even if this Pete was a physical threat, he wasn't going to be foolish enough to do something with Jude right here. It would be too risky. And more foolhardy than he could guess.

Jude glanced at the gun still at his side, then decided it was safe to return it to his room. Not to mention, no matter how many times it might have been done in movies, he wasn't about to stick the pistol in the waistband of his pants. That was a good way to lose what was already in his pants. And he was pretty fond of what he had in his pants, even if he didn't use it nearly as much as he'd like. With that thought, his mind was back to how Ellina looked in her tiny pajamas, and she was in that minuscule garment with this guy named Pete.

He gritted his teeth and headed to his room via the bathroom. Pausing at the end of the bed, he considered quietly approaching the door that led back to the living room, but he caught himself. He quietly stashed the weapon, then went back to the kitchen.

The bowl of waiting eggs suddenly didn't represent the peaceful Sunday zen they had before. Jude went back to work, this time not being nearly as quiet as he'd been before. Disrupting Ellina now seemed like a good idea.

"I'm so sorry," Ellina said, wincing as another pan clattered loudly from the kitchen. "He's a little overbearing."

Peter made a face, widening his eyes in an expression of intrigue. "Who is he? All the details, please."

Ellina shook her head, feeling some of her irritation fade. Leave it to Pete to enjoy being manhandled first thing in the morning.

"He's . . ." She really didn't know what to say. She didn't want to tell Pete that Jude was a bodyguard. That would prompt an endless string of questions, which would inevitably lead to subjects she couldn't answer.

Pete had been her neighbor for nearly two years, but he

didn't have a clue that she was half demon. They were tight. He was her closest friend, but she wasn't sure she could ever be tight enough with anyone to tell them about her hellish family.

Her thoughts turned to Jude, who in one day knew more about her life than Pete. Then her thoughts strayed to the look on Jude's face as he'd looked at her in the hallway. His eyes had roamed down her body, and he'd looked positively . . . hungry.

Parts of her tingled just remembering that look, but she quickly thought of something else, before her body could react in ways that would certainly make her demon side a little hard to hide.

"Why are you here so early?" she asked, avoiding Pete's last question.

"He's what?" Pete prompted, not to be dissuaded from his question. How very Pete.

"He's . . ."

Pete widened his eyes, waiting, an almost impatient look in his blue eyes.

"He's just a friend."

Peter collapsed back against the couch cushions, clearly not pleased with her answer.

"Well, you might think you're friends," he said, "but he definitely thinks you're something else. A man doesn't slam another man up against a wall like that unless he's feeling all alpha about something."

She laughed. Pete was right about that. "Oh, he's pretty alpha. But not about me. Well, not about me in *that* way."

But she's wasn't sure about that. That look in his eyes earlier . . .

She shivered, then cleared her throat to compose herself.

Peter rolled his eyes. "Come on, Ell, there has to be more to this than just a friend."

Ellina frowned and then laughed. "Ell again. What's up with this little nickname you've suddenly given me?"

"Uh-uh," he said, sitting up again, watching her intently. "I'm not letting you avoid this. Dirt, girl. Dirt."

Ellina laughed. "There isn't any dirt."

"Well there haven't been any men around here since I've known you." He raised his eyebrows as if he wanted her to confirm that fact.

She nodded, laughing again, this time a little uncomfortably. "That would be true."

"And now there's one staying with you." He lounged back against the overstuffed cushions of her sofa.

"Just for a while."

"Really?" For a moment, Ellina thought she saw something like annoyance in his eyes. But why would Pete care?

"He's a friend of Maksim's," she added.

"Why isn't he staying at Maksim's then?" he asked sharply, then Pete must have realized how curt he sounded, because he added with a little smile, "I still feel like there's more to this story."

"Not really."

"Really? There nothing behind that reaction when I came in here?"

"Well—he knows about the break-ins, so I think he just—overreacted."

Pete nodded. "That also explains the fact that he's wandering around in nothing but sweatpants?" He paused, listening. "And he's apparently making you breakfast?"

As if on cue, another pan clanged.

He raised an eyebrow.

"You are relentless—as ever," she said with a laugh. "Yes, he is staying here. But he's staying in the guest room. And he just happens to like to cook. Nothing more to tell than that, I'm afraid. I don't even know him that well, to be honest."

Pete smiled, this one somehow easier than the previous smiles. "Well that's too bad. I'm sorry to be pressuring you like this. You know I just want to see you happy."

"Ah, sweetie, how could I be unhappy when I have you?"

She leaned in to hug her dear friend, but before she could embrace him, Jude's voice interrupted her, booming and clearly not pleased.

"Breakfast is nearly done."

She pulled away from her friend to find Jude in the hall doorway, glowering.

"I've made coffee," he said. "Why don't you come help yourselves."

Ellina glanced from Jude to Pete, feeling awkward. Why was Jude acting this way? It was ridiculous.

Pete sat up again, bracing his hands on his knees as he started to stand. "Oh, you know, I think I should probably go."

"Oh, no," Ellina insisted, automatically placing her hand on his. "Please stay—we haven't had much time together lately."

Pete glanced at Jude, then back to her. He nodded. "Maybe for a little while. I have missed our lazy Sunday mornings."

Ellina smiled, squeezing his fingers before releasing them and standing.

"I'll get us both some coffee," she said.

Pete shot Jude another look, then nodded. He was no fool; he knew he was safer remaining right there.

Ellina had to admit she was reluctant to go with the glowering hulk of a man in front of her too. But she needed to talk with him. He was here to protect her, but he couldn't attack her friends. That just wasn't going to fly.

Before this moment, if anyone had asked Jude if he understood the phrase "seeing red," he would have said he did. But he really hadn't. Not until this moment.

With the frittata in the stove, he couldn't keep himself away from the living room. He'd intended to remain out of sight, maybe do a little research about this "friend" of Ellina's.

That was until he heard Ellina's sweetly said words.

. . . How could I be unhappy when I have you?

He'd wanted to gnash his teeth at her words . . . what those words seemed to imply. And he hadn't been able to stop himself from barging in on them. Thankfully, it worked.

He waited for Ellina to pass him, then turned to follow her, watching her movements, fluid even though she was clearly angered. He couldn't focus on the obvious anger, though. He was too lost in the slight sway of her hips. The curve of her ass. Her bare legs long, perfect. God, even her feet captivated him.

And she'd been sitting with that man, in that tiny shorty pajama. He'd been close to all those lissome curves and bare skin.

Had Pete been even closer? Had he ever seen Ellina without even that small barrier of silky material shielding her?

The idea made him want to growl. Howl.

She disappeared into the kitchen, and he followed her. In fact, when she turned, he was right behind her. Her pale eyes flashed as if she was going to confront him. She even opened her mouth, but he beat her to it.

"Who is this Pete?"

She snapped her mouth shut, taken off balance by this curt question.

"My friend," she finally said, but nothing in her tone gave him any hint of just how friendly they were.

He stepped closer, just inches away. He knew he was using his size and the small space to intimidate her, but he wanted answers. Needed them.

"How well do you know him?"

"Jude, this is ridiculous—"

"How well, Ellina? Didn't our talk last night help you understand anything?"

She put down the coffee decanter that she'd just pulled from the maker, the glass clacking loudly on the tile countertop.

She glared up at him, folding her hands across her chest.

The action pulled the thin, silky material closer to her lithe form, her pert, rounded breasts, the curve of her hips.

"Don't tell me you are looking at Pete as a potential threat too?" Her hushed volume didn't mask her irritation.

Oh, Pete was a threat all right. Jude just didn't know whether he was a threat to her safety or a threat to Jude as his rival.

As soon as the thought whipped through his mind, he froze. What was he doing? What the hell was he thinking? Rival?

His eyes moved over her body again. God, she was beautiful.

He grimaced, disgusted with his lack of control. He was here to protect her.

A job. A job, damn it!

She made a noise of frustration, mistaking his appalled expression for a reaction to her and her question.

"Peter and I have known each other for years," she said, stepping closer to him, her small chin jutting up in the air. "So if he'd ever wanted to hurt me, he's had plenty of chances." She seemed to realize her voice was rising, growing more heated.

She stepped closer still, lowering her voice. "He wouldn't have had to break in. He has a key. He didn't make those calls. I'd have recognized his voice. He couldn't have attempted to run me down. He doesn't have a car. And I don't know if you could sense it when you were slamming him against the wall, but he's human, so I suspect putting me into a cat would be rather difficult for him."

Jude knew she had a point. He could concede all her points, but at the moment, they weren't the ones bothering him.

At this moment, his biggest concern was the electricity sizzling between them, heating him with blind lust. Desperate, wild lust. And this uncontainable need to make sure the man in the other room didn't have any claim to her.

She stared at him for a moment, and when he didn't respond, she shifted back to the coffee, pouring two mugs, then adding a dash of milk to both.

He noticed her hands shook as she completed the task, but he couldn't guess what emotion caused the tremors.

She picked up both cups and glared at him.

"I'm not going to let you bully people I care about."

Jude breathed in. He heard her words, but all that seemed to matter was her scent, her heat.

As if tugged by an invisible pulley, he moved closer to her. Ellina didn't back away, but some of her anger faded, morphing into something else. Awareness?

Did she feel it too? This powerful bond between them.

Before he could catch himself, he reached out and brushed a wayward strand of her hair away from her face. His fingers connected with nothing but her hair. Yet even that touch caused the air between them to crackle.

He dropped his hand, afraid of what he might do if he continued to reach out to her.

She stared at him for a moment longer, totally still as if she were holding her breath. Then she looked away. She edged past him. Her back was to him, not allowing any part of herself to touch him.

"I'm serious, Jude," she said, once she was in the doorway, but she still didn't meet his eyes. "I won't let you intimidate those I love and trust."

Love.

The word echoed in his head.

She loved this Pete.

Chapter 11

Once Ellina was a few feet away from the kitchen, she paused, leaning against the hallway wall. She had to pull herself together.

He'd been so close to her, his big body caging her. She had been angry that he was trying to intimidate her, both physically and verbally. But she'd also been aroused. She could feel the evidence of that arousal throughout her, instant and violent like a sudden summer thunderstorm pounding through her.

She glanced toward the living room. She couldn't go back there—not yet. She could feel the change, right there, waiting to appear, given freedom by her arousal.

She turned back and headed toward her room, not glancing toward the kitchen as she walked past. She couldn't even look at Jude. Her body wanted him too much.

Once inside her room, she used her elbow to close her door, then set the two coffee mugs on her dresser. She stared into her mirror. She wasn't surprised to see her eyes glowing—the color of red neon, but in the bright light of morning, they weren't too dramatic.

Oh, Pete would notice something wasn't right, but they weren't too bad. The skin of her bare shoulders and arms was still pale, normal. That was good.

She rooted around in her dresser drawers, finding jeans and a long-sleeved T-shirt. Finally a bra and panties.

She stripped, relieved to find the rest of her was fine—human. Shocking. Because even now, desire filled her. It was as if Jude was right there with her. She could feel his heat on her skin. She could smell him, that clean masculine scent that she hadn't even been aware she knew until this moment.

She closed her eyes, feeling like she was losing her mind. She'd felt attraction before, but it was nothing like this.

Still Ellina couldn't hide out in her room all day. Not with poor Pete left out there. And God only knew what Jude would say to him.

That prospect sobered her enough to focus on the clothes still clutched in her hands. She dropped them on the bed, then picked up her bra, putting it on quickly, ignoring the way the lacy material abraded her puckered nipples.

Just dress. You cannot leave Pete alone with Jude.

He was probably grilling her poor friend right at this very moment.

She snatched up her panties and stepped into them, almost gasping when the cool cotton hit the hot dampness at the apex of her thighs.

She growled, frustrated with her body—a body that no longer felt like her own.

How could this be? How could she want this man—this preternatural? He would be the last man she'd imagine igniting so much lust in her. The last man she'd fancied herself attracted to was an independent bookstore owner with glasses, a nice smile that revealed his slightly crooked front teeth, and perpetually wrinkled khaki pants.

Nothing like Jude. Jude was too untamed. Too masculine. Too beautiful.

Her body started to react just imagining him.

She closed her eyes again, clutching her shirt to her chest, willing away her longing.

Think about poor Pete. He was a sitting duck with a man like Jude.

Ellina threw on the rest of her clothing and pulled her hair into a messy bun on the top of her head, using a clip to hold it in place. She picked up the coffee mugs and gave herself one more quick perusal.

She looked fine. And she could do this. She could repress her desire. And when Pete left, she'd talk to Jude about what was going on between them. Hell, maybe she'd tell him he had to go.

These feelings were too much for her. And her reactions to him . . . she just couldn't deal with it. And she certainly couldn't deal with his reaction when he realized what happened to her when she was aroused.

Imagining that reaction was as effective as being pushed into a icy mountain lake. Her lust disappeared, replaced by dread and regret.

One more breath and then she headed to the door, transferring both cups to one hand as she opened it.

Practicing a calm little smile, she started back to the living room. She glanced into the kitchen as she passed, greeted by the smell of something delicious and an empty room.

Her stomach lurched as she realized that Pete and Jude were indeed together. She could hear them talking as she approached, Pete's voice light, Jude's chocolaty dark.

She paused just out of sight to listen.

"This is wonderful," Pete said, and Ellina could hear the click of utensils on plates.

"Thank you," Jude replied, his tone perfectly polite.

That was encouraging, right?

"Where did you learn to cook?"

"I'm self-taught."

"Ellina is a terrible cook," Pete said.

"Yes, she's informed me of that."

Pete laughed. "She made me shrimp étouffée a couple

weeks ago, and it was like greasy wallpaper paste with some shrimp and a few chunks of onion bobbing around in it."

Jude didn't say anything.

"She's got a pretty good deal here," Pete said.

There was more silence.

"What is a good deal?" Jude's voice was still polite, but there was an edge to it. A forced politeness.

Ellina decided this was the point to make her entrance.

"Sorry, guys," she said brightly as she strolled into the room, coffee mugs lifted in the air. "I just wanted to get dressed. I didn't think the food would beat the coffee here."

She handed Pete his mug, noticing that he'd changed places and was now sitting in one of the wing-backed chairs. Jude sat on the sofa with his plate on the coffee table in front of him. Another plate of food sat beside that. And while she knew he had a big appetite, she didn't think that plate was for him.

When he saw her, he patted the sofa. "Here's yours, dear."

Dear? Oh crap. What was he up to?

"Pete was just telling me something about you having a good deal," Jude said, offering her a smile. She was quickly learning that most of his smiles were reserved for moments of deception.

Even knowing that, she still found it breathtaking.

He tapped the sofa again and gestured to the plate he'd prepared for her. Reluctantly she took a seat on the sofa, making sure there was plenty of space between them.

"Yes," Pete said, his curious gaze going back and forth between the two of them. "I was just about to tell Jude that you have quite a good deal here. A houseguest who cooks like an actual chef."

He raised his fork. "Jude, this really is some good stuff."

Jude thanked him again, then mercifully returned his attention to his food.

Ellina picked up the plate of food and took a bite even though she didn't feel a bit hungry. But despite herself, she moaned with appreciation. The eggs were fluffy and flavored with cheese and tomato and spicy bits of jalapeño.

"Wow, this is wonderful," she said scooping up more.

"It really is," Pete agreed. Then he set down his fork. "So come on, tell me how long you are going to let this perfect guy stay with you?"

Still chewing, she shot her friend a withering look. Wouldn't he just let this go?

Pete had always fancied himself a bit of a matchmaker, at least to his other friends, but thankfully he'd been hands-off with her. Apparently he'd decided to rectify that fact now.

Before she could answer, Jude answered for her. "Oh, I'm staying indefinitely."

"You are?" Pete gave Ellina a curious look. "Because Ellina's being sort of noncommittal about the whole thing."

She hurried to swallow the eggs that suddenly felt like a large wad of dough in her mouth. "Well—I—we—"

Suddenly Jude's strong arm was around her, pulling her without any difficulty against his side. "Ellina, you've got to stop being so shy about this."

Ellina gaped at the man beside her. What? What was he doing?

"Go ahead and tell him, darling." He grinned down at her and squeezed her.

Thankfully he'd put on a shirt while she was gone, otherwise she'd be pressed tight to his bare chest. As it was his black T-shirt didn't do much to shield her from the hardness of his muscles and the heat of his body.

"Oh—I don't know if we—we should talk about that now," she managed.

"Of course we should, sweetheart." Jude's smile widened, so his dimple was deep and adorable. For a moment, she was mesmerized. Then she snapped out of it.

That smile might be truly beautiful, but it would never

lead to anything good. Thus far, Jude's smile had been the predecessor to, at best, odd things to come.

She shook her head, unable to speak as she was caught between finding him terribly attractive and living in fear of what he was going to say next.

"You're being silly," Jude told to her, his voice low and teasing.

She half expected him to tweak the end of her nose like an amusing little child. But when she met his eyes, she saw the warning there. A silent rebuke.

Don't give me any trouble.

Then he turned to Pete.

"Ellina is afraid to tell you, because she doesn't want to upset you. Given the past you've shared."

Pete raised an eyebrow, still chewing away, still thinking his breakfast tasted delish, and only a little puzzled by the cryptic comment from the lunatic next to her.

No, there was none of the churning dread in Pete's stomach, at least not like the kind that twisted hers into suffocating knots.

She swallowed again, bracing herself for what she suspected was to come.

"Ellina and I are actually seeing each other."

Ellina wanted to groan. Why, why had she started this stupid lie? She couldn't do this.

Jude kept his smile unwavering. Even as he felt Ellina, who'd been rigid in his arms, sag back against the sofa as if she wanted to disappear. She was not pleased.

He supposed he couldn't blame her. He was potentially messing up an existing relationship. She'd said she loved this man. She might be truly devastated.

He waited for regret to follow that realization, but none came. All he cared about was making sure this man knew that any relationship he and Ellina may have had was over. At least until Jude was out of the picture.

What the hell are you doing, buddy?

Keeping her safe, he told himself.

But he watched the other man's reaction carefully. Acting as her boyfriend was the perfect cover. He'd told her that before. He was planning to go with that plan, and he expected her to go along with it too.

"Really?" Pete said and Jude saw a flash of something akin to annoyance simmering in his gaze. As he was trying to look unaffected, he nonchalantly took another bite of the frittata.

Maybe they did have feelings for each other. Jude felt that irrational anger rise up in him again.

"And, Ell, you led me to believe he was just a friend of Maksim's crashing here for a little while," Pete said, a hint of scolding in his tone.

Ellina straightened. "Well, he is, but—"

"But we've realized we have a lot in common," Jude finished for her, giving her his best semblance of a fond smile. He pulled her tighter to him. She made a little noise and he relaxed his grip.

Pete set his plate on the coffee table, then frowned at Ellina. "But you just told me that you don't even know him that well."

Jude's anger flared. Why had she said that? Was that her way of appeasing this guy? Making sure he knew that she wasn't interested in Jude?

Or could she have been just speaking the truth?

He ignored his logical mind.

"Did you say that?" Jude said, smiling down at her, infusing his look with as much fond amusement as he could muster.

Ellina stared back at him, her eyes wide and utterly befuddled. Her expression would have been humorous, but despite his feigned appearance, he wasn't feeling very amused at the moment.

Jude hugged her again, this time with much less force. "That's Ellina for you. She's so shy about these things."

Jude looked back to the other man, who regarded the two of them, skepticism narrowing his eyes—skepticism and something Jude couldn't quite read. But he was fairly certain it was, indeed, annoyance.

"Well," he said, "that's—great."

Jude's smile broadened; this time the action was genuine. He suspected ole Petey-boy thought it was anything but great.

"It is, isn't it," Jude agreed, feeling very smug. Then before he thought better of his actions, he leaned toward Ellina and kissed her.

Ellina didn't comprehend Jude's intent until his lips brushed against hers. Even then she didn't react; it was as if her mind had literally ground to a halt. All the gears slowly winding down to a standstill.

Then he deepened the kiss, his lips moving masterfully over hers, controlling her. And she went along willingly, opening her mouth for him, letting his tongue brush against hers.

Her hand came up to his cheeks, feeling the stubble along his jawline.

Her mind kicked back on, but all she could seem to process was . . . this was wonderful. Just . . . wonderful.

Then he pulled away.

She swayed slightly, staring up at him. Dazed. Shaken. Wanting more.

"Well," Pete said loudly, drawing her attention to him, although through her scrambled thoughts she was only vaguely aware of him. Pete then stood and clapped his hands, clearly uncomfortable with the situation. Then she was painfully aware of him and what he'd just seen.

"It looks like you two are ready for some alone time."

Ellina immediately stood too. "No . . . no, you don't have

to leave." She couldn't actually say she wanted him to stay, because she was far too mixed up to act even remotely normal.

At the same time, she hated to see her friend leave in a huff, which he seemed to be doing as he strode to the door.

"No, I think it's time I made my exit," he said, his expression harsh, and for a moment he didn't even seem to look like her usually easygoing friend. Then he buffered his tone with a slight smile. "Breakfast was great. And I'll see you later."

Ellina nodded, completely confounded by everything that had taken place this morning. It was probably best he leave. She needed to talk to Jude. That much she could comprehend.

"I'll call you later," she told him.

He smiled. "Not if I call you first."

Pete's teasing tone put her at ease. At least about him.

"Nice meeting you," Jude said, his tone normal and totally unaffected by what had just transpired not even minutes before.

Pete returned the sentiment, although Ellina only barely registered it. Anger was replacing some of the bewilderment that had muddled her mind.

She welcomed the anger; it was a much more straightforward emotion. It made her thoughts more lucid.

Once Pete left, she waited a few moments, then she turned to Jude, who still sat on the sofa, looking calm and smug like a well-pleased aristocrat.

"Why did you do that?" she demanded, hoping she would wipe away some of his self-satisfaction with a mere glare.

It didn't work. He raised an eyebrow, looking even cockier than before.

"Which *that* are you referring to?"

"All of them," she cried, his demeanor making her more and more furious. How dare he look so composed when she felt totally out of control? Totally out of control wasn't good. But she didn't feel the demon. Also good.

"I was just going with the boyfriend scenario," he said. "I told you I thought that was a good plan."

"It's a stupid plan," she said, her voice, much to her dismay, rising an octave higher.

"No," he said calmly, "it makes a lot of sense. I mean, look how curious he was about why I'm here. And look how easily he bought the explanation."

"He didn't buy it easily. He was upset when he left. He doesn't understand how I went from being single one day to having a live-in boyfriend the next."

Jude shrugged. "People do things like that every day."

"I don't," she shouted.

How could he be so blasé about the whole thing? She was overwrought. She was angry. She was confused. And even amid all that, she was still attracted to the arrogant jerk.

"Well, for my purposes, now you do," he said, irritation evident in his voice.

"*Your* purposes. How is this about you?"

He didn't speak for a moment, then said quietly, "You're right. It's about you. And this little story is a good way to keep you safe. To keep me close to you without raising suspicion."

"Maybe I don't want you close."

Finally his calm composure changed. His eyes narrowed slightly and a muscle in his jaw ticced as if he were clenching his teeth. They glared at each other, neither speaking for a few moments.

Then Jude said, "Listen, when we figure out who's trying to hurt you, then you can go back to your life. And back to Pete."

She frowned, confused by the way he said Pete's name. Almost as if he was jealous of him.

That was ludicrous. Pete had been her friend for years. How could Jude, who she'd known for less than twenty-four hours, be threatened by her friend? Why would he be threatened?

"So we'll stick to this plan, right?" he prompted when she didn't say anything.

She didn't want to stick to this plan. Not if she had to actually get close to him. She couldn't do that. And the only reason wasn't about turning demony at this point.

She considered telling him she wanted him to leave, but she knew he wouldn't do it. The only way this man was going to go was if Maksim fired him, or he discovered who was supposedly after her.

Why had she ever agreed to this? Damn it.

"You'll stick to the plan, right?"

Ellina nodded. She would, until she talked to Maksim. Then they were going to think of a different plan.

"Good," he said, the smugness returning.

Her irritation returned too, and she couldn't help asking, "Why did you kiss me, though? We could have pulled off the plan without that."

"I wanted him to know this is real. I don't need some jerk who's always carried a torch for you deciding to profess his love now. That's an added problem we just don't need."

She laughed then. All of this was ludicrous.

"First of all, Pete isn't a jerk. And he certainly isn't carrying a torch for me."

"You can't be sure of that," he said.

"Oh, I'm pretty sure," she said, her own smile turning smug. "Pete's gay."

Chapter 12

Jude stared at Ellina.

Pete was gay?

Suddenly his behavior of the whole morning seemed even more absurd. He'd been acting like an alpha wolf—which, of course, wasn't out of the realm of possibility for him. But even he had to admit it was over the top.

He still felt that Pete was a threat. There was something about him that just agitated Jude, yet now that Pete was gone, he couldn't figure out what or why.

He started to open his mouth to tell her . . . what? He wasn't sure. But his need to find the right words, an excuse, was saved by the bell. Or rather by a jingle.

Ellina's phone.

Ellina started as if the sound startled her too, but she was just as relieved as he was for an escape. Without a word to him, she hurried out of the room. He debated whether he should follow her, then decided against it. He needed to give her a little space at the moment, and he couldn't blame her. He'd overstepped his bounds.

Especially with that kiss. In all his years of taking jobs, he'd never kissed a client. He'd claimed it was for her own good, to create a believable pretense, but he knew as well as she did that it hadn't been necessary.

He'd just wanted to kiss her. He'd wanted to stake a claim over her in front of her human friend.

Whether it made sense of not, he had sensed a threat from the human male. Right away something had rubbed him the wrong way about the smaller man. Now that he was gone, Jude couldn't say what it was, but something had made him act that way.

Was it . . . jealousy? Or was it something more?

He didn't know. He didn't understand himself this morning.

As he sat there contemplating his weird reaction to the man, Ellina returned.

Her brow was creased, her eyes gray with worry.

"That was Maksim. He says that Jo is having a very difficult delivery. He would like me to come to the hospital."

Jude rose, noticing that she already had her purse and her usually bare feet were clad in black boots.

"Just give me a minute." He stood, starting toward the guest bedroom.

"There's no need for you to go," she said. "I'll just take a cab."

He glanced at her. She regarded him with grave eyes and a firm set to her mouth. She still didn't get that she was potentially in danger. She also didn't get that he didn't have any choice but to go with her.

She was his job.

You'd do well to remember that too, buddy.

"I'll drive you there," he said evenly, trying not to sound as authoritarian as he had most of the morning.

She looked as if she were planning to argue, then she nodded. Probably because she didn't want to waste time debating with him.

He nodded too, then strode to his room. Once there, he

pulled out his Glock, laying it on the bed as he went to the duffel beside the bed and pulled out a pair of jeans. He then pulled out the case under his bed. He took out the Kel-Tec-P-II and the ankle holster. This gun was easier to conceal.

He placed the Glock back into the case and stashed it under the bed. Quickly he pulled on his jeans, then buckled the holster. One last trip to his duffel materialized his sunglasses and he headed back to the living room.

Ellina was perched on the edge of one of the wing-backed chairs, her hands clutched on her lap. She popped up as soon as she saw him.

"Ready?" he asked and she nodded.

As she passed him, he could see how tense she was, how rigid she held her body, and he nearly reached out to place a hand at the small of her back. But he caught himself. She didn't want his comfort, and really he didn't know how to comfort her.

Still he wanted to soothe away the tension he saw in her. He wanted to help.

Of course keeping his distance was probably what would help her most right now. That was the best plan for him too. He didn't want to be agitated and distracted now. They were going out in public. He needed to be centered. He needed to be aware of what was going on around him.

He waited on the sidewalk as Ellina locked her doors, and he wondered after even the second break-in why she hadn't installed an alarm system. But of course he knew the answer.

When would she take these events seriously? He was afraid it would take something really bad to get her attention.

She came down the steps and he gestured toward his black van. If she found anything odd about his vehicle/mobile home, it didn't show on her face. She simply climbed into the front seat and waited for him to start driving.

"Turn right at the next stop sign," she said. Then she told him to turn right again several streets later. And that was how the drive went. No conversation except to direct him to the hospital.

Even when he asked what was wrong with Jo, she just shook her head and repeated what she'd said in the living room, "Maksim said she's having a hard delivery."

He didn't press her further, realizing she didn't want to talk. He understood that. There were plenty of times in his past when he was more than content to just be silent.

Especially when he was worried.

They pulled into the hospital parking lot, and Ellina had her door open even before he'd shifted the van into park.

He hopped out just as quickly, realizing she wasn't going to wait for him. As it was, he had to jog a bit to catch up with her.

As soon as the automatic doors slid open, the distinct smell of disinfectants and blood and sickness enveloped him. He knew hospitals had a definite smell to humans as well, but he imagined it was even more marked and overwhelming to preternaturals.

He knew he didn't like it. It made him uneasy, like a small animal catching a whiff of a predator. In this case, the predator was illness and death.

While neither predator would get him, certainly not illness, it didn't make it any less uncomfortable to be around. It was odd, because he was no stranger to death, or maybe it was because he was no stranger. The smells here triggered too many memories. Painful ones.

"Maksim said labor and delivery are on the third floor." Elina beelined to a set of silver elevators, pressing the Up button.

While they waited, Jude pulled off his dark glasses and watched the people milling around. Hospital staff in white.

Humans pushed around in wheelchairs. Still others visiting sick loved ones, and, of course, the patients who were there to get well. Maybe to get well. Maybe to die.

No, he didn't like it here.

The elevator dinged and the doors slid open. It was empty, so they stepped right in. Neither spoke as they made the short trip upward.

When the doors slid apart, he saw the secured doors that led into the maternity ward. They followed the necessary procedures to get into the area; fortunately they didn't detect his gun. Then Ellina went to the nurses' station to ask where to find her brother and sister-in-law.

Jude paced, waiting. A couple walked past him, the woman clearly in the early stages of labor. Her young husband, with his arm around her, looked harried.

Another couple, both appearing tired but beaming with almost euphoric smiles, strolled to a large windowed room. They stood arm in arm, talking quietly, pointing, grinning.

Jude wandered in that direction to look as well. He stopped, staring at the tiny inhabitants of the white room. Babies in clear-sided bassinets lined the room. They all wore matching little pink- and blue-striped caps. Some were covered with pale blue blankets, others with pink. Some cried, their tiny faces screwed into expressions of utter rage. Others slept. A few just blinked with small unfocused eyes, bemused expressions on their faces as if they were mystified as to how they had ended up here.

Jude stepped closer, memories tugging him.

"He's little, but he's strong."

"Of course he is. He's my son."

"The nurse told me they are down this way."

Jude blinked, turning to find Ellina beside him.

He nodded, trying to shake away his thoughts. His memories.

"Lead the way."

* * *

Ellina glanced over at Jude as they walked down the hall. His eyes looked ahead of them, but they seemed to be focused on something beyond the hallway, and he'd had the strangest look on his face as he'd looked in the nursery window.

"Are you okay?" she asked.

He started, drawn back from wherever he'd been.

"Umm—shouldn't I be asking you that?" he said, offering her a slight smile. The smile didn't touch the strange, almost haunted look in his eyes.

She frowned, ready to ask him more, when Maksim appeared. It actually took her several moments to recognize him. Her usually polished brother was a mess. His hair stood out all over his head as if he'd spent hours running his hands through it. His usual designer clothing was covered with pale green scrubs, ill-fitting and wrinkled. Dark circles shadowed under his eyes and his lips were set into a grim line.

"Ellina."

He pulled her against him, hugging her so tight she couldn't manage a full breath. She didn't try to loosen his grip. She simply hugged him back with the same force, knowing he needed comfort.

"I'm so glad you're here," he muttered against her hair, his voice gravelly with emotion.

"What's going on?" she asked as soon as he released her.

"They had to take the baby," Maksim said.

Her heart lurched, afraid of what that meant. She looked toward Jude, who stood to one side, watching them. Their eyes met and held for a second. And she knew he was wordlessly telling her it was going to be okay.

Her gaze returned to her brother, waiting for him to continue. It was clear Maksim was exhausted and not thinking clearly. He seemed to be struggling to organize his thoughts.

"Jo's labor started intensely almost as soon as we got here. She was in a lot of pain, but the labor seemed to be going along fine. Then the baby's blood pressure dropped and Jo was in so much pain."

Ellina took Maksim's hand, squeezing his fingers, offering him as much comfort as she could, although he didn't seem to register her touch.

She looked back to Jude. He watched her, his gaze giving instant comfort.

Maksim pulled in a shuddering breath and continued, "They did a cesarean, and the baby's fine, but Jo kept bleeding. She's stable now, but . . ."

Maksim's eyes darkened, taking on a haunted quality.

Ellina glanced at Jude again, but this time he wasn't watching her. He stared at Maksim, a similar expression on his face. He understood what Maksim was going through. He'd been there. She knew it as sure as if he'd told her with words.

Her heart ached just seeing their pain.

"I was really terrified," Maksim said, his voice hoarse, as if he was trying to squelch the emotions rising inside him—and he was losing. "I still am. I feel so goddamn helpless."

Ellina hugged him again.

"She will be okay. And the baby is fine. Jo will get stronger every minute. She has too much to live for to let this slow her down. She's a tough gal."

She pulled back to smile at her brother. "After all, she agreed to take you on."

He managed a smile of his own, although it didn't quite banish that tormented pain shadowing his gaze.

"She did do that," he agreed, trying to sound light, but failing. "I'm going to go back in with her. You will stay?"

Ellina nodded. "Of course."

He squeezed her hand, then started back down the hall.

"Wait, Maksim," she called to him. He turned back to her.

"Is your baby a boy or a girl?"

Maksim face relaxed then, just for a moment. And instead of torment, she saw love in his eyes.

"It's a boy. Barrett James."

Tears filled Ellina's eyes even as she smiled at him.

"Go see him," he told her.

She nodded, the action causing the tears to spill over onto her cheeks. But her grin never wavered.

"I will."

Maksim disappeared through a set of doors at the end of the hall.

"Are you okay?"

Jude stood next to her and again she was struck by how much she liked his silent strength. How with a look or a few words he could make her feel safe.

How could that be when just earlier this morning, she'd found him to be an overbearing jerk?

But right now—this moment—she appreciated him being there.

"I'm fine," she said, giving him a watery smile. "Just a little emotional because Maksim and Jo named the baby after me. Barrett's my middle name and my mother's last name."

Jude smiled too. One of the few genuine smiles she'd received from him, it made her heart skip a beat. Even more than one.

"Come on," she said, grabbing his hand. "Let's go see my new nephew."

Chapter 13

"Can you tell which one he is?" Ellina asked, peering from one wizened little face to another. "I can't make out what any of the name cards say. And I thought it was supposed to be doctors who have lousy handwriting."

Then she added in a whisper, "And frankly, they all look like eighty-year-old men who have been morphed with baby birds."

A surprised laugh escaped Jude.

"I mean cute old men and cute baby birds," she amended, smiling over at him.

Jude scanned the rows of infants. "He's in the back. The third one in from the left. With his cap on crooked."

"Oh," she immediately cooed. "Look how jaunty he looks with his hat at an angle."

Jude smiled, amused by her excitement and her take on the hat.

"He's definitely the cutest one," she said decisively.

"Cutest of the geriatric baby-bird men?"

She laughed. "Yes. He's perfect."

As if she couldn't contain herself any longer, she tapped the glass to catch the attention of one of the nurses monitoring the infants. The nurse, a lady in her mid-fifties, was clearly used to overexuberant new parents and other family members. She smiled and opened the nursery door.

"Can I help you?"

"Yes. I was hoping to see the Kostova baby. I'm his aunt."

The older woman smiled again. "I can't let you take the child out of the nursery without one of the parents present, but I can push him up to the window so you can have a better look."

"Okay," Ellina agreed, but Jude could tell she was disappointed. She sighed. "It seems sort of silly to keep him away from his own family."

"I think it's pretty good, the level of security they have here. You can't be too careful."

"Spoken just like a man who mistrusts everyone," she said, but smiled slightly to buffer the words.

"It's in the job description," he said.

"I know." Her tone held none of the brightness of just moments earlier. "It just must be a hard way to live."

He didn't speak for a moment, then he said, "It is."

Ellina didn't know what to say. She was surprised that Jude had been even that candid. Sharing was something that very clearly made him uncomfortable. Yet that comment admitted a lot.

The nurse tapped the glass, drawing Ellina's attention back to the nursery and little baby Barrett.

Both she and Jude gazed at the child.

Ellina didn't have much experience with babies. None, really. So she found every wiggle, every twitch fascinating. She smiled when his eyebrows moved up and down like Groucho Marx. She sighed when he yawned. She laughed out loud when he flailed his arm around like the appendage had a life of its own. That is, until his fist quite unintentionally found its way to his mouth.

"He's amazing."

Ellina looked at Jude and was surprised at the raw emotion in his voice. He watched the baby, but none of her joy was on his face. She only saw hurt, loss.

"Are you okay?" she asked softly.

He breathed in slowly. "Yeah. I . . ."

She waited for him to say something more. She could feel he wanted to, but the words wouldn't come.

Instead he said, "Yeah."

She watched him for a moment longer, wondering what could have happened to cause that distant, haunted look in his eyes.

But she didn't press. She simply reached out a hand and touched his arm, offering comfort the only way she could.

"So, the rumors are true."

Ellina spun around, gaping at the person who just spoke from behind her.

"Daddy."

Jude had to admit that Viktor Kostova, also known as Valafar, was not exactly what he'd expected. He was dubbed the Grand Duke of Hell, and Jude had imagined him to appear like a stern, imposing grandfather. And while the demon was indeed imposing, standing as tall as Jude, although with black hair and dark eyes, he seemed more Hollywood than Hell. Old Hollywood to be exact.

His hair was perfectly coiffed, and his eyes were shrewd and intense. He wore a charcoal-gray suit with a blue ascot, and Jude was immediately reminded of Errol Flynn or Sir Laurence Olivier.

And he was much younger looking than Jude had imagined. Of course, that shouldn't have surprised him. Demons usually aged normally until their late teens, then they acquired control over how old they wanted to appear.

Apparently Viktor Kostova had decided somewhere between thirty-five and forty was a good age range for him. But
even if age-wise he didn't appear that he could be Ellina's father, his lecturing tone as he spoke to her left little doubt that
he was her pater.

"So your phone doesn't work? I have to rely on your
brothers to find out anything that's going on in your life."

"I'm sorry, Dad."

He nodded, but he was still not pleased. His gaze moved
over her.

"Really, Ellina. You come to the hospital to meet the
newest member of the Kostova family and this is what you
wear. You look like a groupie for a rock band."

He raised an eyebrow at her faded jeans. And from his
continued expression clearly the vintage Rolling Stones T-shirt
and boots that looked like the female version of biker boots
didn't pass muster either.

This time Ellina didn't apologize, but she did fidget under
his scrutiny, tugging at the hem of her shirt and looking every
inch the scolded child.

Jude decided right then that he did not care for
Viktor Kostova—and *that* didn't surprise him in the least.

Viktor, after giving him a quick once-over, which didn't
reveal what he thought of his jeans and long-sleeved black
shirt, extended his hand.

"You must be the beau that my sons told me about." He
looked pointedly at Ellina. "Not my daughter, mind you. But
my sons."

Jude gave his hand a quick shake, trying to avoid too
much of that creepy, clinging feeling, but alas it coiled up his
arm like a snake curling itself around a tree limb. And Viktor's was particularly unpleasant, indicative of an older,
stronger demon.

He dropped his hand down at his side, opening and closing it into a fist, trying to shake away the feeling. He looked to Ellina, waiting for her to give the answer to her father's question, and noticed she was watching him. Or rather his hand.

Then she looked back to her father.

"Dad, this is Jude."

Ellina gave Jude a look that silently told him to leave it at that.

Jude didn't say anything, although he did give her a slight smile. She managed to get around that question without a real answer. Her way was certainly more subtle than his this morning.

His gaze dropped to her lips. Then again, he'd enjoyed his method while it was happening.

Stop it.

Things were nice between them, a sort of unspoken truce, and he didn't want to ruin their camaraderie by being over-bearing.

"Well, I suppose we should take a look at this child," Viktor said, not sounding anything like a proud granddad.

He stepped toward the nursery window, but not before he gave Ellina a look down his aquiline nose and added, "Your brother does actually contact me with his news."

Ellina again didn't say anything. Instead she just moved aside so her father could have a better view.

"Well, he's a tiny little thing, isn't he? Human babies are always smaller." He looked over his shoulder at Jude. "Half-breeds are too."

Jude didn't react to the man's words. When Viktor turned back toward the nursery window, he did look to see Ellina's reaction. Her expression was placid, her eyes as emotionless as a doll's.

"Half-breeds are born totally human," Viktor continued, watching the baby, oblivious to either of their reactions.

"Their demon traits don't appear until they reach puberty. Or in some cases, like little Ellina here, they never really appear."

Viktor shot a grin over his shoulder as if his comment was delightfully funny. As if he hadn't just criticized his daughter. He was essentially, although not in so many words, telling her she wasn't quite good enough to be his daughter.

"Dad."

Maksim appeared, looking calmer than when they first arrived.

Jude didn't know if Ellina felt relief, but he did. Maybe the arrival of the new father would put them on a more positive track.

"Maksim," Viktor greeted, giving him a hug.

There had been no hug for Ellina. Just indirect criticisms intermingled with outright ones.

"Have you seen him?" Maksim asked, looking from one person to the next.

"He's small," Viktor said.

Nope, no positive track here.

"Well, I expect he'll grow," Maksim said undisturbed.

"They brought his bassinet right up to the glass," Ellina said with an encouraging smile. "We couldn't hold him without you here for security purposes."

Maksim nodded, but Viktor gave a snort of derision.

"Like that child needs to be protected from his own family," he said, shaking his head at the foolishness of it all—and undoubtedly of humans in general.

"I think it's a good idea," Ellina said softly. "You really can't be too careful."

Jude shot her a surprised look, and her lips curled in a half smile just to let him know she'd said the words on purpose. A private joke.

"I'll get him now," Maksim said, leaving them to knock on the nursery door. The nurse from earlier answered, talking quietly with him, then checking the hospital wristband he wore.

Within minutes Maksim held his son, squirmy and bundled in light blue.

Maksim directed them over to a more private section of the waiting area and settled on a tan vinyl couch, holding his son close to his chest. Ellina sat down beside him as if she couldn't wait to get her hands on the baby.

"He really is so beautiful," Ellina said, leaning in to push aside the edge of the blanket for a better peek.

Together, she and Maksim gazed down at him.

Jude watched Maksim, wondering if he'd ever sported that same silly grin, that same glow of delight. Or had it all been too bittersweet for that?

Pain, so intense it stole his breath away, tore through him like a ricocheting bullet. He looked away, trying to compose himself. Hell, simply trying to breathe.

When he looked back, Maksim had passed the baby to Ellina, and she cradled him in her arms, gazing down at him with love in her pale eyes. The image was beautiful.

He couldn't bear it.

Jude stood abruptly, wandering over to a water cooler in the corner. He took his time filling one of the paper cups. Then he took a long swallow, even though he wasn't thirsty.

"How is Jo?" Jude heard Ellina ask.

"She's doing okay. They gave her a sedative, and she's sleeping. But there was a lot of tearing. She'll have to stay here for a few days."

"That's the problem with human mothers," Viktor said, from where his chair was set away from his children as if he were some lord overseeing them, "they can be such—delicate creatures."

Jude got the feeling delicate wasn't the actual word he'd wanted to use.

"That's why Jo's going to cross over. Now," Maksim said.

Jude frowned, curious about the announcement. Crossing over usually referred to a human becoming a vampire or a werewolf. Was that their plan for an eternity together? That was certainly a much less selfish, self-important reason than his, wasn't it?

Ellina stopped stroking the back of her finger over the infant's chubby cheek.

"I thought Jo wanted more children."

"She did—probably still does. But honestly, I don't know if I can go through this again," Maksim's voice was rough with worry and exhaustion.

"So tell me," Viktor said as if his son hadn't just said anything of importance. Certainly not revealed that he'd been terrified for the life of his wife and child. "What have you named the boy?"

"Barrett James," Maksim said.

Silence filled the room. Even little Barrett, who'd started making hungry snuffling noises, was quiet.

Jude watched the array of reactions with curiosity.

Maksim sat regarding his father with a strange look of unrepentance on his face. Ellina's eyes remained on the baby, but Jude could see discomfort on her face. And from the firm set of Viktor's jaw and the hard cast in his eyes, it was pretty easy to tell he was fuming.

Just then, Barrett let out a plaintive cry and started rooting against Ellina's chest.

"I think it's dinnertime for this one," Maksim said with another proud fatherly smile at his son, totally ignoring his father's dour expression. Ellina carefully placed the baby back in his father's arms, then stood.

"I think maybe we should go," she said, casting a worried glance at Viktor. Clearly she was not able to ignore their father's mood as easily.

"Stay a little longer," Maksim said. "Just until Jo wakes up. Please."

Jude could see that Ellina wanted to leave—she wanted away from her father—but she offered her brother a sweet smile.

"Of course."

"Thanks, sis." Maksim gave her a quick one-armed hug and then hurried back to the nursery to get his son a bottle, Barrett was letting it be known that he'd had enough family time.

Jude could tell Ellina had too, but she braced herself, her shoulders straightening, her head up. She faced her father.

"Are you going to stay too, Dad?"

Her father's expression was still grim. "I need a drink."

"They probably have a cafeteria."

Viktor grimaced. "That wasn't quite what I had in mind."

Chapter 14

Ellina really just wanted to go home. Not that she wasn't worried about Jo and Maksim. Not that she couldn't stare at her new little nephew indefinitely. But dealing with her father, she could do without. Especially right now. Although she agreed a stiffer drink than tea would be nice.

She should have known Maksim's name choice wouldn't go over well with her father.

"Is this okay?" she asked Jude and her father, pointing to a small square table near the window. The cafeteria was relatively empty. One round table was surrounded by a half dozen older women, and two hospital staff members sat at another table on the other side of the room.

"Sure," Jude said, offering her a slight smile. A hint of a dimple for support—as she was coming to think of it.

Her father followed behind them, a Styrofoam cup held out in front of him like a live hand grenade. But even with that disdainful look, his dark, austere handsomeness garnered him much attention.

The woman at the cash register, with her plastic gloves and hairnet, gazed up at him as if he were a god—not some persnickety demon who was never satisfied—even after he requested a venti, extra hot, double espresso made with springwater.

She'd just smiled apologetically, and flirtatiously, Ellina

thought, and pointed to the square machine with three spig-
ots, regular, decaf, and hot water.

"What civilized establishment doesn't have espresso?" her
father muttered as he pulled out one of the chairs surrounding the table. He grimaced as he sat down. "One with folding
metal chairs, obviously."

Ellina sat down too, and was oddly relieved when Jude took
the spot beside her, rather than across from her. She could feel
his heat, his strength, close to her, and that gave her courage.

Odd that he could do that for her. This man she'd just met.
This man could make her so aggravated with his mistrustful
and domineering personality, yet he could also make her feel
so safe. But right now, she wasn't going to question her reaction. She needed the reinforcements.

Her father took a sip of his coffee, then scowled. He set
the cup down and pushed it away from him.

"So why on earth would your brother name that child
after your mother?"

Ellina stopped midsip of her tea and set down the cup.
Well, that certainly hadn't taken long. She knew it was coming, but she'd expected him to work his way up to the subject.

He must really be peeved.

"Well, I think Maksim and Jo actually named him after
me," she said, keeping her voice even. "Barrett is my middle
name."

He considered that. "I suppose that it's better they named
him that. After all, he isn't a true Kostova. If Maksim had
named his real child after Kitty . . . well, I would have had to
speak up."

Ellina bit the inside of her lip, then took a drink from her
cup to keep from saying anything, but even the burn of the
overly hot tea couldn't seem to stop her wayward tongue.

"Maksim considers Barrett his true son, Daddy."

Her father raised a contemptuous eyebrow.

"He can consider him that all he wants, but it still doesn't make the boy his child. He's . . ." he dropped his voice because the group of older women sat nearby and were, of course, looking at him, "human."

Ellina tried not to roll her eyes. Honestly, her father was pretty much the Archie Bunker of the underworld.

"And what is this about Maksim's wife?" Again he dropped his voice, "She's crossing over?"

"That's really their business, Dad."

He was silent for few seconds, then he muttered, "I don't agree with all these cross marriages. All these half-breed children. His children even will not really be a part of the demon world."

Even though that wasn't the first time she'd heard a comment like that from her father, the words still hit her like pellets from a gun, stinging, trying to draw blood.

"Pardon me, sir," Jude said, his rich, low voice surprising her.

For some reason, she hadn't expected him to say anything. Watching him wide-eyed, and a little nervously, she waited for him to speak.

"But how can you have such a low opinion of integration when your own daughter is a creation of such a union?"

Her father had the decency to look a little uncomfortable, but then he straightened in his hated folding chair and said, "I'm not of a low opinion, I'm just concerned."

Ellina frowned, having no idea what that really meant.

"Besides, having a child with Kitty Barrett was not my intention."

Well that revelation certain makes me feel better, she thought bitterly. Thanks, Dad.

Ellina closed her eyes for a moment, amazed at how her father could carelessly toss out harsh words with little thought as to who they might wound.

Then she felt Jude's hand on her leg, his fingers curling around her knee, the gesture meant to comfort her. To tell her he was there.

Jude was there.

And while she did find his touch reassuring, she also felt shame. He was seeing exactly what her family thought of her. The family she'd defended to him. She couldn't help wondering if, were the tables turned, they would defend her.

Sadly she was pretty sure she knew that answer already.

"I intended to steal Kitty's soul," her father said as nonchalantly as someone else might say, "I intended to borrow her car" or "I intended to ask her to loan me a twenty." "But she had such a sweet little personality and pretty face. And she was such a good cook that I ended up staying with her much longer than I planned."

"Who knew a mean beef bourguignonne and berry cobbler could save your soul?" Ellina said.

Jude smiled at her, then surprised her by adding, "And I thought it was good fiddle playin'."

"And a chicken in the bread pan, picking out dough," Ellina said.

Her father looked unimpressed with their jokes.

"'Devil Went Down to Georgia' is not a factually based song," he informed them, condescension dripping from every syllable. "Nor is 'Sympathy for the Devil.' Or 'Friend of the Devil.' And for your information, Satan prefers to play slide guitar."

Ellina glanced at Jude, trying not to laugh. He squeezed her knee, clearly sharing her amusement.

Her father sighed as if dealing with them was just exhausting.

"Anyway, back to what I was saying," he said to Jude. "By the time I decided to go for Kitty's soul, Ellina was on the way."

Ellina supposed she should be glad that her mother's pregnancy had stopped his nefarious plot. It still amazed her that it had.

Jude squeezed her knee again and gave her an encouraging smile.

Then the table fell silent.

Really, how did one follow a touching story like that?

"So Jude, tell me about yourself." Her father's tone was that of a concerned father, as if he hadn't just revealed he never really cared for Ellina's mother, and he was not pleased with his daughter. "What are you? I'm having a hard time reading you."

Jude smiled, one of his wide grins with dimples coming out in full glory. "I'm a half-breed, sir."

Her father's eyes darkened and narrowed. "What are you then?"

"I'm half vampire/half werewolf."

"Vampire and werewolf. Now how and why does that happen?"

Jude's smile didn't waver. "Well, I made it happen. I chose to become both."

Ellina stared at him. He said it was an accident.

His father raised that eyebrow of his again. "Interesting."

Ellina was surprised he didn't say more. That seemed like something he'd have an opinion on, since he had an opinion about everything. But she needn't have worried. He just moved onto one of his other favorite things to criticize.

"I suppose you know about Ellina's books?"

Ellina fought the urge to bang her head on the tabletop.

"I do." Jude said with a nod.

"I can't tell you how many times I've told her what silliness they are. A demon-fighting pastry chef. So ridiculous."

Ellina breathed in slowly through her nose, telling herself she could get through this. She'd listened to his derogatory diatribes many times before, although he was in rare form today.

And the attacks were usually for her ears only. Not in front of someone else. Jude's opinion mattered to her. She didn't understand why, but it did. Very much.

"Have you actually read her books, sir?"

Ellina's gaze flew to Jude, again surprised by his question.

"Because," Jude continued, "I think you would find them very good. They are smart and well written with wonderful characters and great plot twists. And actually the lead character is a baker and cake decorator."

Ellina was stunned by Jude's words. Did he really think that? She didn't even know he'd read any of them. He even knew Jenny Bell was a not precisely a pastry chef—but a cake maker.

She glanced to her father, who didn't look nearly as impressed with Jude's review.

"They are about demons. Demons as villains. She should be more loyal to her own kind."

Jude nodded as if he understood the man's point and agreed. "But," Jude said, his dark brows drawn together as if he were genuinely confused, "didn't you basically say earlier that half-breeds aren't really a part of the demon world?"

Her father's expression grew darker, then he looked at his wristwatch. "Well, this has been an interesting visit. As always."

He gave Ellina a pointed look.

"But I have to go. Please tell Maksim that I will be in touch."

He started to leave, then paused, looking back to Ellina.

"Maksim told me about the break-ins. Be careful. And call me if you need help."

Ellina nodded, utterly confused. Her father had done

nothing but say one hurtful thing after another, and now he was showing concern for her. She'd never understand the man.

He cast his dark, intense gaze to Jude. "Take care of her."

"I will," Jude said, his tone resolute.

Her father didn't look back as he crossed the cafeteria, his back stick straight, his demeanor one of being inherently better than everyone around him. People watched him as he passed, and from their admiring stares, they seemed to believe the same thing.

Jude's hand left her knee. Cool air replaced the warmth his large arm had created. But his touch didn't leave her for long. He caught her hand instead, his fingers curling around hers. His thumb brushed the back of her hand with a velvety roughness that managed to touch deep inside her.

She suppressed a pleased shiver.

"Your father is a piece of work."

Ellina nodded with a humorless chuckle. "That he is."

She met his gaze and saw something that looked an awful lot like pity in his green eyes. She didn't want pity.

Yet before she could control it, tears welled in her eyes.

Oh God, she wouldn't cry.

All the pent-up pain and humiliation from her own father's words hit her, becoming even more glaringly ugly when seen through Jude's eyes.

To her utter dismay, she began to sob.

Jude watched Ellina crumble and wondered how she'd held up under the weight of her father's thoughtless censure this long.

He squeezed her hand, although he wanted to pull her onto his lap and hold her like a small child. He wondered if anyone had ever done that for her during her youth. Had she ever been protected? Comforted?

She cried quietly for a few moments, her head down, her shoulders hunched forward, trying to shield her breakdown from others. From him

"I'm sorry," she managed, her voice hoarse with emotion. "Don't be."

She cried quietly for several more seconds, then said with a watery, choking laugh, "I feel like an idiot."

She subtly gestured to the table of women a few feet away from them.

The women watched Ellina, sympathetic expressions on their faces. One even offered an empathetic smile to Jude.

"This is a hospital. I'm sure people cry here all the time," he told her, squeezing her delicate fingers.

"Not," she sniffled, "because of their bully fathers, I bet."

Jude noticed a couple in their thirties had joined the women as spectators, although they seemed more curious than sympathetic. They even looked away guiltily when they realized Jude saw them.

"Let's get out of here," Jude suggested. He stood and tugged her finger, gently urging her to stand too.

She did, allowing him to lead her along. The hallway outside the cafeteria was busy, and he knew being around others wasn't what Ellina wanted.

He ushered her through a few hallways, eventually finding one that was empty and quiet. At the end were double doors and a sign that read CHAPEL.

"Chapel?" Ellina said, wiping her damp cheeks with the back of her free hand.

"It should be quiet. And some say a good place to gather your thoughts."

He smiled at her, and he noticed her eyes flicked to his lips. She nodded.

He pushed open the door and peeked inside. His eyes adjusted easily to the dim lighting that radiated from stained-glass wall sconces and onto the gleaming oak quarter-paneled walls. Matching oak pews lined both sides of a burgundy carpeted aisle. At the end was a small altar with a round stained-glass window casting a myriad of colors on the oak floor and walls.

The room was empty.

He pulled her inside and they sat down in the back pew, both silent, just taking in the colors, the quiet, the peace.

"This is better than the cafeteria," Ellina decided with a nod.

"It is."

They fell quiet again.

Then Ellina swiveled slightly toward him. She'd stopped crying, but eyes were still moist, her lashes clumped, thick and dark from her tears. Instead of detracting from her beauty, the effect reminded him of a waif, lost and alone.

The protectiveness that was becoming an ingrained part of him since meeting her flamed.

"I'm sorry you had to witness that," she said managing a wan smile. "My dad is always overbearing, but he's not usually that—well, that bad."

Jude nodded, but didn't quite believe her.

"You know, he's just annoyed with my books. And it bothers him that I don't really have any demon qualities. And—"

Jude caught her hand to stop her. She was taking on her father's criticisms as if they were real flaws. They weren't. She needed to know that.

"His opinions about those things are just that, his opinions. You are fine." He squeezed her fingers. "Perfect, in fact."

Her eyes searched his, and he could tell she was gauging his sincerity. Then her gaze dropped to their joined hands.

"Well, you were right though. Last night."

He shook his head, not sure to what she was referring. "About what?"

"When you asked if my family considered me one of them. They don't. The only one who accepts me is Maksim."

"What about your mother?"

"Kitty Barrett," she said mimicking her father's affected accent. "She lives in a commune somewhere in Nova Scotia. I haven't seen her in years. It's hard for her to get away, you know, what with all the chores and whatnot."

"A commune? Really?"

She nodded, flashing a quick smile. "Some sort of back-to-nature, holistic type thing."

"Was she a good mother when you were little?"

Ellina pursed her lips as she considered his question.

"Yes. She was pretty good. Of course, she was obsessed with my father. That was definitely her primary concern. She lived to please him. She really believed that eventually he'd come to his senses and realize he loved her."

"So your parents were never together?"

"They were off and on. Daddy was definitely attracted to her. At least sexually. And apparently to her cooking too," she half smiled. "But he never really respected her. He basically used her. When I was about twelve, she seemed to realize that he wasn't going to be with her. Not in the way she wanted. She became more—eccentric after that."

"The commune?"

"Oh, that was just one stop along her way to self-discovery, as she called it. There was her stint as a stripper. Learning to embrace her sexuality. Then she decided to clean up her act and become religious. She actually attended five different churches every week. But she didn't get what she wanted from that, so she joined an all-girl biker gang. Really, the commune is the most moderate of her interests."

Jude shook his head, trying to imagine what it must have been like to grow up in such an erratic, extreme environment. Ellina must have been left to her own devices—the consequence of having two parents who were essentially obsessed with themselves.

Suddenly Ellina's pretty laughter filled the paneled room, incongruent with his thoughts.

His brows came together, a puzzled smile on his lips.

"What's so funny?"

She giggled. "I suddenly feel like I'm in confession or something. At least as close as I've ever been. Well, aside from the time, during Mom's religious phase, when she converted one of our showers into a confessional. She wanted me to confess my sins, but every time she'd make me try, I'd just turn on the water. It was worth getting soaking wet, clothes and all, to get out of that."

She laughed again, the sound urging him to join in.

"I'm sure it was."

"See, I'm confessing things that I've never told anyone. Even Maksim doesn't know about the confessional shower."

Jude smiled, oddly pleased by the admission.

"Although I'll gladly trade places and let you be the confessor now. I think you've learned enough about me and my warped family for the time being."

Her laughter faded, and she relaxed against the pew, a smile curling her pale pink lips. She looked at ease.

Her father's harsh judgments seemed to be gone from her mind. He hoped he'd helped with that. He looked down at their hands, still linked.

Serenity filled him too, so he had no idea what prompted him to make the admission he did, but he heard himself saying it before he could stop himself.

"I was a father."

Chapter 15

Ellina laughed. That was a pretty good joke, a funny play on her confessional observation and her crazy story about her mom.

"Father Anthony? It does have a nice ring."

Her chuckle faded as she realized he wasn't sharing in her amusement. She leaned away from him to better see his face, her eyes roaming his features.

No mirth there.

"He was born in 65 BCE."

She gaped at him. He was serious. He had a child and . . .

She blinked. Wow, Jude was really, really old.

And he was a father. That was amazing. And surprising. And . . .

Her swirling thoughts grasped onto what he'd actually said, and why his face was so somber.

He *was* a father. He wasn't any longer.

Oh God.

She met his gaze, silently urging him to tell her more.

He breathed deep into his chest. Then he looked away, suddenly fascinated with the stained-glass window at the head of the chapel.

She tightened her hand around his, and his eyes moved to their joined fingers.

He inhaled again, then spoke.

"My wife, Livia, always loved children."

Wife. Of course he'd had a wife. Somewhere in the all those centuries, which were really *a lot*, she thought again, still amazed, there had to be a wife or two, right? Maybe a hundred. That idea so didn't please her.

"She had been desperate for a child of her own. It took us a while to conceive, but when we finally did, she was ecstatic. People talk about women glowing with pregnancy, that was her. She just shone."

The haunted shadows she'd seen in his eyes back at the nursery returned. He was silent while lost in his memories.

Something sharp and bitter flared in her chest. An emotion that shocked her. An emotion that wasn't fair or reasonable.

He was telling her about a woman he loved. His wife. Ellina's irrational jealousy had no place here. But it was there, tightening her chest nonetheless.

She ignored it, waiting for Jude to continue.

"She had a difficult labor like Jo, but of course at that time there was little that could be done to help her. She never even regained consciousness to see our son."

Now Ellina felt even pettier for feeling envious of this woman. Livia never got to see her child. She couldn't imagine that. Never seeing the child she'd carried for nine months. Never getting to see him walk or talk or grow into a fine young man.

"That's awful," she said, moving her free hand to rub his arm, to offer any comfort she could. Although she wasn't sure he noticed; his thoughts were gone to the past, lost there for the moment.

"And your son? Did you raise him alone?"

He shook his head, his eyes darkened to the color of a remote, desolate forest.

"He died too. Four days later."

"Oh, Jude."

She hugged his arm, resting her head on his shoulder, feeling his pain as if it were her own. That explained the look on his face as they'd watched the babies in the nursery. That must have been so difficult. All the memories and emotions that must have flooded back.

Suddenly her father's disapproval seemed so insignificant. Her twin brothers' ridicule. Those things didn't compare with a loss like that.

Poor Jude.

Ellina ran her hand up and down his arm, willing away his pain.

"Jude, I'm so sorry," she whispered, her voice full of sorrow.

She nuzzled her cheek against his shoulder, hugging him, unsure what else to do to help him.

Then the world seemed to shift on its axis, and she found herself sitting on Jude's lap, his strong arms holding her there.

"Ellina," he murmured, touching her hair, his eyes searching hers. Then his mouth found hers.

Jude hadn't intended for the kiss to happen.

He realized that, even now, as his lips moved over hers.

One minute he was remembering the most excruciating times of his life. The one thing he regretted so much that he'd never recovered. Never stopped punishing himself.

The next minute, Ellina was hugging him. Her hand stroking his arm, her touch meant to offer him comfort. But then somewhere amid his memories and her consolation, he became aware of her nearness. The way her touch felt, so good, so different from any other woman's touch. Even Livia's—as much as he hated to admit it.

And before he thought it out, before he weighed the repercussions, he pulled her onto his lap and kissed her.

And consequences be damned, there was no way he could stop now. Not when her lips clung so sweetly to his, sculpting to his as if they were made for him.

He nibbled the softness of her lower lip, hearing her gasp at the small bite. He took her gasp into his mouth, using her response to deepen their embrace.

She moaned again, her arms coming around his neck, her firm breasts pressing to his chest. A tremor ran through him. He had to taste her, to be inside her in any way he could.

His nudged her mouth open, mingling her tongue with hers. Hot, moist, raspy touches.

He groaned, pulling her tighter to him.

"God, Ellina," he murmured again her lips, "you taste so good."

He angled his head, taking her mouth again, when he felt her freeze. Her body went rigid under his hands; her mouth closed, unyielding.

He lifted his head to ask her what was wrong. Had he done something to scare her?

But before he could get the questions out, she wriggled out of his hold, dashing toward the chapel door.

He rose.

"Ellina!"

He sprinted after her, his movements much faster than hers, but she still managed to reach the door before he could catch her. The door slammed behind her, but he had faith he could stop her in the hallway.

He yanked open the door and charged out, only to run full

speed into someone. His hand shot out and caught the person before they could fall to the floor.

Aside from the automatic save, he didn't acknowledge the person, his attention focused on which way Ellina would go once she reached the end of the hallway. She paused for a second, looking both ways. Jude moved to follow.

"You could kill a person."

Jude hesitated, looking back at the man he'd hit. A frail man in his eighties, if he were a day, slightly stooped with a few sprigs of gray hair on an otherwise bald pate.

His clouded eyes were narrowed until he saw where Jude's gaze had been directed. They both watched as Ellina chose to go right and dashed away. Out of sight.

"Chasin' your girl," the old man stated rather than asked. "Mine always makes me chase."

It was hard to imagine this man chasing anyone. But something in the man's tone, maybe a hint of sentimentality, made Jude realize the old man was heading to the chapel to pray for his girl.

"Yes, I'm chasing my girl," Jude told the man.

"Then go, man."

Jude nodded. "Are you okay?"

The old man pursed his lips together, giving him a look of gritty gumption. "I reckon I made it this long, I don't think a pup like you is going to slow me down any."

Jude smiled slightly, liking the man's pluck. He nodded and started down the hall after Ellina.

"I hope your girl is making you chase her again soon," he called back to the man.

"She will."

Jude smiled to himself as he turned right. The man had given him a strange sense of resolve.

My girl.

*   *   *

Ellina ran into the women's room, heading directly to the largest stall at the end. It was marked handicapped, and at the moment she was definitely feeling like that term applied to her.

As she hoped, the stall was not only larger to accommodate wheelchairs and walkers but also contained its own sink. She latched the door and headed directly to the sink.

Bracing her hands on the cold porcelain, she peered at herself in the soap-splattered mirror above the low-set sink.

She let out a small whimper.

Thank God she only encountered that one little old man during her mad escape. She'd averted her head and she didn't think he'd seen anything. She hoped.

This was the worst reaction she'd seen in a long time.

The skin of her neck was layered in the scales that crept upward and onto her cheek like gills. Her eyes glowed so red they looked like stoplights affixed above too prominent cheekbones.

Stoplights. Ha! Too bad she hadn't heeded the stoplights. Instead she'd driven right through them without even braking. She'd allowed the kiss to go on much, much longer than she should.

And if that wasn't evident enough from the creeping scales and the beacon eyes, then the crowning glory to her stupidity was the two small red horns poking through her *champagne fizz*–colored hair (at least that's what she thought the dye box had said).

Like she needed to be thinking about that now!

She couldn't remember the last time she'd gotten so aroused or agitated that the horns had actually appeared.

Reluctantly, she touched one of the slight curved protrusions. It was hard and seemed to quiver under her fingertips like her scales did.

She stilled as she heard the restroom door open. A woman in worn brown flats went into the stall beside hers.

Ellina turned on the water to make it less obvious that she was just standing at the sink. Hiding out. Freaking out.

The woman was finished, hands washed and out the door before Ellina's eyes had even dulled from stoplights to Christmas bulbs. Of course the fact that she could still taste Jude on her lips and feel his strong arms holding her close to his solid chest didn't help her cause.

Why had she allowed him to do that?

Because you wanted him to, you fool.

She sighed. It was time to face the facts. She couldn't control her attraction. She was just kidding herself to think she could.

She looked at her monstrous reflection. Clearly kidding herself.

So now it was time to legitimately think of a solution. Because the truth was she could not let him see her this way. It would kill her to witness the revulsion in his eyes. Just another one in her life who couldn't accept her. And he did seem to be accepting her, so to lose that . . .

You barely know him, you ninny. But she had shared more with him in the short time they'd been together than she ever had with anyone else in her life. Even Maksim. Even Pete.

That fact didn't change what she had to do. She had to tell him that he had to go. She couldn't risk him seeing—she stared at herself—*this*.

Especially not now that she knew he'd experienced real love in his life. He'd had a wife and child and known something genuine and perfect. Even if only for a short time.

The image that greeted her in the mirror was so far from perfect. She looked like a demon with mange. Half scale. Half skin. All hideous.

"Ellina?"

She started as Jude's voice echoed off the tile walls, seeming to come at her from every angle. For just a moment she even wondered if she'd imagined it.

"Ellina? I know you are in here."

She cleared her throat, but her voice still sounded croaky. "Yes. I'm here."

"Are you okay?" He sounded almost sheepish.

Or maybe it was regret. Her eyes returned to her reflection. He'd really regret that kiss if he only knew.

"I'm . . ."

Scaled? Horned? Glowing?

"I'm fine."

"Okay. I'll just be waiting out here."

"Okay," she said.

She heard the door close, the sound almost like that of air being sucked from the room. Seeing as she was having difficulty breathing, that seemed apropos.

She braced her hands back on the sides of the sink, willing some control over her disobedient body. Over her rebellious demon.

But after several seconds, she gave up. Concentration wasn't working, and she couldn't hide out in here indefinitely.

She turned on the faucet, running the cold water, then pulled several paper towels from the dispenser. Testing the temperature of the water, she prepared herself.

Surely splashing cold water on herself would get rid of this burn in her body—and thus her demon side. A makeshift version of a cold shower, and those supposedly worked.

She cupped her hands under the stream and leaned forward. She splashed several handfuls of the cool water over her face and neck. She lamented that the neckline of her shirt would be wet, but that was a small price to pay to be a normal texture and color and hornless.

She'd just tell Maksim that she felt unwell. That wasn't exactly a lie. This whole thing had her stressed and sick to her stomach.

Just then she heard the bathroom door whoosh open again. She paused, remaining over the sink, her face dripping, eyes screwed shut. She listened. Footsteps echoed on the tiles. Not Jude—his tread was too quiet, almost silent, like the agile gait of a wildcat.

Just someone using the facilities.

She ladled one more handful of water over her cooled skin, then shut off the faucet. Feeling around, she found the paper towels where she placed them, on the edge of the sink. Straightening, she pressed the rough paper over her face. She couldn't feel any scales on the underside of her jaw or on her neck.

Thank God, she thought and opened her eyes.

At least she was pretty sure she opened her eyes. But everything was still black. She blinked as if it must be her. But nothing changed.

Was there a power outage? Surely a hospital had backup generators.

Then she heard it, a sound not far from her. A shuffling. A slither.

"Hello?" she called, turning toward the sound. She'd heard someone come in. Was that what she was hearing? A disoriented woman, fumbling in the dark to find the exit.

She heard another shuffle. Except the person wasn't moving toward the exit. She was moving toward her. The poor woman must be disoriented.

"Hello?" she said again, not even realizing she was backing away until the back of her legs hit something hard.

She gasped, then told herself to calm down. It had to be the toilet. She slowly back up again. She bumped into the object again. Yes, definitely the toilet. She stepped away from it.

Again, she heard that shuffling sound.

"Who's there?" she demanded, trying to stay calm, but she knew her voice was tinged with panic.

Then it was almost as if the darkness shifted, becoming a living thing, moving around her. Or rather something in the darkness was moving around her. Inside her stall with her.

Terrified, she opened her mouth to scream when something came around her waist, clamping so tight it forced the breath out of her, stealing her shriek. Another thing—an arm— came around her head, a large hand slapping over her face, sliding roughly around until it found her mouth.

"Hello, Ellina."

Chapter 16

Jude leaned against the wall, several feet from the bathroom. He didn't want to appear like some weirdo, lurking—as Ellina would say—right outside the ladies' room.

As it was, one of the nurses had seen him sticking his head in the door to talk to Ellina. He'd told her that his wife was feeling ill, and he was just checking on her. The nurse informed him that without an appointment he'd need to take her to the emergency unit.

He'd thanked her and had been trying to remain unobtrusive ever since.

"Where's your girl?"

Jude smiled as soon as he saw the old man from the chapel shambling toward him.

"In the ladies' room." He gestured toward the door with his head.

The man stopped, peering up at him with those opaque eyes that still managed to see everything.

"Women love to primp," he announced. "Especially when they think they have a reason to."

Jude nodded. "I suppose that is true."

"And your girl knows she's got a reason, don't she?"

Jude gave him a questioning frown. He wasn't quite following.

"Well, she had you chasin'. And now that you've caught her, she's expecting some special treatment."

Special treatment. Jude didn't know about that, but he was pretty sure she was going to expect an apology at the very least.

"Oh, lordy-be."

Jude snapped out of his thoughts to see that the old man had reached out to steady himself against the wall. His wrinkled skin looked somewhat gray. Jude immediately went to his side.

"Are you all right?"

"Ahh," the man growled, pulling an irritated face. "Just the world gettin' away from me again."

Jude wasn't sure exactly what that meant, but since he'd barged into the man and probably hadn't done him any favors, he wasn't going to let the poor old guy take a tumble now.

"Where are you headed?"

"Back to the waiting room." He smiled up at Jude. "Eloisa should be out of surgery soon. Eloisa. That's my girl's name. What's your girl's name?"

"Ellina," he said, amused by how similar the names were.

"Nice name." The man nodded approvingly. "I'm Cliff."

"Jude."

They shook hands, the old man's palms dry and callused, his fingers gnarled. Like time was literally drying him out.

Concern moved Jude to ask, "Could I walk with you?"

Then he added, because he knew the codger was too proud to accept his help, "I'd like to hear how things went with Eloisa."

"That would be nice." The man levered himself off the wall, swaying a little before he regained his balance and started shuffling down the hall.

Jude glanced at the bathroom door, hoping Ellina wouldn't come out while he was gone, although he trusted she'd go back to the maternity ward.

But as he walked away, he had a sense he shouldn't dawdle. He glanced at the door again. He couldn't say why, but he felt a strange sense of apprehension.

"Hello, Ellina."

A mouth was right next to her ear. She could smell the man's breath. Sour like stale coffee and garlic. There was another smell too. Something earthy. Something she thought she'd smelled before, but couldn't quite place.

"I imagine you've been expecting me."

She made a noise against his hand, attempting to answer him, but he didn't loosen his grip to hear what she had to say. He'd probably have been quite upset to know she hadn't been expecting him at all. She hadn't believed there was a *him*.

"Waiting is a bitch, isn't it?"

He forced her head up and down, making her agree.

"Yes, it is. I've waited a long time myself."

Ellina told herself not to panic. She needed to file away every detail she could about this man.

He seemed relatively tall, although it was hard to tell in the pitch black. She was disoriented with no focal point, no frame of reference.

His voice was strange. Oddly muffled, as if he had something over his mouth. He also wore gloves. Leather ones. She could tell from the texture against her face.

"I'll try to make this quick."

Fear snaked, cold and needling, down her spine. What was he going to make quick? Somehow she didn't think it was going to be something pleasant.

He started walking her forward. She tried to struggle, to

drag her feet, but he only lifted her, his arms brutally tight around her waist.

Then he pinned her against something. The wall. Her face, at an angle, smashed against the cold hardness.

The stall door she realized from the way the surface shook under his pressure. She tried to open her mouth to scream, but the odd angle and his hand painfully against her cheek only allowed a muffled croak.

He laughed and pressed harder.

Using his weight to pin her body, he moved his other hand. She could tell he was leaning down to reach for something. On the floor? In his pocket? She couldn't tell.

But she knew this was her chance to escape. She began wiggling, using her now free arms, although the way he had her head trapped and his body against hers, she could only reach behind her and claw at his head.

She made contact with something knit. A ski cap? She pulled, tugging as hard as she could.

He made an angry noise low in his throat, tightening his grip. But she managed to yank it off, and then claw at his face, his cheek, grabbing at his ear.

"Stop it, bitch," he growled.

Grabbing a large hank of her hair, he jerked her head back. Viciously. Then he slammed her face against the door.

She saw flashes of light, and she squeezed her eyes shut against the shooting pain in her nose and forehead.

When she opened her eyes again, she still saw light.

"Hello?" a female voice said.

Suddenly the weight at her back was gone and she was being hurled across the stall. She lost her footing, falling heavily between the toilet and wall.

She tried to right herself to see who had attacked her, but by the time she levered herself around, the stall door was open and the man was darting through the bathroom.

All she could make out was black clothing. It looked like the cap covered his head again.

"Hey," the woman who'd just entered cried, and then she screamed as he shoved her aside to get to the door.

Ellina managed to get to her feet and head toward the door herself, joined by her accidental rescuer.

They both ran into the hall, looking around them. The hall was empty.

"Are you okay?" the woman asked her.

Ellina realized she was a nurse from the scrubs she wore. She nodded, even though the adrenaline coursing through her was making it impossible to really know how she felt.

"Thank God I came in when I did."

"Yes," Ellina agreed.

"I was actually coming to check on you."

Ellina shook her head, confused.

"I saw your husband talking to you from the doorway," the woman said. "He said you were feeling ill, and since I hadn't seen either of you pass the nurse station, I decided I better check on you."

The nurse glanced around. "Where is your husband?"

Ellina, who was starting to feel a little light-headed, started to say she didn't have a husband, but stopped. Was the woman talking about Jude? Where was he?

"I don't know."

She swayed. Oh dear, she really didn't feel good.

Then she heard Jude's voice.

"Ellina?"

She saw him coming down the hall, his steps hastening as he saw her.

"Jude?" she said, taking a step toward him, but then everything closed in like she was seeing him through a key-hole.

"Ellina!"

She saw Jude reach for her, then everything went black.

Jude caught Ellina just before she crumpled to the floor.

"Bring her in here," the nurse he recognized from earlier said, pointing to a room on the right. He followed the nurse inside, placing Ellina's limp body on the examination table.

"I'll get a doctor," she said rushing from the room before giving him any explanation as to what happened. But from the look of Ellina, something bad.

He pushed back a tangle of hair that had fallen out of the loose knot she'd been wearing. He spotted a lump on her forehead that was already turning purple. A droplet of blood trickled from one of her nostrils.

He stepped over to a counter where the examination supplies were lined up and grabbed a tissue. Carefully, he blotted away the blood.

What the hell happened?

Then disgust filled him. He should have been there. He should have listened to that strange sensation when he'd walked away with Cliff. Hell, he had a damned gun. This guy could be dead now. Or at least hurting.

He'd told himself that the agitation was because of the kiss. That he was concerned she'd keep avoiding him. Or that the job would have to end. She'd want someone else to act as her guard.

God, who would blame her now? He gently touched her cheekbone, which was turning a sickening shade of purple.

He'd come back, telling Cliff that he had to go, but he'd come back too late. He'd definitely sensed it, but he'd been too late.

He lightly dabbed her nose again, but this time she flinched away from the pressure. The paper covering the exam table crinkled as she moved. Her eyes flickered open, staring up at him.

"Hi," he said softly, brushing another lock of hair away from her eyes.

She frowned, clearly confused, then tried to sit up.

He gently pressed her back down.

"Don't move, sweetheart. You just passed out. And it looks like you have some pretty nasty bruises."

She frowned, still bewildered, then dawning memory lit her eyes.

"I was attacked."

He nodded. "I guessed as much."

"He shut off the lights, then attacked me in the bathroom stall. A nurse came in and that scared him off."

"Did you see him?"

Ellina shook her head, then winced as he touched the lump on her forehead.

"He wore all black."

"Maybe the nurse saw him," Jude suggested, and she nodded again, this time more gingerly.

"Where were you?" she asked, and while her tone wasn't accusatory, the guilt already tight in his chest threatened to suffocate him.

Just then the nurse returned with a woman in a white doctor's coat.

"Hello," said the doctor, who seemed to be in her mid-thirties, "I'm Dr. Hamilton. Janice just filled me in on what happened. We've called the police, and now let's see what we can do for you."

Jude moved out of the way to allow the doctor access.

"Would you mind waiting outside for me?" the doctor asked him.

Jude nodded, but Ellina stopped him.

"I would prefer if he stayed." Her gaze sought his. Fear made her eyes glitter. "He's my husband."

That possessive feeling came through him again. Jude held her gaze, trying, with his eyes, to tell her that she would be okay. That he wouldn't leave. He'd already failed her once today. He wouldn't do it again. Ever.

The doctor said he could stay, and he took a seat in a chair in the corner.

The doctor's examination revealed lots of nasty bruises, but otherwise she was fine. No concussion. She'd probably passed out more from fear than her injuries, and she could go home once she talked to the police.

"Until then, I recommend you just lay here and try to relax," Dr. Hamilton told her, with a kind smile.

As soon as the doctor left, Jude moved back to her side. He took her hand, his thumb soothing over the back of her palm and fingers.

"You were right," she said, her pale eyes bleak. Her skin was pale, making the bruising on her forehead and cheek more pronounced. "He knew me. He was specifically after me."

Even though she hadn't had a chance to tell him that until now, he wasn't surprised. Any attack would have shaken her. But there was such stark fear in her pale eyes.

She'd been terrified. He'd seen it every time she'd sought him out throughout the doctor's exam. Crystalline terror glittered in her eyes as cold and unyielding as diamonds.

He was disgusted with himself. He'd failed her. This guy had come into a hospital and attacked her. That was pretty damn brazen. And that made this guy even more dangerous than Jude would have guessed.

He squeezed her hand, thanking every god he could think of that she was okay. That had just been pure luck this time. But it wouldn't be luck next time. It would be him, keeping her safe. And finding out who the hell this guy was.

Then killing him.

Fuck!

He'd had her. He'd had the herbal mixture ready. He'd memorized the incantation until it was like reciting the alphabet. He had a silver dagger, pointy and ready to kill.

The whole thing should have been over in seconds. He'd already covered himself in the powder. He'd just needed to say the words, then slit. And he would have been free.

Done deal.

But the bitch had fought. Then some hospital bitch came in and really fucked it up.

He threw the paper grocery bag with his "killing" clothes onto the bed and collapsed beside it.

He knew the hospital wasn't ideal, but he'd seen his chance and taken it. He'd been following her. Seeing where she might go if she'd ever get away from that damn Neanderthal she now had by her side every minute.

He'd actually been considering giving up for the day. Then a stroke of luck. On his way out of the hospital, he'd just happened to see her running down that hallway. Alone. And going into the restroom.

So he'd gone into the men's room right beside it, readied himself, and made his move. Except when he'd poked his head out, there was the goddamn Neanderthal.

But again, luck had been on his side. Along came some old geezer, and miracle of miracles, the oaf went off with man. And he'd made his move.

That's what the Neanderthal got for being a good Samaritan.

He stretched, exhilaration coursing through him. He felt better than he had since this horror began. He felt alive. Strong.

He'd failed. But he'd been so close.

Next time, the key was to get her alone. He was taking the wrong tactic. After all, it didn't matter if anyone knew he'd killed her after the fact. He'd be long gone by then.

So he would just get her alone quite straightforwardly. That shouldn't be too hard. After all, she already trusted him.

Chapter 17

Ellina had never been so happy to be home in her life. She'd always loved her home. But now . . .

She released a sigh of relief as soon as she stepped through the door.

They'd had to wait quite a while to talk to the police, and she'd made the whole event sound like a random act of violence. Given this was New Orleans, and crime was almost as common as Mardi Gras beads, the police hadn't doubted her story or questioned why she was the target.

She agreed with Jude's assessment that the police wouldn't be of any help, especially if the attacker was supernatural, so she'd been as vague as she could. It was best to give them as little as possible.

In truth that hadn't been that difficult. The whole thing had happened so quickly and been so disturbing, the details were hazy at best.

She'd told Jude more on the ride home. But not much more. Just that the attacker seemed to have some sort of plan, but she wasn't sure what it was, or why she even thought that.

In truth, there just wasn't much she could tell.

Then, rather than going to see Maksim, who already had

enough to worry about, she'd just called him and said she was not feeling well.

Fortunately, Jo had woken up and seemed to be feeling better, which made coming home easier for Ellina.

"I think I will go take a shower," she said to Jude.

She'd wanted one since the assault happened. It was strange—she'd heard that rape victims' first instinct was to go shower after the attack was finished, to wash away the violence, the brutality.

She understood why now. Her attack hadn't been that invasive, or even that brutal, but she still wanted to wash the whole thing away.

Jude, who, since the hospital, had been watching her as if she might break, nodded. "I'll see what I can find for dinner."

She gave him a forced smile, leaving him in the living room. She didn't have the heart to tell him she couldn't even imagine putting anything in her stomach. She was too tense to think about food.

But cooking seemed to be therapeutic to him, and he looked like he needed some calming too. She could tell he felt guilty that he hadn't been there. She supposed that made sense. Her safety was his job.

But she didn't think anyone could have predicted that attack. And she'd been the one avoiding him.

As she wandered down the hallway to her room, some of her peace at being home faded. She glanced into her office, realizing that man had been here. He'd walked her floors. He'd searched through her stuff.

She shivered. Now that made her feel even more violated.

She walked into her bedroom, flipping on the light as soon as she walked in. The room wasn't dark; it was early evening, but even the shadows seemed to unnerve her at the moment.

She pulled some flannel pajama bottoms and a sweatshirt

from her bureau. That seemed to be another side effect of the attack. She couldn't get warm.

Once in the bathroom, she turned the hot water on full blast in the tub. Then she fished a tiny manila envelope from her pocket, and dumped the contents into the palm of her hand. Two Valium.

The doctor had given them to her, and she hadn't thought she'd use them. But after thinking about that monster being in her house . . .

She popped one in her mouth, then moved to the sink and used her hand as a makeshift drinking cup.

As she straightened, she caught her reflection in the mirror. A bruise marred her left cheek and a pretty nasty goose egg bulged out from her forehead. Her nose had swelled as if it didn't quite fit proportionately between her eyes.

And here she'd been lamenting her demon looks. Now her human appearance wasn't much better. Most of the damage would be gone by tomorrow. That was one demon trait she had—one that she could actually be happy about too—especially now. She healed fast.

She stripped off her jeans and shirt, letting them fall to the floor in a pile. She examined the rest of herself. She had some bruising around her rib cage. And another big bruise on the outer thigh of her right leg, where she must have hit the toilet when he'd pushed her aside to make his escape.

She grimaced at how sore she felt as she crouched down to look under the sink. She had some lavender and mint shower gel that she'd purchased with the intent of using it to help minimize her stress over her writing and deadlines. Suddenly today's events seemed like a much more important use of aromatherapy.

As she searched she happened to glance at her clothes lying next to her. Then she did a double-take.

Frowning, she touched her shirt. The black material was speckled with something white. Picking it up, she held the garment out by the shoulders. The whole back was peppered with white, powdery specks.

Was that from her attacker? She lifted the shirt to her nose and sniffed. She instantly recognized the scent as the one she'd smelled on him, the one that seemed oddly familiar, yet not.

She stood and tugged on her sweatshirt, hurrying out to find Jude.

"Look," she said, finding him sitting in the living room, working on his computer. She waved the shirt at him.

"This was on my attacker."

Jude frowned as she waved something at him again, more insistently. Then he realized it was the T-shirt she'd been wearing today. He reached for it, holding the garment closer to the light. White spots dotted the material like someone had sprinkled baby powder down her back.

"Smell it," she said.

He did. It had a musty, earthy scent.

"I noticed that smell when he was restraining me. I remember thinking it was somehow familiar, but I couldn't place it. I still can't. But that's definitely what I smelled."

Jude examined it further, trying to figure out what it could be. It was chalky. More gray than white, really.

"I think we should save this," he said, rising. He went to the guest room and placed the garment in one of the empty bureau drawers. "We can take it somewhere and have the powder tested. I'll look for a lab online."

"Do you think that could lead to anything? Help us figure out who this guy is?"

"I don't know, but it can't hurt to try."

She nodded, leaning heavily against the door frame as if the excitement of the discovery had suddenly drained her last vestiges of strength.

Exhaustion made her so pale her skin looked almost translucent.

"Why don't you go shower," he said. "I've ordered a pizza and opened a bottle of wine. Did you take those pills the doctor gave you?"

She smiled and nodded, but even that seemed to test her limits.

"Just one. So it probably wouldn't hurt me to have one glass of wine, right?"

She looked so wistful, he laughed.

"I'm not a doctor, but I don't think one glass would hurt you."

"Could I take it with me now? Drinking in the shower isn't a sign of a bigger problem, is it?"

A surprised chuckle escaped him. He hadn't expected her to have the energy to joke.

"After today, I think that's fine. But just one." He waited for her to turn and head toward the kitchen.

She did, and he followed behind, trying not to let his gaze slide downward. And failing miserably. Her long legs bare beneath her oversized sweatshirt were simply too much of a temptation. Even exhausted, frazzled, and mussed, she was still the most beautiful woman he'd ever seen.

"Oh good. Red," she said when she entered the kitchen.

Guiltily his gaze snapped up to her face. He struggled to comprehend what she was saying.

"Oh yeah," he finally said, realizing she was talking about the wine. "I figured that was the best pizza wine."

She spun the bottle to face her. "Shiraz. Good call."

He again tried not to watch as she stood on her tiptoes to

reach into the cupboard for a glass. The sweatshirt rose up, promising a hint of panties.

Then she was flat-footed again, holding out a glass to him.

He took it. He definitely needed a drink. Badly.

She filled her glass.

"Okay, the shower is calling." She walked past him, and this time he managed not to look. He even breathed out a sigh of relief when he heard the bathroom door shut, closing her away from him.

He filled his own glass, then decided to take the whole bottle with him as he headed back to the living room. He set his glass and the bottle on the coffee table, then told himself to focus on something else.

The powder on her shirt. He went back to his room and opened the drawer. He pulled it out again.

He couldn't place the scent. He put it back, deciding to do an Internet search for a lab right now.

Then he heard Ellina pushing the shower curtain open. Against his better judgment, Jude approached the bathroom door. He listened to the sound of the water. The change in the resonance as she moved under it.

He imagined the water sluicing over her bare skin. Her hands moving over herself as she washed. Soap bubbles sliding from the tips of her nipples, clinging to the curls between her thighs.

He groaned, resting his forehead against the door.

He had to stop this.

Then his thoughts shifted to the old man from the hospital. Cliff. And his Eloisa.

He could have that with Ellina. He wanted that, he realized. He'd known she was different from the moment he walked into the house. There was no explanation why he felt this strongly, this quickly. But he did.

But look at how she reacted to your kiss, buddy.

He forced himself to leave the doorway.

Search. For. A. Lab.

He'd do some research, wait for the pizza, and not focus whatsoever on his desire for the woman in the bathroom.

He sat down on the sofa and started typing word combinations into his computer's search engine. Then, after a few moments, he pushed the computer aside.

Okay, maybe he'd wait for the pizza, drink his libido numb, and then not focus whatsoever on Ellina.

He took several gulps of the red liquid, then topped off his glass again.

When Ellina returned to the living room the next time, she was covered from neck to ankle in fleece and flannel. Her wet hair was wrapped in a towel. Despite the much more demure look, it did nothing to temper Jude's attraction to her.

Neither did the half a bottle of wine he'd drunk.

She smiled as she noticed the bottle, then lifted her now empty glass that she'd taken to the shower with her.

"And I thought I was going to be ahead of you."

"Well, you had the sedative," he pointed out. He held out a hand to take her glass. It was wet from the shower, and he pictured her under the spray, drinking it.

He gritted his teeth. He was making himself crazy.

She settled on the other end of the sofa, curling her legs underneath her.

"Mmm, what a day," she said. Ellina sighed and leaned her head against the back of the couch, closing her eyes. She lifted her head again and tugged off the towel. Her wet hair fell in curls around her face. Her . . . red hair?

"What did you do to your hair?" he asked, stunned.

She frowned, touching the damp locks. "What? You don't like it?"

She looked hurt.

He studied her for a moment. "That's not it. I'm just surprised."

She smiled sleepily. "I'm a bit of a chronic hair dyer. I do it when I'm feeling stressed or bored or upset."

He considered that—it was an interesting trait.

"I think it's a control thing."

He could see that.

"Or a way of re-creating yourself." He wished he'd kept that thought to himself, but she simply nodded.

"Could be."

Her acceptance of his theory surprised him, then he noted how tired she looked, her eyes barely open. But the shower had helped her coloring. Her cheeks were pink and actually looked quite lovely against her new red hair.

Jude turned his attention to the pizza, flipping open one of the boxes.

"Want a slice?" he asked.

She shook her head, her eyes now closed.

"I'm good." Then she opened one eye and said, "I would take another glass of wine, though."

"I don't think so," he said. He was serious about her not drinking any more. Plus she looked pretty relaxed already.

She sighed again, looking at him from beneath heavy lids.

He ate quietly, listening to her low, even breathing. She was probably out for the night, which was good. She'd had enough excitement for the day.

"Why would anyone want to hurt me?" she asked suddenly, surprising him.

He shook his head. He wished he had an answer for her. It would make things easier all the way around.

"I'm not sure."

She nodded as if that was a good answer. It wasn't.

She fell silent again. He ate another piece of pizza and was reaching for more, when Ellina chuckled.

He half-suspected that she was just giggling in her sleep, but then she opened one eye and smirked at him.

"You know, I was planning today to tell you that you should go, but now that doesn't seem like such a wise idea."

She giggled again, then made a face. She closed her eyes. "Wow, that was a dumb thing to say, wasn't it?"

"No," Jude said, "it wasn't. I suspected you were feeling that way after the kiss."

She sighed. "The kiss. I liked the kiss."

Jude blinked. Did she even know what she was saying? Or were the drugs and wine and stress of the day speaking?

But still, he said, "I liked the kiss too. A lot."

She smiled, her eyes closed. "It was fun, wasn't it?"

He nodded even though she couldn't see it.

"Until I got all horny." She giggled.

He gaped at her, then chuckled. Oh hell, she didn't have a clue what she was saying.

Then to his surprise, she opened her eyes, leaned over, and kissed him. She tasted like red wine and smelled like lavender. His penis hardened instantly.

The kiss was short, but utterly sweet. She leaned back and bit her lip, the action coy and sexy as hell.

Then she giggled again. "You do make me horny."

She giggled once more, and he smiled, amused by her silliness.

"Horny," she repeated, laughing harder. Then she actually put her fingers up to her head, pointing her index fingers upward in the impression of horns.

He frowned, suddenly pretty sure she wasn't referring to horny as a term for aroused.

She sobered slightly. "How do you feel about that, Jude? You could have a real demon in bed. Literally."

She giggled again.

Chapter 18

"Can I kiss you again?" she asked Jude.

Oh, she was going to regret this tomorrow. And he was already regretting what he was about to say.

"I'm not sure that's a good idea, sweetheart."

Ellina frowned. "It's the demon thing, isn't it? You haven't liked that from the very beginning, have you? You don't like touching demons, do you? I've seen how you react when you do."

Her observation surprised him.

"I don't," he agreed. "But that doesn't apply to you."

"I don't believe you," she said, her tone suddenly petulant.

Jude laughed. "Oh Ellina, I've liked everything about you from the beginning. Too much."

He was being too candid, but it was easy to do with her being so open. Too bad it was under the influence.

Her frown deepened. "Then why did you want to leave almost as soon as you met me?"

He laughed again. "Well, I didn't leave, did I?"

"That's because Maksim offered you any price to stay." She pouted slightly, until an idea occurred to her. "Wait, I have plenty of money. I could pay you anything too."

"For what, sweetheart?"

Because he wasn't taking any amount of money to leave.

"For you to sleep with me."

Okay, he didn't see that coming.

Ellina smiled, proud of the idea. Why hadn't she thought of this sooner? If it was a business transaction, then her little demon issue wouldn't be a problem. He'd be paid to ignore it.

She tilted her head. Wait. Was that a good idea? She was getting confused now.

She blinked, focusing on Jude. He wasn't smiling anymore.

"Why aren't you smiling? I like your smile. I like your dimples."

She reached out and touched his cheek. She could feel the stubble on his jaw. She liked that too. He had such a beautiful face, sculpted and almost a little harsh until he smiled. Then the dimples. They made him look boyish, sexy.

He caught her hand, holding her palm to his face for a moment, then lowering both their hands. But he didn't let go; instead he stroked his thumb over the inside her wrist. Warmth pooled in her belly. She liked that too.

She sighed.

"Ellina, I think you should go to bed."

She nodded. She was feeling awfully strange. She started to stand, but the room seemed to tilt and she tumbled back down onto the sofa.

She was laughing, then she was squealing, because Jude had picked her up, high against his solid chest. She looped her arms around his neck to keep her balance.

"I feel all dizzy and funny," she told him, leaning in to nibble his ear. Wow, she'd never done anything like that before. She nibbled it again, worrying the soft lobe between her teeth.

Jude trembled. Or at least she thought he did. It might just be her dizzy feeling again.

The next thing she knew Jude had brought her to her bedroom.

"Are you going to sleep with me?" she asked as he placed her in bed.

"I certainly hope so," he said, and she grinned. "But not tonight."

She pursed her lips, not happy with that answer. Jude pulled her comforter over her and tucked the edges around her as if she was a small child.

"I'm going to get you some water," he said, "Stay here."

"Okay," she agreed with a yawn. She stretched, deciding that her bed felt pretty wonderful. Not as good as Jude's arms, but still nice.

"I'll be right back," Jude told her again.

She nodded, letting her eyes drift shut while she waited.

Paying him to have sex with her. That was a pretty great idea.

Wasn't it?

Jude stood outside Ellina's bedroom door, trying to fathom what the hell just happened. Was she honestly telling him that when she had sex she turned into a demon? And did she really want to pay him to have sex with her?

He shook his head, utterly confused.

Clearly he'd been wrong to think that one glass of wine with a Valium wouldn't affect her that much. That girl was lit.

He headed to the kitchen and filled a large tumbler with ice water.

"Here you go," he said as he came into the room. "I think some water will make you feel better."

There was no response from the bed. He walked over to find Ellina with her eyes closed, her arms crossed over her chest in the perfect imitation of a vampire at rest.

"Ellina?"

Her only answer was a slight snore.

He shook his head again, smiling with amusement. Ellina *was* entertaining.

He set the glass on the nightstand, then went to get the book he'd been reading the night before from his room. He returned, taking a seat in the feminine little chair she had in the corner.

He didn't want to leave her alone tonight for two reasons. One, he wasn't sure what type of creature had attacked her at the hospital and he couldn't risk the guy coming into her room. And second, she was so gone he had no idea what she might do if she woke up again.

He didn't want her going out and offering some other man money to have sex with her.

He chuckled, opening his book.

One thing he did know for sure—she was going to be embarrassed as hell come tomorrow morning.

If she remembered it.

Ellina groaned, throwing an arm over her face to block out the light. Why the hell was it so bright? She started to roll over, but the movement made her head ache so badly that she remained on her back. Perfectly still.

What was wrong with her?

Then she remembered the attack. But she didn't think the bumps and bruises she'd sustained would make her feel like this. She thought harder, although that seemed to make her head throb more.

Then everything returned with full, vivid, awful clarity. She'd taken the sedative the doctor gave her. She'd had a glass of wine.

She'd kissed Jude.

Oh God.

She'd told Jude about the demon issues.

Oh God.

She'd offered him money to have sex with her.

"Oh God."

"You're awake."

She gasped, sitting up to see Jude at the end of her bed, lounging in her yellow gingham chair, his feet up on the windowsill, legs crossed at the ankles.

He smiled serenely, looking for all the world as if he belonged there.

"What—what are you doing here?"

She dreaded the answer. Had he taken her up on the money for sex offer?

"I didn't think it was a very good idea to let you sleep alone last night."

She made a small noise of dread in her throat. Oh no, he had slept with her. She didn't remember.

"So I sat here and read all night."

She relaxed slightly, but still had to ask, "So we—we didn't . . ."

He smiled. "So you remember, do ya?"

She could feel the heat burning her cheeks, but she didn't respond. She was mortified.

He rose then, setting down the book he'd been reading on the chair. He crossed to the bed and sat down on the edge.

"Let me assure you," he said with a smile, "no money exchanged hands last night."

She let out a pent-up breath. "Oh, good."

Then another horror hit her.

"We didn't . . . do it? You know, without money?"

He chuckled, then shook his head.

"No. We didn't."

Again relief washed over her. Until he leaned in and kissed her. Then relief was not what was washing through her.

The caress was different from the other kisses they'd shared. This one was gentle and sweet, but no less arousing for its tenderness. In fact, more so, in some ways. A whisper of lips touching, breaths mingling.

She couldn't stop the tremor that shook her.

He pulled away, looking deep into her eyes. Then he cupped her cheek, his thumb running lightly across her lower lip.

"I want to make something very clear to you," he said his voice low and velvety. "You don't have to worry about my attraction to you. I'm desperately attracted to you. Everything about you. But you have to trust that. You have to decide you can trust me."

Ellina stared at him, unsure what to say. He rose then.

"I already put on coffee," he said. "That will probably help your headache. I'm going to jump in the shower."

She nodded, still dazed by what he'd just told her. He disappeared through her bathroom door, closing it behind him.

She sat there, too overwhelmed. Jude was telling her he wanted her. All of her, even the demon. Something like exhilaration danced through her, only to be squashed by doubts.

He said that, but he hadn't actually seen her. He didn't know what he was agreeing to, not really.

She pushed back the covers and crawled out of bed. Her body felt okay, not too sore, but her head was another story.

Valium and wine. Bad. Very, very bad.

And not just because of the headache. Dear Lord, the things she'd said.

She trudged to the kitchen and fixed herself some coffee, praying Jude was right. She needed something to drive away this headache. She didn't have an answer for the mortification.

She'd just settled down on the sofa with her mug and her television remote, because TV was about all she was going to be able to handle this morning, when someone knocked on the door.

She started, her stomach sour with dread.

Like your stalker is going to knock on your front door, she admonished herself. But she still didn't move. She heard the shower running and worried Jude wouldn't be able to hear her if something happened.

But you can't live in fear of everything, she told herself. She stood, but pushed back her curtain to see who was there before she actually headed toward the door.

She released the breath that she hadn't even realized she was holding. Her body sagged with relief.

It was Pete.

"Hi," she smiled as she opened the door.

"Good morning," he smiled back, but then his smile slipped. "What happened to you?"

At first, she thought her friend referred to her unfortunate mixture of sedatives and alcohol, then she realized he couldn't know about that.

The bruises, she realized. She touched a hand to her cheek, suspecting it actually looked better this morning than last night.

She considered making up a story, but then opted against it. This was Pete. Aside for her little demon secret, she told him everything. Well, most things.

"I have a stalker," she told him.

"What?" Pete instantly caught her elbow and led her to the couch. Clearly he wanted to settle in and hear all the details.

"Remember the break-ins?"

He nodded.

"Well, those seemed to have been done by the same person. And that person attacked me yesterday."

"Oh my God. Where?"

"At the hospital while I was there to see Maksim and Jo's baby."

Pete shook his head, clearly shocked.

"They had a boy, by the way," Ellina added.

Pete brushed aside that information. "He attacked you at the hospital? That's pretty ballsy."

Ellina nodded, although she was a little surprised by his disinterest in the sex of Maksim's child. They'd had a bet on it, since she'd told Pete about the pregnancy. And he'd lost. That meant he had to buy her a meal at K-Paul's Louisiana Kitchen. Not cheap.

But then, he was concerned about her.

"Yeah, it was pretty ballsy," Ellina said. "I really think the only reason I'm sitting here is because a nurse happened to come into the bathroom. It was really scary, Pete."

"I bet. Do you have any idea who it might be? Did he say or do anything that you recognized?"

"No. But I did notice this smell. A strange sort of musty, earthy scent. And when I got home I had this strange powder all over my shirt. Jude put it in the guest room to take to a lab. Maybe we can find out something."

Pete frowned. "Powder? Really? That's weird."

She nodded.

"And where was the boyfriend?"

She frowned for a moment. Who? Oh, Jude.

"Out in the hallway."

Pete nodded. She got the feeling he wanted to say something but was holding back.

"Why?"

"Well . . ." He shook his head. "No, it's nothing."

She frowned. What was he going to say?

"I mean, I was in a ladies' room. He wouldn't have been with me anyway, if you're wondering why he didn't help me."

"Of course," he agreed with a smile, but again she detected an undercurrent to his response.

"Okay, Pete," she said. "What are you thinking?"

He looked reluctant to say anything, then he sighed. "Well, Ell, I'm just thinking that you don't know him very well. Are you sure you can trust him?"

She stared at her friend. "Of course I can trust him."

Pete nodded. "Okay. I know you certainly know him better than I do. It was just a thought."

Then he offered her his usual perky smile. "I was actually stopping by to see if you wanted to go get beignets. It might be good for you to get out around people. And in the sun."

Ellina couldn't restrain her look of disgust. "I'm afraid my stomach can't take all that fried dough and powdered sugar this morning."

Pete raised a curious eyebrow.

She rolled her eyes. "Let's just say I've discovered first-hand that Valium and wine do not mix. But coffee's made. Would you like a cup?"

He debated. "Sure."

She left him in the living room as she went to prepare him a cup. She was surprised Pete would even consider something like that about Jude. Her friend was usually far more trusting than she was. It made her think maybe Pete sensed something about her houseguest.

She shoved the thought aside. Jude was here to protect her, so he'd sort of dropped the ball. It was an accident, and he'd felt awful.

When she came back to the kitchen, Pete was in the guest room doorway.

"Pete?"

He started and closed the door with an impish smile.

"Sorry, you know me. Just being nosy. Seeing if he really

was staying in the guest room. And maybe sneak a peek at some post-shower towel action."

Ellina laughed. That was the Pete she knew.

"You are so bad."

He wiggled his eyebrows as he accepted the coffee.

She paused, looking at her friend. "It's funny, Pete. But you look different to me. Did you get a haircut?"

Pete laughed. "Not recently."

She shrugged. "I guess you just look different when you're up to no good."

She smiled.

"Could be." He joined her on the sofa.

"Post-shower towel action," she repeated, with a chuckle. "Bad, bad, bad."

"Who's bad?"

Ellina turned to see Jude standing in the hallway door, wearing nothing but faded jeans, still drying his hair with one of her lilac-colored towels. He could even make lilac look masculine. Not the towel action Pete was referring to—but still good.

"Umm, we were just talking about the incident at the hospital yesterday," she said.

Jude nodded, keeping his expression impassive as he watched Ellina's friend.

Pete shook his head, looking thoroughly dismayed. "That is just so scary."

"It was," Jude agreed, looking at how closely they sat together. He still didn't understand why, but something about this guy made him feel like he needed to make the boundaries around Ellina very clear. It made even less sense now that he knew about Pete's sexual preference.

It wasn't like this guy was planning to move in on his girl. Unless, of course, Ellina was wrong about him. Maybe she was, because for whatever reason, ole Pete just rubbed Jude the wrong way.

Jude walked over and touched Ellina's shoulder, squeezing it gently.

"Feeling any better?"

She stiffened under the touch, but didn't pull away. She nodded.

"A little."

Pete took a drink of his coffee, then set it on the coffee table. "You know, I think I will go get beignets by myself. I seem to have a craving for them today."

Ellina gave him an apologetic smile. "Sorry. I wish I felt like going."

Pete waved a hand. "Don't worry about it. You need to look out for you right now."

He headed to the door, and Jude would like to say he was disappointed to see him leave, but he couldn't.

Then Pete turned back. "I don't suppose you'd be interested in coming along, Jude?"

"Oh no," Jude said automatically but managed to buffer his quick rejection with a somewhat believable smile and thanks.

Pete smiled back, his expression perfectly amicable, but Jude still got a vibe from the guy.

He didn't like him.

As soon as the door closed, Ellina stood.

"I think I should get some work done," Ellina said, picking up her coffee mug.

She glanced at him, her gaze dropping surreptitiously to his bare chest. Then she hurried out of the room, not waiting for Jude's response as she disappeared down the hallway.

He couldn't say he was nearly as pleased with her departure as old Pete's.

In fact, he was very disappointed. Apparently she wasn't going to address his earlier confession. But he wasn't going to pressure her. She had to decide what she wanted for herself. He was serious about her needing to trust him.

That being said, he wasn't above subtly trying to sway her.

He looked down at himself. His lack of clothing wasn't *just* because he'd sensed someone in the house and he was in a hurry to see who it was.

He whistled to himself as he headed to the kitchen to make a little breakfast.

Chapter 19

Given all the things that Ellina had weighing on her mind—stalkers, hangovers, scandalous proposals—she was surprised to discover that by the time her house phone rang at around noon, she'd actually written about fifteen manuscript pages.

And even then, she didn't have to stop working. On the second ring, Jude answered, and she could hear the low rumbling of his deep voice as he conversed with whoever was on the other end. But when, after several minutes, he hadn't come to tell who called, she ventured from her office to find out.

As she walked past the kitchen, she smelled something delicious cooking. Chicken and onions with a hint of garlic.

Jude sat on sofa, working at his computer again. Much to her dismay, he still had on no shirt. And despite herself, she couldn't help admiring the lean muscles of his shoulders and chest. She was again reminded of an Olympic swimmer. Her fingers twitched with the need to touch him.

"Hey," he greeted easily, when he saw her. "There's chicken soup on the stove, if you are starting to get hungry. Not my best effort, just jazzed-up canned soup, but it's edible."

She ignored that, irrational annoyance flaring in her chest.

He was so relaxed it was as if he hadn't said anything earth shattering to her. Of course admitting he was attracted to her probably wasn't earth shattering to him. He'd probably done it millions of times before.

While she'd never gotten past heavy petting.

"Who was on the phone?" she asked, her tone not hiding her irritation.

"Oh, just a grocery delivery service. I placed an order online and they were just calling to confirm the address."

"You ordered my groceries?"

He raised an eyebrow, surprised by her curt reaction. "Well we needed food, so I figured that was probably the easiest way. You were working, and I wasn't about to go shopping and leave you alone."

Even though it made no sense, more irritation rose up in her. Why was he being so rational, so considerate? She didn't want that.

She didn't say anything more. She just spun on her heel and headed back to her office. She sat down behind her desk, determined to focus on her writing, but it wasn't working any longer.

He claimed he wanted her. Well, he didn't seem overcome with the need now.

Make up your mind, girl. Do you want him to want you or not?

Giving up on work, she headed to the bathroom, locking the doors. Then she turned on the shower, but instead of preparing to take a shower, she sat on the closed toilet seat and dropped her head into her hands.

Why was she so angry? Jude wasn't doing anything wrong. He was being helpful, considerate. He was being kind.

And she didn't know what to do with that, she suddenly realized. Because if she allowed herself to just accept it and trust him, and then he rejected her, she'd be devastated.

She sat there, for how long she didn't know, trying to decide how to handle him. What to do about the words he'd said to her this morning.

Beautiful words. But not ones she could believe. After all, even the people who did love her—Maksim, Pete, Jo—they didn't know everything about her.

And she just didn't believe Jude could really be attracted to her, care about her. Not when he saw the real her.

Suddenly an idea came to her. She had to take him at his word. Then once he rejected her, as she knew he would, she'd stop being attracted to him too. It would hurt like hell, but it would have the hope of him off the table once and for all.

Right now, she was enchanted with the idea of him. The protector, the caregiver, the most beautiful man she'd ever seen. But once she saw he had the same weaknesses as all the others in her life who should care about her—well, then she could move on,

Taking a deep breath, she went to her room to ready herself.

"Jude. Could you come here?"

Jude frowned, striding to Ellina's room. She'd been so upset with him, he was surprised she'd be calling for him. Something must be wrong.

Although he hadn't sensed anything.

He pushed open her door, scanning the room, not immediately seeing her, because the last place he'd expect her to be was on the bed.

But there she was, reclining amid her fluffy comforter and many lace-edged pillows. Her head rested on one hand, while the other toyed with the hem of the tiny little scrap of fabric she wore. Each movement of her wandering fingers revealed a glimpse of her thigh, only to cover it again.

Erotic peek-a-boo.

He stepped farther into the room, unable to stop himself. "Ellina?"

He was confused. What was she doing?

"I've thought about what you said," she told him, her voice low. "And I've decided I do want to trust you."

His body reacted instantly to her words, even as his mind sent up warning flares. This wasn't the Ellina he knew. The Ellina he knew was not forward with anything but her opinions and her questions. This wasn't right.

But still he moved closer to her as if she had a leash on him, and she was slowly reining him in. When he reached the edge of bed, she rose on her knees, her newly red hair billowing around her bare shoulders like a brilliant, glorious sunset. Her pale eyes were hooded, but he caught a hint of uncertainty there.

That was his Ellina. The unsure wanton.

She ran her hands over her nightie, and he realized it was the scrap of material he'd seen in her closet. Silky black with tiny polka dots. His eyes roamed over how the material clung to her lithe curves. It looked better than he could have imagined.

Knotting her fingers into the skirt, she eased the material higher and higher, stopping just below the soft mound that he ached to see. Touch. Taste.

Even as he told himself something wasn't right about this, he went to her. His hands captured both of her arms just above the elbows, tugging her toward him.

His mouth found hers, his lips molding to hers hungrily, tasting her. He nipped at the soft flesh of her lower lips, then his tongue flicked over the places he'd bit, teasing her. She moaned, the low sound vibrating through him, making him groan in response. She was driving him wild.

Her beautiful body. Her sweetness. Her flowery scent. Her taste like warm sugar. Part of her cotton-candy room.

His hands slid up her arms, to cup both sides of her head, his fingers tangling in her hair. He gently angled her head so he could better taste her, his tongue finding her. Tasting her velvety heat. Feeling her every shiver.

Ellina could feel herself changing, and she kept telling herself to pull back, let him see who—or what—he was making love to, but she couldn't. His mouth felt too wonderful sculpted to hers. The hot rasp of his tongue, the tiny nips of his teeth.

Then his hand slid out of her hair and down her torso, finding her breast. His thumb swirled around the hardened nipple, teasing it.

She gasped, the sensation too much, too good, and she knew she had to stop him now. She had to be the one to show him her demon self. She couldn't risk him being the one to pull away. The one to reject her, while she was helplessly responding to him.

So even though every cell in her body wanted to tug him closer, to allow him to continue the wonderful things he was doing, she shoved him away. Then she rose up on her knees, defiantly letting him see what she'd become.

She didn't look down at herself, but watched his face.

His eyes widened as he looked her; they roamed over her in a combination of horror and fascination. Then he frowned, his brows coming together, and next she saw exactly what she knew she would.

Disgust.

Even though she told herself she knew it was coming, his look shattered her, splintering her into millions of broken, ruined pieces.

She had to get away.

She scrambled off the bed, shoving past him, racing into the bathroom. She slammed the door shut and locked it.

Then she backed away, staring at the door as if she could still see him out there. Repulsed, sickened.

Her back hit the wall, and a sob escaped from her throat. Slowly she slid down the wall to the floor into a heap of tears and heartbreak.

Jude was furious. How dare she do that to him? She'd set him up, already knowing what he would see. Nothing about her seduction had been about attraction or affection.

It had been about proving a point.

Damn her.

He crossed to the bathroom door and pounded, the whole frame shaking under his fist.

"Let me in, Ellina."

"Go away," she cried, and he could hear tears in her voice. Tears she'd created herself. He refused to feel sympathetic about this. Those tears were her own self-pity. She wouldn't get his pity.

He pounded again.

"Damn it! Open this door now."

She didn't answer this time. Instead he heard the shower hiss to life.

More rage filled him. He wasn't going to let her ignore him. But he also knew breaking down the door wasn't going to do anything but scare her.

And scaring her was not what he had planned.

He turned and searched for something that would help him. On her dresser, he spotted a business card.

Erin McCarthy
BESTSELLING AUTHOR

Sorry, Erin, but right now you are my lock pick.

He returned to the door and slid the laminated card underneath the latch. Then he wiggled it back and forth. It took him several tries, but eventually he heard a little click. He just hoped Ellina didn't.

Thanks, Erin.

He tossed the card back onto Ellina's bureau.

Quietly he twisted the knob and pushed the door open. Ellina was not in the room proper, which meant she had to be in the shower, because he could feel her there. That electrical bond that always drew him.

Silently he stepped to the shower and eased the curtain open. She stood with her back to him. He stared at her, amazed. Her skin was deep red and iridescent. It shone in the light and glimmered through the streams of water almost as if she were a mermaid.

It was beautiful. But even more beautiful than her skin was her body. The long length of her legs, the curve of her backside, the shallow indentation of her spine.

He closed the curtain and carefully shucked off his jeans. Then, fully naked, he stepped into the shower behind her.

Ellina's tears fell silently, mingling with the shower spray. She didn't want to see herself, so she kept her face turned up, letting the water wash over her, even though she could tell it wasn't washing away her demon self. That wasn't happening, because, despite her hurt and anger, she was still aroused. Still turned on by the man out there who'd damned near broken her heart.

Hell, he had broken her heart. Because, whether she wanted to admit it or not, she was falling for him.

She pulled in a deep breath, willing herself to stop crying. She braced her arms over her head and rested her head on the cool tile wall.

She'd be okay. She would.

Suddenly she felt hands on her, sliding around her sides,

over her stomach. She froze, terror choking her. She tried to turn, to see her attacker, but she found her front pressed against the tiles. The hard length of a male body caged her against the wall. A nude male body.

"Shh, it's just me."

Jude's low, rich voice was next to her ear.

"Jude." Her voice was uneven. She trembled, and she wasn't sure if it was with fear or delight. His hands still rested on her belly, his chest tight against her back.

What was he going to do? She'd really angered him, and she was afraid what payback might be.

"That was a pretty nasty trick," he said. His hands grazed up and down over her stomach. Her skin, scales, seemed to vibrate under his touch.

"I'm sorry."

"Mm-hm," he said, his lips right beside her ear. She couldn't tell if that was acceptance of her apology or not. All she could really tell was his breath was warm, even in the steamy mist of the shower.

"Really not fair," he said. His hands moved higher, his thumbs brushing the underside of her breasts.

She nodded, but that was mostly just a mindless bobbing of her head. She would likely agree to anything with him pressed against her like this.

Then his hands cupped her breasts and she *knew* she'd agree to anything. His fingers moved to her nipples, swirling around and over them. Her breasts felt heavy, aching. He teased them, making her arch into his palms.

"Not fair at all," he said.

Then he squeezed both nipples and she cried out. Something between pleasure and pain shot through her body.

His hands left her breasts and she whimpered. She wanted more. She started to tell him that, but he bit the side of her neck, his teeth sharp and delicious. She whimpered again.

His hands skimmed over her stomach, slowly slipping lower and lower, until he found the small nest of curls between her thighs. One hand remained there while the other moved back up to her breast.

As he swirled and tweaked her nipple, the fingers of his other hand parted her, slipping inside her. One finger going deep, his thumb stroking the little nubbin at the top of her sex.

Ellina cried out again as he continued to stroke her. Another finger joined the first, stretching her. She writhed against him.

"Please," she begged.

"Please what?" his voice whispered against her ear.

She shook her head, not sure what to say, what to ask for. But she needed something. Whatever it was, it was close, but she couldn't quite reach it.

Then he spun her around to face him. His eyes roamed over her, and she could see they weren't filled with disgust. Or revulsion. Or even pity. His eyes were burning hot, like green fire.

Jude lowered his head and sucked one of her nipples. She cried out his name, her hand locking in his wet hair. He turned his head and lapped the other one.

She whimpered. God, he was killing her.

Then she watched as he sunk down to his knees. She stared in amazement as he parted her and buried his face in the thatch of curls.

Then his tongue was where his thumb had been, swirling around her clitoris, licking her, tasting her. Her knees shook at the intensity of it, and she had to use his shoulders to steady herself.

"Oh God," she cried as she felt that rising feeling again. The thrust upward toward something . . . something . . .

She screamed, pushing his face harder against her. Her orgasm shook her whole body, surging through her like shock wave after shock wave.

"Jude," she murmured, but he didn't give her time to recover or even fully understand what had happened, because he rose and turned her back around. Then using his own body like a mold, he bent her forward, bracing her hand against the wall under his.

"Spread your legs," he said, his mouth back next to her ear. She did as he asked, loving how exposed she felt to him. He straightened and stroked a hand over her bottom, then down the crevice between her cheeks, down farther still to her vagina.

"God, you are sexy," he said, his finger dipping inside her. He thrust in and out, stretching her, teasing her. Then he repositioned himself over her.

She gasped as she felt his penis, the shaft much, much thicker than his finger. He nudged her and she arched against him.

"Do I want you?" he asked, his voice rough with desire.

She nodded.

"Do I want you?" he repeated, his hands locking on her hips.

"Yes," she said, her voice breathy, desperate.

"And do you want me?" He leaned over her and bit her shoulder blade, the nip causing her whole body to vibrate.

"Yes," she cried. "Oh God, yes."

Jude tightened his hold on her hips and thrust into her. She cried out, her orgasm hitting before he even began to move.

Chapter 20

Jude gritted his teeth, trying to remain in control as Ellina's vagina pulsed around his erection, squeezing him, stroking him with every swell of her still-occurring release.

God, she felt good. She felt perfect.

Then just as her orgasm seemed to calm to small ripples, he began to move, stroking in and out of her tightness, deep and smooth. He curled over her; his hand over hers pinned them to the wet tiles.

"Ellina," he muttered roughly, his pace becoming more and more frantic. He drove into her, feeling that electricity they shared snapping around them. Snapping in his blood, building and building, urging him harder and deeper, until he cried out, curling over her, his chest to her back, his penis still deep inside her.

They remained that way, breathing heavy, the water pounding on them for seconds, minutes. Jude didn't know.

Finally he straightened, carefully pulling himself from her. She made a small noise, then stood too.

He turned her in his arms and kissed her. The pressure of his mouth was possessive, and she moaned, leaning into his possession.

He broke the kiss to turn off the water, then he kissed her

again in the steam, letting the air cool their still burning bodies. After several seconds of tasting each other, claiming each other, he stepped out of the tub and grabbed two towels from the cabinet. He unfolded one and wrapped it around Ellina's flushed body.

Then he looped his around his hips. Holding hands, they left the bathroom. Once in her room, he moved behind her and positioned her in front of him, his arms wrapped around her middle. He rested his chin on her shoulder.

"Do you have any idea of how beautiful you are?"

She nodded.

"Both sides of you?"

Ellina tried to turn in his arms, but he held her fast and directed her toward the mirror over her bureau. They both stared at her reflection.

She didn't say anything for a moment, then she reached up to touch her face. "It's normal me."

He nodded.

"I change back after I—orgasm?"

"You changed back about halfway through."

She shook her head. "How?"

He shrugged. "Maybe because you weren't so worried about it."

Ellina thought about his theory. Maybe he was right. She knew she shouldn't ask, but she couldn't stop herself.

"Which do you like better?"

Jude caught her chin gently between his finger and thumb. His green eyes peered deep into hers. "You will believe what I say, right?"

She nodded.

"I like both sides of you. My angel and my demon."

She stared at him, seeing nothing but sincerity in his expression. Then she squeaked as he scooped her up and carried her to the bed. He placed her on the center, then followed her down.

They curled in the middle, their arms and legs intertwined. Both of them quiet and peaceful.

"I was your first, wasn't I?" he asked almost hesitantly.

"Well, with my little sexual quirk, what do you think?"

He lifted his head to look at her, then he stroked her cheek, regret in his eyes. "I should have been—gentler. But I was angry. Hurt."

She winced. "I know. I'm sorry."

"But it's still no excuse for being so rough," he added.

"You were making love to a demon," she said giving him a saucy smile. "I think I can handle it."

Then she leaned in and kissed him, lingering for a moment. "It was perfect."

They were quiet again.

"I think you are right," he said suddenly, and Ellina lifted her head to look at him.

"Probably," she agreed, "but about what?"

"I think your father doesn't like the books because of the relationship between Jenny and Dante."

Ellina laughed. "What made you think about that?"

"I was just reading the fifth book last night, and Dante is pretty harsh. Pretty unlikable. He's based on your dad, isn't he?"

She nodded. "Yes."

"I bet that's hard for him to read."

Ellina laughed humorlessly. "He doesn't read them."

"He must have to react to them so strongly."

She'd never considered that. She'd just assumed he'd heard about them from others and formulated his own opinion based on that.

"And why did you use real spells in the stories? It wasn't really necessary."

"I don't know," she said honestly. "Maybe—maybe because I felt a need to understand that side of myself. Since I didn't get any of the demon abilities, I think I felt even more need to really know them."

She rolled over, so she was resting her chin on his chest. "Why all the questions?"

He smiled at her, tucking a strand of hair behind her ear. "I happen to find you intriguing."

She smiled back. "How intriguing?"

She ran a hand over the smooth skin of his chest, feeling his muscles tense as moved lower . . . lower . . . lower still.

"Very, very intriguing."

She laughed, loving the sudden freedom she had with this man. It was all new, but it felt so right, so natural, it was easy to just go with her desires. He'd seen all of her—quite literally—and if the reaction that she was seeing under the covers was any indication, he'd truly had liked what he'd seen.

"So do you think we could have a replay of what happened in the shower?"

"Oh, I think we can do that," he said, breathing in sharply as her fingers curled round his already erect penis. "After all, you've waited a long time for this."

She nodded, and it was on the tip of her tongue to say she'd waited a long time for him. But she didn't, afraid that might be too much.

This was all way too new.

It was almost evening when she and Jude actually managed to crawl out of bed, and only because Maksim called.

"I feel like such a selfish jerk," she announced as soon as she hung up the phone.

"Why?" Jude asked, coming out of the guest room, pulling on a shirt.

"I spend the day having sex, when I should have been with

my brother. Jo is doing much, much better. They are even saying she can go home in the next day or so."

"Do you want to go see them?"

Ellina wanted to stay here, alone with Jude. But she did want to see her family too.

"Maybe we could just go for a little while," she said, even as her hand stroked down over his chest, fiddling with the waistband of his jeans.

He smiled at her, catching her hand and bringing it up to kiss her fingers.

"You told me you'd be a demon in bed, but you didn't say you'd be an insatiable one."

She smiled. "I thought that was implied."

But she did force herself to leave Jude and go freshen up.

As soon as they got to the hospital, Jude wished he'd not been the decent, selfless guy and he'd taken Ellina back to bed. When they walked through the door of Jo's room, he and Ellina were greeted by the evil twins.

Pasha stood by the window, looking bored. Andrey talked to Maksim and Jo was sitting up at an angle in her hospital bed, the baby nestled beside her.

"Oh, look it's sis. And her boy-to—friend. Boyfriend."

Maksim glanced at the doorway, clearly bewildered. "Ellina's boyfriend?"

"Yes, I brought Jude," she said quickly, smiling in what she hoped was a natural way.

Maksim frowned, but simply nodded. "So Jude has met the twins."

"Yes, I have. They made quite an impact too."

Both Pasha and Andrey smirked at Jude's comment.

Ellina decided it was best to speak with Jo for a moment, then leave.

"Jo," she said, going to sit in a chair beside the bed, and on the other side from the twins. "You look good."

Her sister-in-law smiled; only hints of exhaustion were on her face. Then she smiled at her baby. "I'm much better. And this little one was worth every minute."

Maksim spoke up then, distracted away from his talk with the twins. "She's insisting we have more."

"Just one," Jo assured him, patting his hand.

Maksim shook his head, obviously still not on board with the idea. But Ellina had no doubt Jo would sway him.

"But you," Jo said with a curious smile, "you look wonderful." Her sister-in-law gave a pointed look at Jude, who was trying to be sociable with her brothers.

Ellina blushed. "Yeah. I'm feeling pretty wonderful."

Jo gave her an approving look.

"And I like the red hair," Maksim said—apparently eavesdropping.

"Very Little Orphan Annie," Pasha said, and Ellina didn't miss his implication. Another stab at her not being a real member of the family.

But the jab didn't hurt. Not like it would have once. Because, as she looked around the small room, she realized she had four people here who cared about her. Three more than the twins.

Well, little Barrett had no opinion yet, but he would. And he'd think she was the greatest auntie in the world.

"I have a favor to ask you," Jo said, changing the subject. "I've been trying to reach Maggie and Erika, but neither of them ever seem to have a cell phone that works, so I was hoping you could go to the bar and tell them what's going on."

Ellina's first reaction was to think of an excuse why she couldn't do that. But she felt herself nod.

"Sure. I can do that."

"Are you sure?" Jo double-checked.

Ellina nodded. "It won't be a problem."

She looked around the room to see Maksim looking worried. The twins looked intrigued—in that way a person was when they expected failure. And Jude looked puzzled.

She smiled at them all. She could do it.

"So what was that back there?" Jude asked once they were outside. "What's so odd about going to this bar for Jo?"

"Well," Ellina started slowly. "You know how the demon comes out when I'm aroused."

"Indeed I do," he said with a lascivious grin.

She laughed. "Well, the other time the demon comes out is in crowds."

Jude paused in the middle of the parking lot to look at her.

"Is that why you don't make public appearances?"

She shook her head. "It's starting to weird me out that you know so much about me. But yes, that's why. At one of my first book signings, I had a huge crowd and, well, you know what happened."

"What did you do?"

"Hid in the bathroom for forty-five minutes, then told the organizer that I was sick. It was mortifying."

"Then do you think we should go do this?"

Ellina considered it, not for the first time since Jo asked, and nodded. "It's a Monday night, so Bourbon probably won't be wall-to-wall people, and I think I'm able to control it now."

Jude pulled his keys from his pocket and unlocked the van with the remote. He opened the door for her.

"You are doing great controlling it with me," he said. In fact that had become a game. Have sex with the angel. Have sex with the demon—a game he quite liked, by the way. "But this is different."

"I know," she said, but then said resolutely, "but I want not to have to hide in my house forever. I want to be in control for real."

Jude nodded. He understood that. Isn't that what he wanted too?

"Okay," he said, closing her door and getting in on his side. "Here we come, Bourbon Street."

"This isn't too bad," Ellina said as she walked down the center of Bourbon, heading toward the bar. Jude had to admit it wasn't too crowded, but it was early too.

"This is the bar."

Before they stepped inside, the sounds of classic rock reached them. Jude listened. "Sweet Home Alabama."

Jude took Ellina's hand as they stepped into the murky neon light of the bar. The dance floor was right in front of them, and there were quite a few people gyrating around in tipsy abandon.

Ellina squeezed his fingers, but continued to walk through to the bar. He directed them to two empty bar stools and they took a seat, watching the band.

Ellina had already informed him on the drive who the band members were—Maggie, Jo's dear friend, and her husband Ren. Vittorio was Ren's brother and married to Jo's other best friend, Erika. They were all vampires—lampirs actually.

And Jude could actually tell that. He could feel the band siphoning off energy from the room. He didn't like that much.

"Oh, I think that's Erika," Ellina said, pointing to a tall female with pale skin and long black hair, sitting at the other bar.

Ellina immediately got up and started toward her. Jude

stood to follow, but not before a drunken man in a business suit caught Ellina's arm and hauled her onto the dance floor.

Jude hurried to follow, getting ready to push the guy away and pull her back to where the bar was less crowded. But then he paused.

He'd expected Ellina to look panicked. But instead she was laughing. And dancing. She waved for Jude to join her.

He did, and she pulled him close. They both swayed to a Journey song.

When they were done, Ellina kissed him.

"Thank you."

He frowned. "For what?"

"For thinking I'm okay," she said simply.

He kissed her. "Oh, sweetheart, I think you are way more than okay."

Chapter 21

Ellina made Jude stay at the bar for hours. She danced and talked to the band. Hell, she talked to everyone. And he had to say she was damned adorable doing so.

"So I've also created a party animal too," he teased when they finally got back to her house sometime after one A.M.

She took his hand and twirled around, grinning. "Is that bad?"

"Only if I don't get you to myself on occasion." He pulled her in close, and she kissed him.

"All yours," she promised. She then took his hand again and led him to her bedroom.

And Ellina wasn't kidding. They stayed in the house for the next three days, doing nothing but making love, cooking, Ellina would work a little, then they'd make more love.

Jude couldn't remember a happier time in his life.

Nor could Ellina.

"Tonight, I want to show you something," Jude said as they lounged in her bed, leisurely stroking each other's bare skin.

"Okay. Is it a surprise?"

"I think it will be, yes."

WHAT A DEMON WANTS   217

"A good one?" she asked, rising up on her elbow to look at him.

"I hope so."

They finally left.

He'd started to think they'd never leave her damn house again. As it was, Ellina was a pathetic homebody. Even finding the times to get into her house and search for the spell had been a long and tedious process.

And now that she had a lover, she could potentially stay there forever.

But they did go out tonight, leaving in the Neanderthal's creepy black van, which gave him a chance to set up his new plan. Made all the more delicious because she'd come running to him, thinking he would protect her. And protect her from whom? That was the really fun part.

He walked into the guest room and began searching. He found what he was looking for almost immediately. Not even hidden. How silly of the Neanderthal. Oh, wait, he was a Neanderthal—he shouldn't have such high expectations for the poor oaf.

He placed the item in his backpack.

And now came the second part of the plan. Time to do a little planting. He pulled a few things from his bag. Now where to sow the seeds? He looked through the room, trying to decide.

It had to be a believable place. His duffel, perhaps. But the oaf might find it before silly Ellina did. He looked under the bed.

Ah-ha. He pulled out a case, lifting it onto the bed. Unzipping it, he let out a low whistle. Wow, this was some serious artillery.

A shotgun. A Glock. Damn.

This seemed like just the place to hide his goodies. In something that was already in hiding.

He chose a pouch on the outside, one that the Neanderthal clearly didn't use.

He carefully zipped it back up and slipped it under the bed, making sure it was in the same position that the oaf left it in.

This was brilliant. And so much fun. Because he could take down two idiots for the price of one.

"So do you actually live in this van?"

Jude thought from what was stored in there that was pretty clear. But he just nodded. "On occasion."

Ellina swiveled in her seat to survey the back. "Why? Don't you want a permanent place?"

"I have had some homes over the centuries. You know, before vans."

She studied him. "Where? I always spill to you. You still don't spill much."

Jude looked incredulous. "What do you mean? I told you about my childhood. My different jobs."

Ellina shrugged. "Vaguely. I want more details. Where was your last permanent residence?"

"I lived in New York City for several years."

"Really? Why did you leave?"

"I got disillusioned."

"About what?"

He hesitated, then decided that if he'd expected Ellina to trust him, he needed to be able to offer her the same thing. "I was the member of group there. I was the vice president, actually. It was called SPAMM."

"Spam?"

"The Society of Preternaturals Against the Mistreatment of Mortals."

"Well, that sounds like a pretty respectable, and wordy, cause. Why did you become disillusioned?"

"Because one of the members was actually using the group to get to humans and kill them. That's when I started to question if there is any point to trying to deny who we are."

"What do you mean?"

Jude paused, not sure he should tell her this. Their relationship was still new, and his past was less than lily white. She might not understand.

"I've always been a fighter," he finally said.

Ellina was silent, and he got the feeling she didn't know if she wanted to know more either.

"What kind of fighter?" The question was asked, but he sensed her concern.

"You name it, and I've probably done it. Bodyguard, boxer, heavy for a loan shark. I worked for the mob." He glanced at her to see if this was okay. "In those jobs I only hurt people who'd hurt other people. But I'm still not proud."

She stared straight ahead at the road.

"What did you do before becoming what you are now?"

"I was a gladiator. I was one of the few who was not a slave or convict. I fought because I wanted to and I could make good money."

She was silent for a long time. "You had to kill people as a gladiator, didn't you?"

He nodded. "I did. I'd like to tell you I didn't, but that would be a lie. And the truth is back then I was a young punk, really. Hungry for success and fame. And I was good. Then I met this group of gladiators who assured me that they had the secret to winning forever. Winning forever? I wasn't going to pass that up."

He put on his blinker and turned right onto a small road off Frenchman's Street. He pulled the van over and put it into park. He turned in his seat to look at Ellina.

She looked both curious and scared. She waited for him to continue. So he did, praying she'd understand.

"So that lure of strength and immortality kept tugging at me. Livia told me I shouldn't get involved. She believed that with anything like great success or great riches, there was an even bigger price to pay."

He took a deep breath. "And of course, she turned out to be right. Except the price ultimately was paid by her. Not me."

"How so?"

"Well, she died because I wasn't there. Once I crossed over, I was obsessed with being the most celebrated gladiator of the time. It was like using steroids—except more powerful, of course. I began to do basically the circuit. Traveling, fights, more fights. That was my life."

"What did Livia do?" Ellina asked.

"Waited for me. Before I came so obsessed, we had a good relationship. We wanted a family and land and a little money. But somewhere along the way my priorities became warped."

Ellina understood that. Hadn't she seen that in her own family? "That happens. It doesn't make you a bad person."

"I was away when she died." His voice grew rough and his eyes distant, like they had in the hospital. "I only saw my son for four days before he passed too."

She reached across the armrest and took his hand. "I know you feel guilt, that's understandable. And you wanted to be there, but would things have gone any differently?"

Jude shook his head. "I couldn't save them. Livia would never have crossed over. She was too principled for that. And Justus was too young."

She squeezed his fingers, then brought them up to her lips and kissed them. He'd just told her those hands had killed, but she couldn't believe he'd do that now.

He was too kind. Too fair. He'd changed. She believed that.

"I know if you could have saved them, you would have."

They sat staring at each other for a few moments.

Then Jude forced a smile at her that didn't quite meet his eyes. "I have something I want to show you."

Jude came around her side of the car and he took her hand as she hopped down from the vehicle. Together, they walked down the uneven sidewalk surrounded by quaint New Orleans–style homes and shops.

Finally they reached a beautiful restaurant with a courtyard and floor-to-ceiling windows that could be opened during the summer to create a full open-air dining area.

"This is beautiful. Too bad it's closed."

Jude nodded. "It won't be for long. I know the owner. He's an old member of SPAMM, himself. He has no interest in the place, and he's selling it to me."

She turned to stare at him.

"This is what you are going to put Maksim's money toward." She grinned. "That is perfect."

Jude shook his head. "I can't take Maksim's money. I'm involved with you—which so goes against employee/employers guidelines."

She made a face. "Whatever."

She walked up to the window and peeked inside. The place really was wonderful. The tables were still there and just in need of new tablecloths. She could easily see Jude running this place. Cooking. That would be perfect for him. And he could stay right here in New Orleans. With her.

She walked around to see the courtyard better.

She found a little break in the courtyard's shrubbery fence and slipped inside.

"Ellina," Jude called in a whisper. "What are you doing?"

She stuck her head of where she'd just entered. "Come on. I want to take a peek."

Jude glanced around to be sure they were alone, then followed her, although wedging through the shrubs wasn't as easy for him as it was for her. But he made it in.

She waited for him and they started walking together. The courtyard wasn't huge. Maybe it would sit ten tables of four, but a portion of it would be left as a garden. There was a fountain and a few benches.

Ellina sat on one of the benches, patting the concrete, silently inviting him to join her. He did, sitting close to her.

She placed a hand on his knee and leaned her head on his shoulder. The small garden was quiet and the sun had nearly set, surrounding them in the blue light of twilight.

Her hand moved on his leg, and the prickling of electricity swirled around him.

He wasn't surprised when she said, "Don't you think we should christen your new restaurant?"

Chapter 22

"I'm not sure if sex in a restaurant would be approved by a health code inspector." His hand moved up her thigh, feeling her heat through her jeans.

Ellina laughed, the pretty sound filling the courtyard, making it seemed more magical. "Well, we won't do it on the kitchen counters or in the walk-in fridge."

Jude smiled, his hand moving upward, but she caught his fingers and motioned for him to shift.

"Straddle the bench," she said. He did, waiting for her to continue. Her fingers moved to the button of his jeans. She leaned in and kissed him, her soft lips nibbling. She flicked the button open, then moved to the zipper. The metal rasped as she lowered it.

Then her hand found his already rigid penis. She smiled as she curled her fingers around his girth, liberating him.

"You are a big boy," she said, and he wasn't sure if that was addressed to him or his cock. But he let his cock answer, as it pulsed eagerly in her palm.

She lowered her head and kissed the tip. Her fingers ran up and down the sensitive underside. She licked the head, her tongue warm and raspy. He jumped, electricity surging from him.

He could feel her smile against him.

"You are like a new toy," she murmured, licking him again.

He pulled in a shuddering breath. He liked being her new plaything. Again her tongue darted out and lapped all around the top, like he was a lollipop. His hips rose up from the bench and she responded by taking him as much of him as she could in her hot, wet mouth.

He groaned low in his throat as she bobbed her head over him, her mouth moving over the top of his shaft, her hands stroking down below. God, nothing had been so wonderful as this woman surrounding him.

As always with her, his arousal became possessive. Suddenly just being in her mouth wasn't enough. He had to be buried deep inside her. The wolf in him. Claiming his mate.

"Stand up," he said, his voice low, little more than a hungry growl.

"Don't you like this?"

"I love it, but I've got to be inside you."

She didn't hesitate. She stood, her own hands going to her jeans. She undid the fasteners, then pushed the jeans and her panties to the ground. He directed her to also straddle the bench.

But he didn't let her sit. He placed his hand between her spread thighs, stroking her.

"Mmm, you are so wet, sweetheart." He dipped his finger into her moist heat. With each plunge of his finger, she grew wetter and wetter.

His hands moved to the hem of her shirt, and he pushed it off over her head. Then he stripped her of her bra. She didn't falter at being outside and totally nude. In fact she seemed to be reveling in it. Her skin was totally red and iridescent in the moonlight. She shimmered and shone as her body writhed under his touch. Her skin was like living velvet under his palms.

Then Jude removed his hand, pushing her to sit on the bench. He laid her back and positioned himself over the top of her.

Ellina arched her back, her breasts rising up, firm and round and perfect.

He spread her thighs wider and lowered his head, lapping his tongue over her core, pleasuring her as if he were her minion.

The idea oddly excited him.

"You are my demon goddess."

She laughed, the laugh changing to a strangled whimper as he suckled hard on her clitoris.

Her hands moved through his hair, knotting there, pulling.

He fed from her, tasting her essence until finally he felt the quaking under his tongue, the building explosion.

She cried out, convulsing under him, but he didn't even let the orgasm finish before he entered, hard and swift. She pulsated around him, squeezing him, urging him to join her.

Her legs came around him, pulling him tighter and deeper. With every stroke, his body seized with pleasure. He plunged deeper, wanting to be closer still. Wanting to reach the place where neither existed alone.

Then his release hit him, coming so hard he couldn't breathe, all he could do was focus on his reaction to her, his surge deep into her core.

She cried out again, joining him.

He collapsed on her, his body limp as if she'd stolen all the energy from him.

When he finally lifted his head, his demon lover was gone— replaced by his sweet angel. And he wondered how he'd lucked out getting a woman who was both.

It was on the tip of his tongue to tell her he loved her, but he hesitated. What if it was too soon for those words, even though he knew, for him anyway, they were true?

Instead he rose up and took her hand to help her up.

"Want to eat now?" he asked with a smile.

She grinned at him, pleased with what they'd just done.

"Yes. I'm ravenous."

Ellina woke early the next morning. Jude had taken her to a wonderful little restaurant on Dauphine. They'd eaten crawfish and jambalaya. They'd come home and had another perfect night. She knew this was all going so fast, but she had to admit, it also felt right.

She'd never been as free with anyone.

She could feel her cheeks burning just thinking about her behavior in the courtyard of the restaurant he planned to buy.

What had gotten into her? Jude had taken to calling her his angel and demon. And around him, she had to admit she could be both, which was quite liberating.

She pushed up in bed to see that Jude was already up. That was the one odd thing about the man. He didn't sleep. Couldn't sleep.

It made her feel guilty when she promptly dozed off after a particularly energetic round of lovemaking. But he assured her that made up for all the men in the world who were doing that very thing to their women.

She'd laughed, supposing that was true enough.

A clatter of a pot sounded in the kitchen and she knew what Jude was doing. All the way around, he was spoiling her. Delicious food. Delightful sex.

She stretched her arms over her head. More than delightful sex. Perfect sex.

Everything about this man was perfect.

Funny, that had been her very first opinion of him, and then he'd promptly changed her mind. And now, here she was back to her original assessment.

There was something to be said for following one's gut instincts.

Just then her cell phone ran. She crawled out of bed to see Pete's number on the screen.

"Hi Pete," she greeted, stretching again.

"Hi Ellina. Are you alone?"

She frowned. "Jude is here, but I'm in the bedroom and he's in the kitchen."

"Okay, good. I have something odd to tell you, and it's just a hunch. Nothing that really points a finger to anyone or anything."

"What is it?"

"Well, yesterday afternoon, I was walking Mrs. Neiderman's dog, you know that little poodle-y thing she has. Anyway, I was walking down the alley beside your house and I saw a shirt on the ground near that Dumpster two houses down from yours."

"A shirt?" she asked. Why was he telling her this?

"Yes, I think it was your shirt?"

Why would her shirt be in a Dumpster?

"You know, your Rolling Stones one with the lips."

Ellina paused. That was the one that had those powder stains on it. The one that was in the guest room.

"I don't think it's mine, but did you pick it up?"

"No," Pete said. "It was all disgusting and unsalvageable. But when I saw it, I started thinking about the shirt you told me about—the one you wearing during the attack—and I started to wonder if that could be it."

Ellina didn't speak.

"I just think you should be careful. Especially with Jude. He seems nice, but you barely know him."

"I appreciate your concern," Ellina said. But she wasn't sure she did. She didn't like what her friend was implying about the man she loved.

"Just keep aware."

"I will," she promised. "Talk to you later."

"And don't hesitate to come over to talk to me if you need a sympathetic or impartial ear."

"Okay, Pete. Bye."

She hung up, not liking that conversation at all.

Setting down her phone, she headed into the bathroom. Once in the room, she kept glancing toward the guest room door.

She was sure the shirt was probably in the same drawer where Jude had placed it. She didn't need to look; she was sure it was there.

She brushed her teeth, then headed to the kitchen.

Jude greeted her with a big smile, his dimples flashing. "Who was on the phone? Maksim?"

She shook her head. "Just Pete."

He nodded, then gestured to the stove. "I just made French toast. Dig in. I'm going to go shower. I managed to get flour all over myself."

He gave her a quick kiss on the way by, and she noticed dots of flour on his dark shirt.

Just like on hers.

Ellina waited in the kitchen, until she heard the water turn on.

This was stupid, she told herself, even as she headed to the living room and then to the guest room door.

Hesitating, her hand on the door handle, she told herself to just stop.

"Go eat some yummy French toast."

But instead, she eased the door open.

Everything was the same as it had been since Jude arrived. His duffel bag was beside the bed. His computer bag next to that.

She wandered over to the dresser, running her hand along

the top. Then before she could think better of it, she pulled the drawer open.

It was empty.

Her breath caught. She tried the next one. And the next one. All of them. But the shirt wasn't there.

Why would it be gone?

She listened. Jude was still in the shower.

She went over to his duffel. Maybe he'd put it in there for some reason. But after searching the whole thing, all she found was his clothing.

She checked his computer bag. Nothing.

Maybe he thought he should hide it in case the stalker broke into her place again. She looked in the nightstand drawer, but all that was there were her odds and ends. Books, tissues, a flashlight.

She looked around her, sure it must be here.

The mattress. She lifted the edge and saw there was something there. Gingerly, she touched the thing.

Oh my God, she yanked her hand away when she realized what the item was. A sword. A huge, long sword. A sword that could easily kill someone.

Have you ever killed someone?

Her mind returned to that conversation in the van. Jude had openly admitted he had.

She dropped the mattress, backing away from it and the long, offensive weapon.

She glanced behind her at the bathroom. Carefully, she tiptoed to the door and listened.

Jude hummed, the water sloshing as he was scrubbing away.

Ellina approached the bed again, bending down to peek underneath. To her dismay, there was a black case under there.

Reaching cautiously, she tugged the rectangular bag out and

put it on the bed. She stared at it like it was Pandora's Box. And maybe in a way it was.

She reached out and tugged at the zipper. When it was undone she still just stared at it.

But then she decided she'd better look. Now, while she could.

She flipped the top open and she was greeted by a large shotgun. There were three more Velcro pouches. One held a large gray handgun. The second pouch held a smaller gun, and the third.

She reached in, not touching a weapon. Instead it was a small packet of something and a folded piece of paper. She unfolded the paper and saw it was a spell, in her own handwriting. And in the little envelope, she carefully broke the seal and opened it.

Powder.

She sniffed it, and sure enough, the same scent she remembered from the hospital bathroom filled her nostrils.

She froze as she heard the squeak of the shower tap being turned off. She fumbled with the package and the paper, shoving them in her pocket. She needed to get out of here. She needed to think about this.

Where to go . . . ?

Pete.

Chapter 23

Jude dried off, his thoughts still on whether he should tell Ellina how he felt. She hadn't offered anything more committed to him than "that feels good" or "I like that."

But he was crazy about her. They had a connection—an electric feeling that seemed to surround them all the time.

He'd never experienced anything like it and he didn't want to risk losing her and that connection just because he was too chickenshit to say "I love you" first.

He pushed open the door to the guest room, heading in to get some clothes, when he spotted his weapons bag on the bed. Open.

He paused, concentrating.

Ellina wasn't in the house.

Panic rose up in him.

He didn't sense anything different about the house. No residual energy of another person.

So she must have found the bag. What would motivate her to look for it? And why wouldn't she just ask him about the weapons?

Then he smelled something. He stepped closer to the bag. The smell definitely radiated from here.

He reached down, noticing a white-ish gray powder on the black nylon of the gun case. He sniffed.

The same stuff from Ellina's attack.

So where was she? Did someone have her?

Suddenly he got a vivid image.

Pete.

Oh God, he couldn't be late again. Not this time.

"Come on in," Pete said, opening the door of his shotgun cottage just two doors down from hers. But unlike her place decorated in fairy-tale colors, her own fairy-tale world, Pete had chosen to go with darker, more masculine colors.

She stepped inside, surprised at the clutter everywhere. Newspapers littered the floor, a teacup and plate sat, dirty, on the coffee table.

She'd never even seen a dirty dish in his sink. He was normally fastidious.

"What's going on?" he asked, directing her to a chair. She sat on the couch instead. She noted his frown, then he joined her.

"After we talked, I decided I should go see if that shirt was still there."

"And?"

"It was gone. But not only that, I found these two things in Jude's stuff." She dug into her pocket and pulled out the paper and packet. She set them on the table. Pete didn't reach for them.

"And he had guns and this awful looking sword."

Pete shook his head. "That's scary, Ellina. Maybe it's time to consider that he might be involved with the break-ins and the incident at the hospital."

Ellina sighed. "I can't really believe that. Not about Jude. Sure, the weapons startled me, and I don't know what to make of the spell, but I should have stayed and asked him."

She started to rise, when Pete reached over and stopped her.

Ellina's gaze narrowed as he got close.

"Listen, why don't you just relax for a second and I'll get us some coffee."

She nodded, watching him go.

She sat up and said in a slightly louder than normal voice, "Can I have extra sugar in mine?"

"Sure," Pete answered without pausing.

Ellina froze. She'd noticed that Pete looked different somehow the last few times she'd seen him. Now she knew what it was—he didn't have in his hearing aids. He'd never been able to hear her without them.

And the man who just left her smelled like coffee and garlic. And that powder. And he didn't even question what she meant when she'd referred to the spell. Pete didn't know about her spells.

This guy intended to sacrifice her, as per the spell.

Ellina rose. Then she paused. That man in the kitchen was not her friend, Pete. But that didn't mean Pete wasn't in there somewhere.

Just then she saw a shadow outside the door. Electricity seemed to fill the air like a lightning storm. She could tell Jude was near.

"Here you go," Pete said, returning with two mugs. He handed her one and again she got a whiff of that powder. She backed away.

"You know, I think I should probably go check on Jude. I shouldn't have left him alone in my house." Ellina made it out from behind the coffee table, sure she could dash for the door, when she slipped on some of the scattered newspaper.

Her slight loss of footing gave Pete time to grab her.

Ellina screamed.

*   *   *

Jude stood on the doorstep, listening. Finding Pete's place had been simple. He followed Ellina's electricity still in the air. He'd actually thought that Ellina was going to make it out of there on her own, but then he heard a scream.

Without further thought he slammed into the door, wood cracking under his force. He entered to see Pete holding Ellina. A dagger to her throat.

Jude aimed his Glock at the human's head, but it was Ellina who shouted, "No!"

"Don't kill him," she cried. "He's possessed."

Jude shook his head. "I don't care. He's also got a fuckin' knife to your throat."

"That's right," Pete said, pressing it a little harder to her skin.

"But killing me won't do you any good," she managed to sound calm, "because you missed a pretty significant word in the spell."

"What's that," Pete sneered.

"You need a human sacrifice. And I'm not human."

And just like that, Ellina morphed into her demon self.

Possessed Pete released her as if he'd gotten burned by her red skin. He backed away from her. He didn't know that she didn't have any real powers, but she certainly looked the part.

She hurried over to Jude, hugging him, even though he still kept the gun trained on the other man.

Ellina turned back to Pete.

"I can help you," she said. "But you've got to stop breaking into my place. And attacking me."

The non-Pete nodded. "Just get me out of the damned human."

She nodded. "I can do that."

Then she looked to Jude, who clearly still didn't trust the other guy.

"I guess you were right about him. He didn't want to just be my friend."

Jude nodded. "Told you."

She laughed. "I love you. Is it too soon to say that?"

"Not a moment too soon." He lowered the gun and turned to kiss his demon girl.

Possessed Pete just sighed and rolled his eyes. His plans never went right.

Epilogue

Ellina curled closer to Jude's side as they lounged on her sofa, watching Jude's new favorite, The Food Network.

"I think your grand opening was a rousing success," she said with a proud smile.

"I think so too," he admitted.

Jude had still refused to accept Maksim's money for guarding her, but he had agreed to let Ellina invest as a full partner.

In fact, she'd agreed to be a full partner in his business and in his life. "I think the wedding will be perfect in the garden at the restaurant," she said.

"Right near my favorite bench."

She laughed. That was her favorite bench too.

"And I have to admit, I'm much happier having the real Pete in our wedding—over the possessed one," he said.

She laughed again. "Me too. I don't need anyone trying to sacrifice me on my wedding day."

"No definitely not. I still can't believe Pete thinks he was in Hawaii that whole time he was possessed."

"Well, if you have to be possessed, that's the way to do it, I guess."

They both laughed.

"Speaking of wedding guests, must we invite the twins?"

Ellina nodded. "They are family. And they didn't put me in the cat. Now that I know that was Orabella, Maksim's hideously evil ex, I feel better about the twins."

Maksim and Vittorio, Orabella's son, had pieced that mystery together based on the things Orabella had done to them both. Orabella had come to Ellina to ask about demon spells, which Ellina had been going to tell Vittorio about, because she'd had a bad feeling about the woman. The cat trick was how Orabella had stopped her.

"Okay," Jude sighed, "the evil twins can come. I don't actually care who's there as long as I get to marry you and get to spend all eternity with you."

She kissed him. "That's a definite." She kissed him again.

"I love you," he said against her lips.

"I love you too. You're just what a demon wants."

They cuddled again, half watching a chef make something with zucchini and squid. But mostly starting to lazily stroke each other's skin while losing themselves in each other.

"You know, it really is a good thing I stopped using real spells in my books," Ellina said. "I never would have thought Pete would try to perform one and get himself possessed."

Jude nodded, but then he said, "But you still have six books out there with real spells in them."

She nodded. "But Pete was a friend and read all my stuff. Really, what are the chances of another human trying to perform one?"

Somewhere in Boston . . .

"I can't believe we are actually doing this," Madison said, rolling her eyes at the other two girls.

Daisy opened the book wider, ignoring her uptight friend.

"I think it's fun," Emma said. Emma was always up for whatever.

"Shh," Daisy said. "We have to be focused. Jenny Bell says spells only work if you focus."

If you liked this book, you've got to try Mary Wine's
IN THE WARRIOR'S BED,
out now from Brava!

S he was a fool.

Bronwyn felt her heart freeze, because the man was huge. The hilt of his sword reflected the last of the daylight. His stallion was a good two hands taller than her mare. It could run her down with no trouble at all. Worse yet, the man wore the kilt of the McJames clan. With her father and brothers raiding their land, he had no reason to treat her kindly. His body was cut with hard muscles, and where his shirtsleeves were rolled up, she saw the evidence that spoke of his first-hand knowledge and skill with that sword. She scanned the ridge above him quickly, fearing that the McJameses had decided to repay her father's raids by doing a few themselves.

But there was no one in the fading light. Her teeth worried her lower lip as she returned her attention to him. She'd never considered that a McJames warrior might enjoy an afternoon ride the same as she.

"Good day to ye, lass." His voice was deep and edged with playfulness. He reached up and tugged on the corner of his knitted bonnet, a half smile curving his lips. His light-colored hair brushing his wide shoulders, a single thin braid running down along the side of his face to keep it out of his eyes. He wore only a leather doublet over his shirt, and the sleeves of the doublet were hanging behind him. There was a majestic quality to him. One that was mesmerizing. Her brother Keir was a very large man, and she wasn't used to meeting men who measured up to his size. This one did. He radiated strength from his booted feet to his blond hair. There was nothing small or weak about him. In his presence she felt petite, something she was unaccustomed to. Almost as though she noticed that she was a woman and that her body was fashioned to fit against his male one.

"Good day."

She had no idea why she spoke to him. It was an impulse. A shiver raced down her back. Her eyes widened, heat stinging her cheeks, her mouth suddenly dry. A shudder shook her gently, surprising her. Beneath her doublet, her nipples tingled, the sensation unnerving.

His gaze touched on her face, witnessing the scarlet stain creeping across it. A flicker of heat entered his eyes. It was bold, but something inside her enjoyed knowing that she sparked such a look in him.

"It's a fine day for riding."

His words were innocent of double meaning, but Bronwyn drew in a sharp breath because her mind imagined a far different sort of riding. Her own thoughts shocked her deeply. She'd never been so aware of just what a man might do with a woman when they were alone, and now was the poorest time for her body to be reacting to such things. It felt as though he could read her mind. At least the roguish smile he flashed her hinted that he could. His lips settled back into a firm line. She had to jerk her eyes away from them, but that left her staring into his blue eyes. Hunger flickered there and her body approved. Her nipples drew tight, hitting her boned stays.

"Ye shouldna look at me like that, lass." He sounded like

he was warning himself more than her, but her blush burned hotter because he was very correct.

"Nor should ye look at me as ye are."

A grin split his lips, flashing a hint of his teeth. "Ye have that right. But what am I to do when ye stand there so tempting? I'm merely a man."

And for some reason she felt more like a woman than she ever had. Something hot and thick flowed through her veins. There was no thinking about anything. Her body was alive with sensations, touching off longings she'd thought deeply buried beneath the harsh reality of her father's loathing to see her wed.

"A man who is far from his home." Her gaze touched on his kilt for a moment, the blue, yellow, and orange of the Mc-James clan holding her attention. "I'm a McQuade."

"I figured that already, but its nae my clan that keeps us quarrelling."

He let his horse close the distance again. The mare didn't move now; she stood quivering as the large stallion made a circle around her. The same flood of excitement swept through Bronwyn, keeping her mesmerized by the man moving around her. Bronwyn shook her head, trying to regain her wits.

"But I'm thinking that we just might be able to get along quite nicely." His eyes flickered with promise. "Ye and I."

"Ye should go. Ye're correct that it is my clansmen that seek trouble with the McJameses. Ye shouldna give them a reason to begin a fight."

"And ye would nae see that happen? I'm pleasantly surprised."

His stallion was still moving in a circle around her. Bronwyn had to twist her neck to keep him in sight. Every time he went behind her, her body tightened, every muscle drawing taut with anticipation. Such a response defied everything that she knew.

"Surprised that I've no desire to see blood spilt? Being a McJames does not mean I am cruel at heart. What is yer name?" he asked.

Fear shot through her, ending her fascination with him. Being the laird's daughter meant she was a prize worth taking. Riding out alone so far had been a mistake she just might pay for with her body. Few would believe her if she told them her father wouldn't pay any ransom for her. Beyond money, there were men who would consider taking her virtue a fine way to strike back at her clan.

"I'll no tell ye that. McQuade is enough for ye to know."

"I disagree with ye. 'Tis much too formal only knowing your clan name. I want to know what ye were baptized."

"Yet ye'll have to be content for I shall nae tell ye my Christian name." He frowned, but Bronwyn forced herself to be firm. This flirtation was dangerous. Her heart was racing but with more than fear. "If ye get caught on McQuade land, I'll no be able to help ye."

"Would that make ye sad, lass?"

"No." He was toying with her. "But it would ruin supper, what with all the gloating from the men that drove ye back onto McJames land. There would be talk of nothing else."

One golden eyebrow rose as the horse moved closer to her. He swung a leg over the saddle and jumped to the ground. Her belly quivered in the oddest fashion. But she had been correct about one thing—this man was huge.

"Are ye sure, lass? I might be willing to press me luck if I thought ye'd feel something for me."

"That's foolishness. Get on with ye. I willna tell ye my name. Ye're a stranger; I dinna feel anything beyond Christian goodwill toward ye."

"Is that so?"

"It is."

He flashed another grin at her, but this one was far more calculating and full of intent. "Afraid I might sneak into yer home and steal ye if I know whose daughter ye are?"

He came closer but kept a firm hand on the reins of his mount. Authority shone from his face now, clear, determined, and undeniable. This man was accustomed to leading. It was part of the fibers that made up his being. He would have the nerve to steal her if that was what he decided upon. There was plenty enough arrogance in him, for certain. She felt it in the pit of her belly. What made her eyelashes flutter to conceal her emotions was the excitement such knowledge unleashed in her.

"Enough teasing," she said. "Neither of us are children."

"Aye, I noticed that already."

Her face brightened once more. His eyes swept her and his expression tightened. Maybe she had never seen a man looking at her like that afore, but her body seemed to understand exactly what the flicker of hunger meant. She stared at it, mesmerized.

"Tell me yer name, lass."

And don't miss Donna Kauffman's
HERE COMES TROUBLE,
available now from Brava!

The hot, steamy shower felt like heaven on earth as it pounded his back and neck. He should have done this earlier. It was almost better than sleep. Almost. He'd realized after Kirby had left that he'd probably only grabbed a few hours after arriving, and he'd fully expected to be out the instant his head hit the pillow again. But that hadn't been the case. This time it hadn't been because he was worried about Dan, or Vanetta, or anyone else back home, or even wondering what in the hell he thought he was doing this far from the desert. In New England, for God's sake. During the winter. Although it didn't appear to be much of one out here.

No, that blame lay right on the lovely, slender shoulders of Kirby Farrell, innkeeper and rescuer of trapped kittens. Granted, after the adrenaline rush of finding her hanging more than twenty feet off the ground by her fingertips, it shouldn't be surprising that sleep eluded him, but that wasn't entirely the cause. Maybe he'd simply spent too long around women who were generally overprocessed, overenhanced, and overly made up, so that meeting a regular, everyday ordinary woman seemed to stand out more.

It was a safe theory, anyway.

And yet, after only a few hours under her roof, he'd already become a foster dad to a wild kitten and had spent far more time thinking about said kitten's savior than he had his own host of problems.

Maybe it was simply easier to think about someone else's situation. Which would explain why he was wondering about things like whether or not Kirby making a go of things with her new enterprise here, what with the complete lack of winter weather they were having. And what her story was before opening the inn. Was this place a lifelong dream? For all he knew, she was some New England trust fund baby just playing at running her own place. Except that didn't jibe with what he'd seen of her so far.

He'd been so lost in his thoughts while enjoying the rejuvenation of the hot shower that he clearly hadn't heard his foster child's entrance into the bathroom. Which was why he almost had a heart attack when he turned around to find the little demon hanging from the outside of the clear shower curtain by its tiny, sharp nails, eyes wide in panic.

After his heart resumed a steady pace, he bent down to look at her, eye-to-wild-eye. "You keep climbing things you shouldn't and one day there will be no one to rescue you."

He was sure the responding hiss was meant to be ferocious and intimidating, but given the pink-nosed, tiny, whiskered face it came out of, not so much. She hissed again when he just grinned, and started grappling with the curtain when he outright laughed, mangling it in the process.

He swore under his breath. "So, I'm already down one sweater, a shower curtain, and God knows what else you've dragged under the bed. I should just let you hang there all tangled up. At least I know where you are."

However, given that the tiny thing had already had one pretty big fright that day, he sighed, shut off the hot, life-giving spray, and very carefully reached out for a towel. After a quick rubdown, he wrapped the towel around his hips, eased out from the other end of the shower, and grabbed a hand towel.

"We'll probably be adding this to my tab, as well." He doubted Kirby's guests would appreciate a bath towel that had doubled as a kitty straightjacket.

"Come on," he said, doing pretty much the same thing he'd done when the kitten had been attached to the front of Kirby. "I know you're not happy about it," he told the now squalling cat. "I'm not all that amped up, either." He looked at the shredded curtain once he'd de-pronged the demon from the front of it and shuddered to think of just how much damage it had done to the front of Kirby.

"Question is . . . what do I do with you now?"

Just then a light tap came on the door. "Mr. Hennessey?"

"Brett," he called back.

"I . . . Brett. Right. I called. But there was no answer, so—"

"Oh, shower. Sorry." He walked over to the door, juggled the kitty bundle, and cracked the door open.

Her gaze fixed on his chest and then scooted down to the squirming towel bundle, right back up to his chest, briefly to his face, then away all together. "I'm—sorry. I just, you said . . . and dinner is—anyway—" She frowned. "You didn't take the cat, you know, into—" She nodded toward the room behind him. "Did something happen?"

"I was in the shower. Shredder here decided to climb the curtain, because apparently she's not happy unless she's trying to find new ways to terrify people."

He glanced from the kitten to Kirby's face in time to see her almost laugh and then compose herself. "I'm sorry, really. I shouldn't have let you keep her in the first place. I mean, not that you can't, but you obviously didn't come here to rescue a kitten. I should—we should—just leave you alone." She reached out to take the squirmy bundle from him.

"Does that mean I don't get dinner?"

"What?" She looked up, got caught somewhere about chest height, then finally looked at his face. "I mean, no, no, not at all. I just—I hope you didn't have your heart set on pot roast. There were a few . . . kitchen issues. Minor, really, but—"

"I'm not picky," he reassured her. What he was, he realized, was starving. And not just for dinner. If she kept looking at him like that . . . well, it was making him want to feed an entirely different kind of appetite. In fact . . . He shut that mental path down. His life, such as it was, didn't have room for further complications. And she'd be one. Hell, she already was. "I shouldn't have gotten you to cook anyway. You've had quite a day, and given what The Claw here did to your—*my*—shower curtain—I'll pay for a new one—I can only imagine that you must need more medical attention than I realized."

"Don't worry about that, I'm fine. Here," she said, reaching out for the wriggling towel bundle. "Why don't I go ahead and take her off your hands. I can put her out on the back porch for a bit, let you get, uh, dressed."

Really, she had to stop looking at him like that. Like he was a . . . a pot roast or something. With gravy. And potatoes. Damn he was really hungry. Voraciously so. Did she have any idea how long he'd been on the road? With only himself and the sound of the wind for company? Actually, it had been far longer than that, but he really didn't need to acknowledge that right about now.

Then she was reaching for him, and he was right at that point where he was going to say the hell with it and drag her into the room and the hell with dinner, too . . . only she wasn't reaching for him. She was reaching for the damn kitten. He sort of shoved it into her hands, then shifted so a little more of the door was between them . . . and a little less of a view of the front of his towel. Which was in a rather revealing situation at the moment.

"Thanks," he said. "I appreciate it. I'll go down—*be down*—in just a few minutes." He really needed to shut this door. Before he made her nervous. Or worse. I mean, sure, she was looking at him like he was her last supper, but that didn't mean she was open to being ogled in return by a paying guest. Especially when he was the only paying guest in residence. Even if that did mean they had the house to themselves. And privacy. Lots and lots of privacy. "Five minutes," he blurted, and all but slammed the door in her face.

Crap, if Dan could see him at the moment, he'd be laughing his damn ass off. As would most of Vegas. Not only did Brett happen to play high-stakes poker pretty well, but the supporters and promoters seemed to think he was also a draw because of his looks. And no, he wasn't blind, he knew he'd been relatively blessed, genetically speaking, for which he was grateful. No one would choose to be ugly. A least he wouldn't think so.

But while the looks had come naturally, that whole bad-boy, cocky-attitude vibe that was supposed to go with it had not. Not that he was shy. Exactly.

He was confident in his abilities, what they were, and what they weren't. But confidence was one thing. Arrogance another. And just because women threw themselves at him didn't mean he was comfortable catching them. Mostly due to the fact that he was well aware that women weren't throwing themselves at him because of who he was. But because of what he was. Some kind of poker quasi–rock star. They were batting eyelashes, thrusting cleavage, and passing phone numbers and room keys because of his fame, his fortune, his ability to score freebies from hotels and sponsors, and somewhere on that list, probably his looks weren't hurting him, either.

Nowhere on the list, however, did it appear that getting to know the guy behind the deck of cards and the stacks of chips was of any remote interest.

And there lay the irony.

Here's a sneak peek at the first in
Bianca D'Arc's new zombie series,
ONCE BITTEN, TWICE DEAD,
coming next month!

Somewhere near Stony Brook, Long Island, New York

"Unit twelve," the dispatcher's voice crackled over the radio. Sarah perked up. That was her. She listened as the report rolled over the radio. A disturbance in a vacant building out on Wheeler Road, near the big medical center. Probably kids, she thought, responding to dispatch and turning her patrol car around.

Since the budget cuts, she rolled alone. She hadn't had a partner in a long time, but she was good at her job and confident in her abilities. She could handle a couple of kids messing around in an empty building.

Sarah stepped into the gloomy concrete interior of the building. The metal door hung off its hinges, and old boards covered the windows. Broken glass littered the floor and graffiti decorated the walls.

The latest decorators had been junkies and kids looking for a secret place to either get high or drink beer where no one could see. There didn't appear to be anyone home at the moment. They'd probably cleared out in a hurry when they'd seen Sarah's cruiser pull up outside. Still, she had to check the place.

Nightstick in one hand, flashlight in the other, Sarah made her way into the gloom of the building. Electricity was a thing of the past in this place. Light fixtures dangled brokenly from the remnants of a dropped ceiling as Sarah advanced into the dark interior.

She heard a scurrying sound that could have been footsteps or could have been rodents. Either way, her heartbeat sped up.

"Police," she identified herself in a loud, firm voice. "Show yourself."

She directed the flashlight into the dark corners of the room as she crept inside. The place had a vast outer warehouse type area with halls and doors leading even farther inside the big structure. She didn't really want to go in there, but saw no alternative. She decided to advance slowly at first, then zip through the rest of the building, hoping no one got behind her to cut off her retreat.

She had her sidearm, but she'd rather not have to shoot anyone today. Especially not some kids out for a lark. They liked to test their limits and hers. She'd been up against more than one teenage bully who thought because she was a woman, she'd be a pushover. They'd learned the hard way not to mess with Sarah Petit.

She heard that sort of brushing sound again. Her heart raced as adrenaline surged. She'd learned to channel fear into something more useful. Fear became strength if you knew how to use it.

"This is the police," she repeated in a loud, carrying voice. "Step into the light and show yourself."

More shuffling. It sounded from down the corridor on the left. Sarah approached, her nightstick at the ready. The flashlight illuminated the corner of the opening, not showing her much. The sounds were growing louder. There was definitely someone—or something—there. Perhaps waiting to ambush her, down that dark hallway.

She wouldn't fall for that. Sarah approached from a good

ten feet out, maneuvering so that her flashlight could penetrate farther down the black hall. With each step, more of the corridor became visible to her.

Squinting to see better, Sarah stepped fully in front of the opening to the long hallway. There. Near the end. There was a person standing.

"I'm a police officer. Come out of there immediately." Her voice was firm and as loud as she could project it. The figure at the end of the hallway didn't respond. She couldn't even tell if it was male or female.

It sort of swayed as it tried to move. Maybe a junkie so high they were completely out of it? Sarah wasn't sure. She edged closer.

"Are you all right?"

She heard a weird moaning sound. It didn't sound human, but the shape at the end of the long hall was definitely standing on two feet with two arms braced against the wall as if for balance. The inhuman moan came again. It was coming from that shadowy person.

Sarah stepped cautiously closer to the mouth of the hallway. It was about four feet across. Not a lot of room to maneuver.

She didn't like this setup, but she had to see if that person needed help. Sarah grabbed the radio mic clipped to her shoulder.

"This is Unit Twelve. I'm at the location. There appears to be a person in distress in the interior of the building."

"What kind of distress, Unit Twelve?"

"Uncertain. Subject seems unable to speak. I'm going to get closer to see if I can give you more information."

"Should we dispatch an ambulance?"

Sarah thought about it for a half a second. No matter what, this person would need a medical check. Worst-case scenario, it was a junkie in the throes of a really bad trip.

"Affirmative. Dispatch medical to this location. I'm going to see if I can get them to come out, but I may need some backup."

"Dispatching paramedics and another unit to your location. ETA ten minutes on the backup, fifteen on the paramedics."

"Roger that."

With backup and medical help on the way, Sarah felt a little better about taking the next step. She walked closer to the corridor's mouth. The person was still there, still mostly unrecognizable in the harsh light of the flashlight beam.

"Help is coming," she called to the figure. From its height, she thought it was probably a male. He moved a little closer. Wild hair hung in limp hanks around his face. It was longer than most men's, but junkies weren't best known for their grooming and personal hygiene.

"That's it," she coaxed as the man shuffled forward on unsteady feet. "Come on out of there. Help is on the way. No one's going to hurt you."

Sarah stepped into the corridor, just a few feet, hoping to coax the man forward. He was definitely out of it. He made small noises. Sort of grunting, moaning sounds that weren't intelligible. It gave her the creeps, as did the way the man moved. He shuffled like Frankenstein's assistant in those old horror movies, keeping his head down, and his clothes were in tatters.

This dude had to be on one hell of a bender. Sarah lowered the flashlight beam off his head as he moved closer, trying to get a better look at the rest of him. His clothes were shredded like he'd been in a fight with a bear—or something else with sharp claws. His shirt hung off him in strips of fabric and his pants weren't much better.

The dark brown of bloodstains could be seen all over his

clothing. Sarah grew more concerned. He had to be in really bad shape from the look of the blood that had been spilled. She wondered if that was all his blood or if there was another victim lying around here somewhere in even worse shape.

His head was still down as he approached and Sarah backed up a step. His hair hung in what looked like greasy clumps. Only as he drew closer did he realize his hair wasn't matted with oil and dirt. It was stuck together by dried blood.

Then he looked up.

Sarah stifled a scream. Half his face was . . . gone. Just gone.

It looked like something had gnawed on his flesh. Blank eyes stared out at her from a ruined face. The tip of his nose was gone, as were his lips and the flesh of one side of his jaw and cheek.

Sarah gasped and turned to run, but something came up behind her and tripped her. She fell backward with a resounding thud, cracking her skull on the hard cement floor.

She fought against the hands that tried to grab her, but they were too strong, and her head spun from the concussion she'd no doubt just received. She felt sick to her stomach. The adrenaline of fear pushed her to keep going. Keep moving. Get away. Survive until her backup arrived.

Thank God she'd already called for backup.

Not one, but two men—if she could call them that—were holding her down. The one with the ruined face had her feet and the other had hold of her arms, even as she struggled against him.

She looked into the first one's eyes and saw . . . nothing. They were blank. No emotion. No feeling. No nothing.

Just hunger.

Fear clutched her heart in its icy grip. The second man looked wild in the dim light from her flashlight. It had rolled to the side, but was still on and lancing into the darkness of the building's interior nearby. Faint light shone on her two assailants.

They both looked like something out of a horror movie. The one from the hallway was, by far, the more gruesome of the two, but the one who wrestled with her arms was frightening too. His skin was cold to the touch and it looked almost gray, though she couldn't be sure in the uncertain light. Neither spoke, but both made those inhuman moaning sounds.

Even as she kicked and struggled, she felt teeth rip into her thigh. Sarah screamed for all she was worth as the first man broke through her skin and blood welled. The second man dove onto her prone form, knocking her flat and bashing her head on the concrete a second time. Stunned, she was still aware when his teeth sank into her shoulder.

She was going to die here. Eaten alive by these cannibals.

Something inside Sarah rebelled at the thought. No way in hell was she going down like this.

Help was on the way. All she had to do was hold on until her backup arrived. She could do that. She *had* to do that.

Channeling the adrenaline, Sarah ignored the pain and used every last bit of her strength to kick the man off her legs. She bucked like a crazy woman, dislodging the first man.

Once her legs were free, she used them to leverage her upper body at an angle, forcing the second man to move. The slight change in position freed one hand. She grasped around for anything on the floor next to her and came up with a hard, cylindrical object. Her nightstick.

Praise the Lord.

Putting all her remaining strength behind it, she aimed for the man's head, raining blows on him with the stick. When that didn't work, she changed targets, looking for anything that might hurt him. She whacked at his body with the hard wood of the stick. She heard a few of the bones in his hand crack at one point, but this guy was tough. Nothing seemed to faze him.

Finally, she used the pointy end of the stick to push at his neck. That seemed to get some results, as he shifted away. He moved enough for her to use the rest of her body for leverage, crawling out from under him.

His friend was up and coming back as she crab-walked away on her hands and feet, toward the door and the sunshine beyond. Her backup was coming. She just had to hold on until they could find her.

The two men followed her, moving as if they had all the time in the world. Their pace was steady and measured as she crawled as fast as she could toward the door. It didn't make any sense. They could have easily overtaken her, but they kept to their slow, walking pace.

Sarah hit the door and practically threw herself over the threshold. She had to get out in the open where her backup would see her right away. She was losing blood fast and her vision was dancing, tunneling down to a single dim spot. She was going to pass out any second. She had to do all she could to save herself before that happened.

Backup was coming. That thought kept her going. They'd be here any second. She just had to hold on.

She crawled into the sunlight, near her cruiser. Leaning against the side of her car, she tried for her radio, but the mic was long gone—probably a victim of the struggle with those two men. They were coming for her. They had to be.

But when she looked up, she saw them hesitate at the doorway to the building. The second man stepped through, but the first stayed behind, cowering in the darkness. The second man's skin was gray in the outdoor light. He looked like some kind of walking corpse, with grisly brown stains of dried blood all around his mouth. Some of it was bright red. That was *her* blood. The sick bastard had bitten her.

The man walked calmly forward, under the trees that shaded the walkway to the old building. Sarah had parked on the street, out in open sun. She watched in dread as the man walked steadily toward her, death in his flat gaze.

Then something odd happened. He stopped where the tree cover ended. He seemed reluctant to step into the sun.

Sarah blinked, but there wasn't any other explanation she could think of. Then she heard the sound of an approaching vehicle. Her backup.

With salvation in sight, she finally passed out.